ASTEROID: DISCOVERY

The Asteroid Series
Book One

A novel by

Bobby Akart

Copyright Information

Other Works by Amazon Top 25 Author, Bobby Akart

The Geostorm Series
The Shift
The Pulse
The Collapse
The Flood

The Asteroid Trilogy
Discovery
Diversion
Destruction

The Doomsday Series
Apocalypse
Haven
Anarchy
Minutemen
Civil War

The Yellowstone Series
Hellfire
Inferno
Fallout
Survival

The Lone Star Series
Axis of Evil
Beyond Borders
Lines in the Sand
Texas Strong
Fifth Column
Suicide Six

The Pandemic Series

Beginnings

The Innocents

Level 6

Quietus

The Blackout Series

36 Hours

Zero Hour

Turning Point

Shiloh Ranch

Hornet's Nest

Devil's Homecoming

The Boston Brahmin Series

The Loyal Nine

Cyber Attack

Martial Law

False Flag

The Mechanics

Choose Freedom

Patriot's Farewell

Seeds of Liberty (Companion Guide)

The Prepping for Tomorrow Series

Cyber Warfare

EMP: Electromagnetic Pulse

Economic Collapse

DEDICATIONS

For many years, I have lived by the following premise:

Because you never know when the day before
is the day before, prepare for tomorrow.

My friends, I study and write about the threats we face, not only to both entertain and inform you, but because I am constantly learning how to prepare for the benefit of my family as well. There is nothing more important on this planet than my darling wife, Dani, and our two girls, Bullie and Boom. One day the apocalypse will be upon us, and I'll be damned if I'm gonna let it stand in the way of our life together.

The Asteroid series is dedicated to the love and support of my family. I will always protect you from anything that threatens us.

ACKNOWLEDGEMENTS

Writing a book that is both informative and entertaining requires a tremendous team effort. Writing is the easy part. For their efforts in making the Asteroid series a reality, I would like to thank Hristo Argirov Kovatliev for his incredible cover art, Pauline Nolet for her editorial prowess, Stef Mcdaid for making this manuscript decipherable in so many formats, Chris Abernathy for his memorable performance in narrating this novel, and the Team—Denise, Joe, Jim, Shirley, and Kenda—whose advice, friendship and attention to detail is priceless.

You'll be introduced to two characters in this story who, through their generous donations to charities my family supports, won the right to have a character named after them. One is a gentleman named Sparky Newsome in Washington, Georgia who bid at a local Rotary Club auction. As it happened, Sparky is the editor and owner of the local newspaper, *The News-Reporter*. This changed the trajectory of my story's outline considerably, and for the better.

The use of Mr. Newsome in the Asteroid trilogy, led to incorporating Washington, Georgia as a location, which then led me to the Deerlick Astronomy Village in nearby Crawfordville. Founded by two astronomers in 2005, the DAV is considered one of the darkest locations in the Eastern United States by DarkSiteFinder.com.

Jackie Holcombe, who donated to a special program at Village Veterinary Medical Center in Farragut, Tennessee that supports people who can't afford extraordinary medical procedures for their pets, was also a named character in the series. She earned a prominent role in the story, alongside Mr. Newsome, as you will see. A huge thank you to both of them for their generosity and allowing me to include them in this series.

The research associated with this project surpassed that of the Yellowstone series. In fact, the premise for this story resulted from my conversations with the team of scientists at NASA's Jet Propulsion Laboratory at CalTech over a year ago.

As I dug into the science, once again, source material and research papers were heaped upon my shoulders. My email inbox was put into circuit overload as so many folks from around the globe contributed to my research. One thing is certain—astrophysicists are uniform in their desire to inform the public as to the threats we face from near-Earth objects, especially those that are recently discovered, or remain undiscovered.

There are so many people and organizations to thank, so let me name a few.

I was fortunate enough to be introduced to some brilliant members of our military at Wright-Patterson Air Force Base in Ohio. The USAF's Aeronautical Systems Division, the ASD, provided me invaluable insight into America's future fighting aircraft. They told me what are capabilities are today, and where they'd likely be ten years from now, and beyond. Literally, the sky's the limit for these folks. Don't be surprised that one day, we'll be flying fighter jets in space.

Also, a great source for the technical descriptions of the aircraft of our adversaries was provided by the US Naval Institute's Military Database in Arlington, Virginia. A big thank you to Melissa Cartwright for helping me navigate through a sea of information. Let me add, anyone who thinks we should be cutting our defense budget is short-sighted, or uninformed. The military capabilities of Russia and China will astound you.

As I've already mentioned, my research regarding the Yellowstone Caldera started with the work of Dr. Brian H. Wilcox, an aerospace engineer at the Jet Propulsion Laboratory in Pasadena, California. Although his proposition that our greatest threat to humankind may not necessarily come from above, in the form of a near-Earth object, but rather, from below, as an eruption from the Yellowstone Supervolcano, he has cautioned that it's the newly discovered asteroids that have the potential to be planet killers. Frankly, I don't know how Dr. Wilcox sleeps at night.

Lastly, I must make mention of the team at NASA's Planetary Defense Coordination Office. The PDCO employs a variety of ground and space-based telescopes to search for near-Earth objects, determines their orbits, and measures their physical characteristics in order to accurately assess the threat to our planet. Their functions including warning our government of the threats, suggesting mitigation techniques to alter the course of an incoming object, and acts to coordinate with multiple agencies as an emergency response is formulated. Thank you to Linda Billings and others in the Public Communications office at the PDCO; Patricia Talbert in the Professional Outreach department; and of course, Lindley Johnson, the Program Executive of the PDCO.

Without their efforts, this story could not be told.

Thank you all!

ABOUT THE AUTHOR

Bobby Akart

Author Bobby Akart has been ranked by Amazon as #35 on the Amazon Charts list of most popular, bestselling authors. He has achieved recognition as the #1 bestselling Horror Author, #1 bestselling Science Fiction Author, #5 bestselling Action & Adventure Author, #7 bestselling Historical Author and #10 bestselling Thriller Author.

He has written over forty international bestsellers, in nearly fifty fiction and nonfiction genres, including the chart-busting Yellowstone series, the pulse-racing Asteroid trilogy, the thought-provoking Doomsday series, the reader-favorite Lone Star series, the critically acclaimed Boston Brahmin series, the bestselling Blackout series, the frighteningly realistic Pandemic series, his highly cited nonfiction Prepping for Tomorrow series, and his latest project—the Asteroid series, a scientific thriller that will remind us all that life on Earth may have begun, and might well end, with something from space.

His novel *Yellowstone: Hellfire* reached the Top 25 on the Amazon bestsellers list and earned him two Kindle All-Star awards for most pages read in a month and most pages read as an author. The Yellowstone series vaulted him to the #35 bestselling author on Amazon, and the #1 bestselling science fiction author.

Bobby has provided his readers a diverse range of topics that are both informative and entertaining. His attention to detail and impeccable research has allowed him to capture the imaginations of his readers through his fictional works and bring them valuable knowledge through his nonfiction books.

SIGN UP for Bobby Akart's mailing list to receive special offers, bonus content, and you'll be the first to receive news about new releases in the Asteroid series:

eepurl.com/bYqq3L

VISIT Amazon.com/BobbyAkart, a dedicated feature page created by Amazon for his work, to view more information on his thriller fiction novels and post-apocalyptic book series, as well as his nonfiction Prepping for Tomorrow series.

Visit Bobby Akart's website for informative blog entries on preparedness, writing, and a behind-the-scenes look into his novels.

BobbyAkart.com

AUTHOR'S INTRODUCTION TO THE ASTEROID SERIES

June 13, 2019
I want you to imagine how vast our solar system is ...

For those of us stuck on Earth, we might gaze up into the night sky and marvel at the size of our solar system, but we'll never get the opportunity to get a closer look. We take for granted the Sun that brightens our day, or the mysterious Moon that appears at night. The trained eye can pick out constellations and even other planets, if one knows where to look.

But just how big is our solar system? Before you can appreciate its vastness, let's consider the units of measurement that give it a sense of scale. Distances are so large that measurements like feet and miles are irrelevant. Most distances are defined in astronomical units, or AUs. One AU, based upon the distance from the Earth to the Sun, is roughly equal to ninety-three-million-miles.

To put that into perspective, if you flew around our planet, you'd cover twenty-five thousand miles. If you traveled to the moon, you'd cover about ten times that, or two-hundred-forty-thousand miles. To reach the sun, we're looking at almost forty times the distance to the moon. And finally, to reach the outer limits of our solar system, where the Oort Cloud is located, is over one-hundred-thousand AUs, or nearly two light years away.

Now, that's a lot of space, pardon the pun. It would take our fastest spacecraft thirty-seven thousand years to get there.

That said, however, space objects travel the vast openness of our solar system with regularity. Over many millions of years, these objects, both large and small, wander the solar system. Some remain within the gravitational orbit of larger bodies, or within the asteroid belt that exists between Mars and Jupiter.

Others, the wayward nomads who are looking for a larger object's gravity to become attached to, float aimlessly, and mostly harmlessly, through space for years and years and years. Until ...

They collide with other objects.

Asteroids are typically material left over from the period of planetary formation four-and-a-half billion years ago. They're the remains of what didn't form into planets in the inner solar system, or often the result of collisions in the past.

They vary in size from only a few feet to the big daddy of them all—*Ceres*, which measures about one-fourth the size of our moon. At almost six-hundred-miles wide, Ceres is about the size of Texas.

This story focuses on the threats our planet faces from a collision with a near-Earth object, or NEO. If you consider an asteroid can be as small as a few feet across, there are an estimated five-hundred-million of them considered to be near-Earth—between us and the Sun. If you limit the number to potentially hazardous asteroids, those within four-and-a-half million miles, then the number is reduced to around twenty-thousand.

That's a lot of traffic in our neighborhood, and yet only ninety percent are accounted for. While NASA and other space agencies around the globe do an admirable job of identifying and tracking these NEOs, the fact of the matter is that they only have identified ninety percent of the threats. That leaves a one-in-ten-chance that an object remains undiscovered.

The big uncertainty is that we haven't discovered many near-Earth asteroids, so we don't know if they are on a collision course with Earth. Now, there is comfort in knowing that the vastness of space might make the odds in our favor that one of these wandering nomads doesn't hit us.

However, because of the size of our planet, and the gravity associated with Earth, asteroids can be pulled toward us. It's happened before, on many occasions.

NEO impact events have played a significant role in the evolution of our solar system since its formation. Major impact events have significantly shaped Earth's history, have been implicated in the formation of the Earth–Moon system, the evolutionary history of life, the origin of water on Earth and several mass extinctions. The famous prehistoric Chicxulub (cheek-sha-loob) impact, sixty-six million years ago, is believed to be the cause of the Cretaceous–Paleogene extinction event that resulted in the demise of the dinosaurs.

Could it happen again? Absolutely. When? Nobody knows. At present, there are only a few potentially close-shaves in our future, at least, that we know of. It's the ones that we haven't discovered that keep astrophysicists and amateur astronomers up at night, watching the skies.

Thank you for reading and I know you'll enjoy the Asteroid trilogy.

REAL-WORLD NEWS EXCERPTS

Weekend Asteroid Flyby Confirms We're Worrying About the Wrong Space Rocks ~ *Ryan Mandelbaum, Space.com, April 17, 2018*

An asteroid (2018 GE3) approximately the size of a football field flew close by Earth only a day after it was first spotted this weekend. This near miss is a perfect example of the asteroids we should worry about, not just the so-called potentially hazardous rocks being tracked by NASA.

But 2018 GE3 was not that small. The 140-meter cut-off was set up because "impacts from objects of that size would only produce regional effects, while larger objects would have corresponding wider effects," according to NASA planetary defense. But an asteroid close in size to 2018 GE3 could have caused the Tunguska event (which leveled seven hundred seventy square miles), and the Chelyabinsk meteor that was only 20 meters in diameter.

Asteroids are Smacking Earth Twice as Often as Before ~ *Seth Borenstein, AP News, January 17, 2019*

Giant rocks from space are falling from the sky more than they used to. "It's just a game of probabilities," said study lead author Sara Mazrouei, a University of Toronto planetary scientist.

Harvard's Avi Loeb said in an email, "this enhanced impact rate poses a threat for the next mass extinction event, which we should watch for and attempt to avoid with the aid of technology. This demonstrates how arbitrary and fragile human life is."

Speedy Asteroid buzzed Earth Last Week, One Day Before Being Detected ~ *Eddie Irizarry, EarthSky.org, April 1, 2019*

A small asteroid measuring 100 feet wide—now designated as 2019 FC1—flew closer to us than the Moon on March 28, 2019 at forty thousand miles per hour. Astronomers detected it one day later. It's the largest of 14 asteroids to pass closer to us than the Moon since 2019 began.

This space rock was almost twice as wide as the asteroid that penetrated the atmosphere over the skies above Chelyabinsk, Russia, on February 15, 2013. For comparison, the Chelyabinsk asteroid was estimated to be 55 feet (17 meters) in diameter, before entering our atmosphere, and generated a blast equivalent to a 300-kiloton nuclear explosion.

U.S. Announces Huge Meteor Explosion Over Earth, Three Months After it Occurred ~ *Paul Rincon, BBC News Space Editor, March 18, 2019*

A huge fireball exploded in the Earth's atmosphere in December, according to NASA. The blast was the second largest of its kind in 30 years, and the biggest since the fireball over Chelyabinsk in Russia six years ago.

What's the significance?

In 2005, Congress tasked NASA with finding 90% of near-Earth asteroids of 140m (460ft) in size or larger by 2020. Space rocks of this size are so-called *problems without passports* because they are expected to affect whole regions if they collide with Earth. But scientists estimate it will take them another 30 years to fulfill this congressional directive.

Epigraph

"Asteroids have us in their sights. The dinosaurs didn't have a space program, so they're not here to talk about this problem. We are, and we have the power to do something about it. I don't want to be the embarrassment of the galaxy to have had the power to deflect an asteroid, and then not, and end up going extinct."
~ Neil deGrasse Tyson, American Astrophysicist
*****

"If the Earth gets hit by an asteroid, it's game over. It's control-alt-delete for civilization."
~ Bill Nye, the science guy
*****

"The second angel blew his trumpet, and something like a great mountain, burning with fire, was thrown into the sea, and a third of the sea became blood."
~ Revelation 8:8
*****

"After great trouble for humanity, a greater one is near.
The Great Mover renews the ages:
Rain, blood, milk, famine, steel and plague,
In the heavens fire seen, a long spark running..."
~ Nostradamus, Centuries II, Quatrain 46
*****

"He who has a *why* to live can bear almost any *how*."
~ D. H. Lawrence

ASTEROID: DISCOVERY

The Asteroid Series
Book One

PROLOGUE

NASA Mission Control Center
Houston, Texas

"Houston, did you see that?"

The words hung in the air of the Mission Control Center at NASA's Johnson Space Center in Houston, Texas, as the flight control communications officer attempted to respond to the question.

Immediately after the American astronaut aboard the International Space Station uttered the question, all communications between flight control and the ISS ceased.

It had been a typical day aboard the recently expanded space station, if you can call living aboard a spacecraft orbiting hundreds of miles above the surface of our planet *typical*.

By design, an astronaut's day was fairly regimented. Free time was usually taken up by ordinary tasks related to hygiene and eating. There was time for exercising, and occasionally the crew of the ISS would play board games using specially magnetized features.

Work consumed most of an astronaut's day, with some tasks more mundane than others. Unlike the days of old when astronauts were recruited from the ranks of Air Force and Navy fighter pilots, today's astronauts consisted primarily of scientists and engineers, who spent their days performing experiments or testing the effects of weightlessness on various ordinary daily activities.

The ISS was a large orbiting experiment designed to prepare future astronauts to travel greater distances and establish a foothold on other celestial bodies.

On this day, there was nothing out of the ordinary as it related to the day's scheduled activities. There were no planned spacewalks. There were no scheduled arrivals or departures via the Russian and French space shuttles. Each of the members of the international team manning the ISS went about their business.

Then the communications failed. The last transmission received was those simple words, *Houston, did you see that?* Yet nobody on the ground had any inkling of what they referred to.

The mostly American and Russian crew were amiable with one another, but a cold war chill had strained relations between the two nations in recent years. Because of budgetary concerns, NASA had reduced the number of its direct missions to the ISS, opting instead to send its astronauts to the space station via French and Russian shuttles.

As a result, the mechanical and technological operations of the ISS had been turned over primarily to the Russians, who continued to lead the charge in terms of space exploration and advancement.

Mark Foster, the director of Flight Control Room One, designated FCR-1, paced the floor nervously as he cajoled his engineering team to find a solution for the communications breakdown. Mission Control workers were divided by those in charge of flight control and ground-team workers. Most were trained to work interchangeably, filling in as needed or, in the present case, assisting in solving a critical failure.

Communications with the ISS had been interrupted in the past, most notably in 2013 for a period of three hours when trouble encountered during a computer software upload prompted a loss of contact.

On that occasion, ISS station skipper Caleb Faust rebooted the onboard, US-designed computer system, clearing the problem after a three-hour cessation of communications and command capability. During a pass over Russian ground stations, Faust was able to report in to Mission Control and assuage their concerns.

However, the Russians were none too happy with the communications blackout. Not because the software caused the glitch, but because Mission Control did not keep them abreast of the situation. After the incident, the Russians insisted upon installing their own redundant communications systems that were directed to their version of Mission Control in Kazakhstan.

Mission Control Director Foster immediately ordered his Defense Department liaison to reach out to the Moscow government and advise them of the situation. Maxwell Robinson, an Army colonel, was the Defense Department's man on the ground at NASA. He stayed in direct communication with the Pentagon, a necessity that arose out of the 2013 incident.

Per protocols, he contacted his team at the Pentagon, who arranged for a secured line to his counterpart in Moscow. The line, of course, was monitored by the Central Intelligence Agency. The Cold War was alive and well, with suspicions running rampant in all aspects of international relations, especially with Russia.

Once the call was made and a connection was established, the Russians equivocated in their response. They provided Robinson the functional equivalent of "we'll get back to you later" and then disconnected the communication.

This both infuriated and puzzled Robinson, who immediately ordered his diplomatic team at the Pentagon to reopen the lines of communication. Two hours later, he was patched through, this time to an unidentified Russian official.

He advised Robinson that their contact with the Russian cosmonauts had also been lost, but they were working diligently to source the problem.

Nine hours later, communications were restored, and those NASA personnel in Mission Control who'd worked tirelessly to solve the problem let out a spontaneous, genuine cheer.

That response became muted when the Russian commander of the ISS announced that NASA had lost one of its own.

4

PART ONE

Three years later …

Sunday, April 1

ASTROMETRY

Identification Number: Unknown

Right Ascension: 19 hours 02 minutes 54.4 seconds

Declination: -34 degrees 11 minutes 39 seconds

Greatest Elongation: 78.0 degrees

Nominal Distance from Earth: 0.41 Astronomical Units

Relative Velocity: 26,822 meters per second

CHAPTER 1

Present Day
Sunday, April 1
Eglin Air Force Base Test Range
Off the coast of the Florida Panhandle

Non semper ea sunt quae videntur.

The motto for the 486th Flight Test Squadron was etched across the outside of the hangar on a remote runway within the four hundred sixty thousand acres that made up Eglin Air Force Base, the largest Air Force installation in the free world.

The squadron's adage, translated as *not always what they seem*, produced a rare smile on the tanned face of Major Gunner Fox as he made the solitary trek across the tarmac. *Nothing ever is*, he thought to himself.

A warm gust of wind blew across the runway, carrying sand particles past him. Instinctively, he looked to the sky and then toward the orange-and-white windsocks to get a feel for the wind's velocity and direction. In a world full of advanced technology, as was evidenced by the sleek and technologically advanced aircraft that awaited him, it was still the cone-shaped textile tube that provided pilots a feel for the atmosphere they were about to enter.

Up ahead, a team of *squires*, as Gunner called them, awaited his arrival. It was quiet on the base, as Sunday was generally a day off for support personnel. Not so for the airmen who'd prepared the gear necessary for his test flight. This was also a rare weekend encounter with *the suits*, civilian project engineers and technicians, who each held the twenty-first century's equivalent of a clipboard—the iPad.

7

Gunner had lived his entire life on an Air Force Base, or within the service of the branch of the military that ruled the skies, and now space. His father had been an airman, just as his father before him. It was the only life Gunner knew, and now, it was all he had.

"Good morning, Major Fox," one of the civilian scientists greeted him heartily. Gunner nodded, but ignored his greeting, opting instead to salute and acknowledge the Air Force technical team who'd ensured that he was properly suited up for the test flight.

Gunner stopped to examine his ride. It was just after six in the morning, and the sun was making its way over the horizon. As it got brighter, the reflection revealed the sleek lines of the jet fighter before him.

The F/A XX.

This bird was the redesigned sixth-generation fighter designed to fly alongside the aging fleet of F-35 Lightnings that had been a staple of America's multirole military jets. In recent decades, the Navy had undertaken the role of advancing the nation's air-attack capabilities with their Next-Generation Air Dominance program.

The program had bogged down in congressional budget squabbling and technical mishaps before being taken over by the Air Force a few years ago. When the switch was made, and Gunner was recruited as a test pilot, he quipped that the Navy should stick to the seas and leave the flying to us, borrowing a marketing phrase from a now-defunct commercial airline.

Gunner walked around the jet, which was more spacecraft than it was airplane. As he walked, the civilian representative of Boeing attempted to chat him up, excitedly extolling the virtues of the F/A XX.

"This will truly be our key to next-generation air dominance," he began, stealing the phrase from the Navy in the process. "An air-superior fighter with multirole capabilities. It has maximum sensor connectivity, allowing the most technically advanced interaction between the aircraft, the ground, and even orbiting satellites. Anything you can imagine needing in a battlefield scenario, the F/A XX can provide you."

Gunner glanced back at the young man and scowled. The civilian sounded more like a car salesman than an engineer. Gunner's glare did nothing to dissuade the Boeing representative from continuing his sales pitch.

"The unique design of the wing makes the F/A XX lighter and more energy efficient. Instead of relying upon movable surfaces such as ailerons to control the roll and pitch of the aircraft, as conventional wings do, the new *smart skin* technology makes it possible to deform the whole wing, or parts of it, using artificial intelligence to maneuver quicker and more efficiently. Really, it's the AI that make the F/A XX so special. In a way, it could fly itself."

Gunner abruptly stopped and turned to address the man for the first time. "Then why don't you?"

"Um, what?"

"Why don't you let it fly itself?" Gunner bristled. He'd heard enough of the sales pitch. "You don't need me."

Gunner began to walk toward the hangar. Confused, the Boeing representative looked around for help as the rest of the team stood stoically at the portable stairwell that patiently awaited its pilot. Another gust of wind caused the F/A XX to wiggle slightly, as if it were emitting a chuckle.

"Major. Major!" The young man panicked as he scurried to catch up with Gunner. "I didn't mean any disrespect, sir. I was simply pointing out the technologically advanced features of this magnificent aircraft. I mean, naturally, a pilot is best—"

Gunner stopped and smirked. He'd tortured the guy enough. Of course he was going to fly the plane. In fact, he was dying to.

CHAPTER 2

Sunday, April 1
Eglin Air Force Base Test Range
Off the coast of the Florida Panhandle

Gunner, with the assistance of the Eglin team, got situated in the cockpit of the F/A XX fighter. His six foot, two-hundred-pound frame was perfectly ordinary by fighter pilot standards, but Gunner was anything but ordinary when he was flying. Flying at supersonic speeds in the world's most advanced aircraft took more than superior physicality, it required a mental acuity that very few possessed. There was very little margin for error when in combat, and Gunner had an extraordinary keenness of thought and vision, making him one of the best fighter pilots in the U.S. Air Force.

He'd spent countless hours in the Boeing simulator taking the bird through its paces in a virtual-reality world. Flight simulation and real-world flying were markedly different scenarios, especially with the planned maneuvers he had in mind. Gunner had flown countless missions in a variety of military aircraft. Only a pilot of his experience knew what to expect in the air, not a scientist.

"Major Fox, I've been told to remind you that—" began one of the airmen before Gunner cut him off.

"I know. I know. Follow the protocols discussed in preflight. Bring the plane back in one piece. Keep in constant communication. Blah, blah, blah." Gunner's demeanor and level of amiability were always at a different level when he dealt with airmen. They, like him, had a job to do. If this airman had been told to give Gunner a lecture, it was because of what had happened in the past, not because what they expected to happen today.

"Yes, sir. Sorry, sir," the airman apologized unnecessarily.

Gunner chuckled. "Have you ever noticed that they never order me to come back alive?"

The young man didn't know how to respond, not that Gunner expected him to.

The Eglin team took Gunner through his final preflight checks, and the group exchanged the traditional thumbs-up. Finally, the tarmac was cleared and Gunner was left alone with his steed, a powerful, shiny toy that was arguably the most technologically advanced aircraft in the world.

He glanced toward the sky, and the sun was now in full view to the east. He wondered who was watching. God? Russian reconnaissance? Someone else?

A shiver came across his body as he studied the cockpit. He glanced to his right and left, marveling at the technology that made this aircraft capable of making faster and wilder maneuvers than ever thought possible. Her agility required multiple onboard computers, the so-called artificial intelligence, to be as responsive as Gunner wanted her to be.

Gunner was ready, and within minutes, he was wings up, soaring high above the Gulf of Mexico. The scramjet technology enabled the aircraft to cruise at supersonic speeds without the need of an afterburner. The smart skin was everything Boeing billed it to be. The sensors and electronics integrated into the fuselage were responsive, and the reduced drag markedly increased the speed and maneuverability.

For the first twenty minutes, Gunner and the F/A XX got acquainted with one another. He followed the script, so to speak, working with those on the ground to run the aircraft through the preplanned maneuvers.

Gunner knew this aircraft was designed to compete with Chinese and Russian technology. In the past several years, proxy wars were being fought around the world. Syria, Iran, and most recently

Venezuela were all hotbeds of military activity as the Russians and Americans squared off in a new cold war era. To complicate matters further, the Chinese took advantage of America's preoccupation with the Russians to make further inroads into the South China Sea.

The Air Force and Navy would need the finest technology in its aircraft to compete with China's J-20 and the Russian Su-35S. Gunner had flown sorties that engaged both of these aircraft, and he'd become concerned about the F-35's ability to hold its own. Therefore, he hoped this new design was the answer.

"Major, we believe we've got everything we need today." A civilian voice came across the comms.

"No, I don't think you do," replied Gunner in a monotone voice. Gunner had piloted an F-22 Raptor on a mission in which he chased a Chinese Chengdu J-20 out of protected airspace near the Philippines. In his debriefing, he'd lamented that the J-20's airframe gave it a much higher speed and operational altitude than the F-22. The pilot of the J-20 on that day was able to climb to an altitude that no American aircraft could achieve.

"Come again, Major?" said the civilian inquisitively. After a short pause in which Gunner didn't respond, the civilian said, "We've performed every programmed maneuver for this test session."

At first, Gunner hesitated. He could return to Eglin and call it a day. Maybe he'd stop by the Bayview Club and have a beer. Or he'd head back to the beach and relax. But that wouldn't help future pilots who might find themselves being pursued by a superior Chinese J-20. He had to know what this bird was capable of, something the simulator couldn't recreate.

Gunner closed off the communications system so he wouldn't be distracted. He checked the aircraft to make sure she was ready. Then he began to climb, forcing the aircraft upward at full power, a steep ascent that resembled a rocket taking off into space.

The F/A XX responded, providing him the thrust he needed to make the vertical climb, fighting through the drag, as the new design was aerodynamically superior to any aircraft he'd ever flown. A smile came across his face as he took the plane toward the stratosphere, climbing to forty thousand feet, alone in the sky, with only space in his field of vision.

The set ceiling height for the F/A XX in its new configuration was fifty thousand feet. He used the aircraft's maximum acceleration to overshoot this ceiling and then some. He'd never reach the one hundred twenty-three thousand feet achieved by the Russian MiG-25 Foxbat, but he'd get close enough. *Close enough to see.*

Gunner was forced into the back of his seat, the gravitational forces taking their toll on his body.

Fifty thousand feet and climbing.

Mach 2.

Gunner pressed forward, shutting out the world underneath him.

Fifty-five thousand feet.

Still faster as the F/A XX began to shudder ever so slightly.

Mach 2.5.

Fifty-eight thousand. Then sixty.

The Russian MiG-29 Fulcrum nearly hit Mach 2 when it achieved an altitude approaching sixty thousand feet. At that height, a pilot could see the curvature of the Earth.

Gunner wanted to see, too. He wanted to experience what *she* experienced. He looked to the Moon. It was sharper, more defined than what the naked eye could see on Earth. The horizon appeared curved. The G-forces were almost unbearable.

Mach 3. Sixty thousand feet. Sixty-five.

The F/A XX climbed higher, through the atmosphere and into the ozone layer that hovered over the planet like a blue fog.

Still holding Mach 3. *Incredible, at this altitude*, Gunner thought to himself.

Seventy thousand feet. The sky began to turn very dark, with the sprinkling of innumerous stars, an incredible view that only a few people had experienced.

Eighty thousand feet, near the stratosphere, where temperatures fell to sixty degrees below zero and winds approached a hundred thirty miles per hour.

Gunner became mesmerized, lost in his thoughts, as he flew the F/A XX to the edge of space, into the stratosphere. It was the screaming of the aircraft's warning alarms that brought him back to Earth.

CHAPTER 3

Sunday, April 1
Eglin Air Force Base Test Range
Off the coast of the Florida Panhandle

I could never understand why someone would want to jump out of a perfectly good aircraft.

If Gunner had said it once, he'd said it a thousand times. Yet he'd done it on many occasions. Oftentimes by choice, sometimes not. To be sure, it was part of his training. He'd performed multiple jumps and followed planned ejection procedures during his years in the Air Force. He'd been shot down in combat twice.

His first jump, while on his honeymoon, he'd dove with his wife's encouragement. He'd almost died that day, but for the quick thinking of his wife, who rescued him in midair when his parachute failed. Otherwise, she would've been widowed and he would've been squashed like a bug on a rug.

"Well, crap," Gunner muttered as he regained consciousness. "The damn thing's falling apart."

The F/A XX was quite literally losing its composure. The onboard computers, the so-called artificial intelligence, were having nothing short of a conniption fit.

As the aircraft began to shake violently, the plane's onboard systems attempted to take over the controls, assuming that its pilot, Gunner, was asleep at the wheel. Granted, he was lost in his thoughts for a moment, so to speak, but he was clearly wide awake and alert at this point.

"Time to go home, girl," he whispered as he began a long sweeping bank to the left in an effort to create somewhat of an orbital trajectory before he returned to Earth.

Relieved that the plane responded, Gunner slowly began a descent before turning a little sharper toward the Gulf of Mexico, which eventually came into view through the haze of the ozone layer.

That was when the F/A XX began to disintegrate.

The single-wing structure, a myriad of tiny subassemblies that were bolted together to form an open, latticelike framework, began to chip away, taking the thin layer of polymer material with it. Thousands of tiny triangles of matchstick-like struts, the aircraft's metamaterial, began to fly off the wings.

Warning! Abort! Warning! Abort!

"No kidding, really?" said Gunner as he focused on the instrument panel, with the occasional glance toward the smart skin that was peeling off before his eyes.

Eject! Eject!

He was still traveling at Mach 2.5, and his descent was approaching sixty thousand feet. And his plane was disintegrating. His probabilities of survival at this altitude and speed were single digits.

He had to stay with her, trying to maintain control while ignoring the AI's pleas to eject. Everything seemed to unfold in slow motion, even though it had only been a few seconds since he'd reached the apex of his ascent.

The disintegration process accelerated, and Gunner had to take the chance. At fifty thousand feet, he ejected and was propelled away from the aircraft into the Earth's troposphere. He somersaulted, tumbling over and over again, momentarily catching a glimpse of the F/A XX as it began to shred, shedding its skin like a snake.

He never saw the explosion when the remains of the aircraft hit the Gulf of Mexico at Mach 1. The rush of air and darkness overwhelmed him. The fact that he was tumbling meant that the initial stabilizing chute had not deployed. The main chute was designed to open automatically at fifteen thousand feet, but Gunner began to doubt whether the automatic-opening function would perform as it should.

Gravity began to pull him back to Earth, causing his six-foot, two-hundred-pound frame to soar at nearly three hundred miles per hour.

Gunner considered opening the faceplate of his helmet, trying his best to gauge his distance from the water. He decided against it, knowing that at this rate of descent, contact with a wayward bird would smash his face, killing him instantly.

Then, without warning, the stabilizing parachute opened, arresting his free fall slightly. It had been two minutes since he ejected, and he tumbled through the atmosphere. Remarkably, he didn't pass out, nor did he become nauseous. He'd never trained for something of this magnitude, but his body seemed to adjust and handle it admirably.

At fifteen thousand feet, the main parachute opened and he slowed to a drift, miles away from where his aircraft had smashed into the Gulf. He could make out the shoreline and quickly identified Apalachicola. The bay and barrier islands were within view now. He was over a hundred miles east of Eglin AFB, the prevailing winds and the jet stream carrying him far away from where his plane probably crashed.

As Gunner's adrenaline calmed, he contemplated this whole skydiving thing. In a way, it was peaceful. There were no honking horns, or lawn companies cutting grass, or any evidence of the human interaction that continuously invaded our private world. He understood the allure.

Naturally, there were those who *jumped out of perfectly good aircraft* for the thrill. You know, the adrenaline-driven, crazed bunch of thrill-seekers for whom a roller coaster isn't good enough.

Gunner was experiencing a freedom that he'd never imagined. It was a feeling that went far beyond the rush. It was a moment, even if for only a minute or two, when you see the world at a completely different angle. From a perspective that was hard to explain.

In his final mile of descent into the turquoise green waters off the Florida Panhandle, Gunner Fox smiled, now understanding why she did what she did.

Every day is a good day when you're floating.

CHAPTER 4

Sunday, April 1
Deerlick Astronomy Village
Crawfordville, Georgia

Since the beginning of man, humans have yearned to live among the stars. With the advent of space travel, followed by the development of larger and more powerful rocket systems, the concept of colonizing the Moon, and even Mars, became a realistic possibility.

While the ability to reside in space, whether aboard the International Space Station or the newly created outpost on the Moon, was unattainable for the vast majority of the human race, there were places on Earth that were so desolate, so devoid of ambient light, that they were ideal locales to study the heavens.

One such place was the Deerlick Astronomy Village in Northeast Georgia. Located just north of Interstate 20 that travels between Atlanta and Augusta, Deerlick was a small planned community development that catered to amateur and professional astronomers alike.

Skywatchers purchased parcels where they could build tiny homes, or live in recreational vehicles, with a minimal number of restrictions. One thing all of the astronomers uniformly agreed upon was to keep light to a minimum. The developers of the community even negotiated with a small nearby town to adjust their public streetlights to point downward, thus protecting the dark skies above Deerlick.

On this night, nearly everyone who owned a parcel within the community was present, using their telescopes to gaze upward at one of the most significant celestial events to occur in their lifetime—the passing of the so-called next *Great Comet*.

Since the turn of the century, two prior Great Comets—Comet McNaught in 2007 and Comet Lovejoy in 2011—had graced the Southern Hemisphere skies while a generation of Northern Hemisphere astronomers made do with photos of these grand events. For stargazers in America, Comet Hale-Bopp, a significant celestial event, but one that fell short of Great Comet status, was the most memorable in recent years.

Until now.

This new arrival to Earth's neck of the universe had a rare combination of brightness, even more so than Comet McNaught or Comet Lovejoy, coupled with an unusually long tail of more than thirty degrees.

Tonight, the world would be treated to its first glimpse of Comet Oort, which was easily going to be the comet of the century and a once-in-a-lifetime event. Coupled with a brightness exceeding famed Comet ISON that was visible during the daylight hours, and the extraordinarily long tail of Comet Hyakutake discovered in 1996, the newest Great Comet had set the world abuzz.

Ordinarily, comets are named after the astronomer who discovered it. Comet Oort, however, was named after its probable source of origin because so many discovered it all at once due to its extraordinary characteristics.

The Oort Cloud, a thick bubble of icy debris that surrounds our solar system, extends a third of the way from our Sun to the next star, or nearly a hundred times the distance from Earth to the Sun.

Every now and then, something disturbs the debris in this icy world and it begins a long fall toward the Sun. This debris, known as a comet, may travel for hundreds of thousands of years in its orbit around the Sun, and on rare occasions, it might come close enough to Earth to be viewed through telescopes.

While this type of scientific discovery bored many, it excited young Nathaniel Phillips of Thomson, Georgia, a senior honor student at nearby Briarwood Academy. His father, the chief of staff at the U.S. Army Cyber Command at Fort Gordon in Augusta, had purchased a parcel at Deerlick for his son, who'd always shown an interest in astronomy. His mother, a plastic surgeon, encouraged her son's interest in scientific endeavors and had given him a new telescope for his birthday the month prior.

Nate Phillips rallied his best buddy, Kevin, and their girlfriends to come to Deerlick that night to observe Comet Oort through his new telescope. He was one of thousands of amateur astronomers around the U.S. who were being trained to study the skies, constantly remaining on vigil for previously undiscovered near-Earth objects.

Several years ago, a small meteor had swept by Earth unnoticed until it crashed into a Russian global navigation satellite in an intermediate circular orbit at twenty-two thousand miles above sea level. The destruction of GLONASS almost caused an international incident, as the U.S. had complained to the United Nations on previous occasions that the satellite was being used for spying, in violation of several international treaties.

Because the meteor that struck GLONASS had not been discovered, the Russians jumped to the conclusion that the Americans had destroyed the satellite using one of their newly deployed laser weapons utilized within the Space Force.

It wasn't until NASA provided uncontroverted, documented evidence that the meteor had destroyed the satellite that the Russians backed off their allegations. The chill between the two countries, however, remained.

"Check it out, Kevin," said Nate cheerily as he finished making the adjustments on his new Celestron EDGEHD 14 optical telescope assembly. Nate stood out of the way and motioned for his friend to look into the lens.

Instinctively, the younger boy grabbed the lens and accidentally altered the eyepiece. He'd already downed two beers and was feeling the effects, as were the two girls who accompanied the teens that evening.

Nate, who'd avoided the alcohol because he wanted to remain focused on watching Comet Oort, playfully pushed his pal out of the way and jokingly admonished his best friend. "Dork! Don't touch, just look."

Kevin laughed and said, "Yeah, that's the same thing you said at that strip club in Panama City during spring break."

"You should've listened to me then, too. You got us thrown out, remember?"

"Yeah, whatevs," replied Kevin as he stepped up to the telescope and took another gander after Nate made the necessary corrections. Within a few seconds, he emitted a genuine *wow*.

"We wanna see," insisted one of the girls. They grabbed Kevin around the waist and pulled him away, a hug the teenage boy truly enjoyed.

The girls took turns studying Comet Oort, commenting on how bright it was and how the tail extended beyond the telescope's view.

"It seems so close," one of the girls commented as she stood and approached Nate. "You'll protect us when it pummels the planet, right?"

Nate scoffed at her remark. Truthfully, he didn't particularly like this particular girl, not like *that*, anyway. She was fun to play with and was never at a loss to show him lots of affection. He wasn't too keen on the drinking aspect, especially when he was driving, but his friends always had a ready supply of cold beer. Tonight was no exception, as was evidenced by Kevin and his girlfriend popping the tops on another round for themselves.

"Come on, Nate, let's party," pleaded Kevin as he and his girlfriend began to kiss each other.

The other girl cozied up to Nate and whispered in his ear, "Yeah, it's too busy around here tonight. Let's go to my sister's place in Washington. She's out of town and I have the keys right here in my pocket. Wanna feel?"

She took his hand and slid it down the outside of her shirt toward her jean shorts. Nate felt the typical stirrings of a high school boy and resisted the urge to engage in a make-out session like Kevin. For now, anyway.

He reluctantly took a beer from his buddy and downed half of it to get the night started. He took another moment to study Comet Oort while he let the alcohol soak into his body.

Then he saw something.

An object. Out of place. Moving.

Nate stood up and looked toward the night sky, rubbing his eyes as if a speck of dirt had caused the anomaly.

"Come on, man," implored Kevin. "The girls are ready, if you know what I mean."

"Yeah, hold on. I saw something."

"What you saw was an opportunity with a hot girl slipping away, probably forever, you dang science nerd."

"Shut up," Nate shot back.

He looked through his telescope again, making minor adjustments so that his field of vision took Comet Oort, and its extraordinary brightness, out of view. Instead, he focused on the tail.

"Kev, something's not right here. I mean, there's something else in the tail, or behind it."

"Man, the only tail you need to worry about is sitting in the passenger seat. Come on, or I'm taking your car and leaving your dumb ass here."

Frustrated, Nate exhaled and swigged down the rest of his beer. He took another look through the telescope and then approached his MacBook. Using the astroimaging camera attached to the EDGEHD, he set the MacBook application to begin recording.

As he locked up his small shed that securely held his equipment, he vowed to come back first thing in the morning to study the recorded footage more closely, using his video-editing software to isolate and enlarge the object that he'd seen.

Nathaniel Phillips never got the chance.

CHAPTER 5

Monday, April 2
The Tap Room
Apalachicola, Florida

"I heard they fished you out of the Gulf yesterday," said Sammy Hart, the longtime bartender at The Tap Room, a neighborhood grill and bar located on the ground floor under its more upscale counterpart, The Owl Cafe. The two restaurants, a part of the Oyster City Brewing Company enterprise developed by a local group of entrepreneurs, had been a mainstay in downtown Apalachicola, Florida, since 2011.

Gunner grinned and shrugged as he pulled out the barstool and got settled in front of Hart. He shook the rain off his sleeves and ran his fingers through his slightly shaggy blond hair. Gunner wasn't much for hats and raincoats. He'd only held an umbrella once in his entire life, at a funeral when they buried his mother. He'd vowed never to do that again.

"Yeah," he replied, accepting a pint of Hooter Brown Tupelo Honey Ale. The rich chocolate and honey flavors of Hooter Brown worked well with Gunner's preferred means of sustenance— Apalachicola Bay oysters. He took a sip of his beer and expanded on his answer. "They told me to push the aircraft, you know, to see what she'd do. So I did. And it fell apart."

"It's all over the news. The reporter said you tried to fly it to the moon and back. Dozen on the half shell?"

Gunner smiled and chuckled to himself. In a way, he supposed he had.

"Better make it two, Sammy. I threw up a lot yesterday from drinking all that salt water. My stomach is pretty empty."

Hart rapped his knuckles on the polished teak bar top and turned to one of the servers, who hovered nearby, to pass along the order. Gunner took a long swig of his beer and glanced at the television monitor that was mounted in the corner of the bar. CNN was providing continuous coverage of Comet Oort, which was a day away from making its closest approach to Earth.

"You wanna talk about it?" asked Hart when he returned to Gunner. He glanced past his only patron as three attractive college-age girls entered the restaurant. It was spring break, and nearby St. George Island was a popular destination for families and the occasional group of college students. Hart shot a glance at the only server on duty, who provided a knowing nod in return. During spring break, the Oyster City family of eateries was especially strict on checking identification to avoid serving someone underage.

"Hell, I don't know, Sammy, might as well. I'm supposed to be in the shrink's office right now for the mandatory post-crash convo, but the weather sucks, so I couldn't take the boat, and I don't feel like driving a hundred sixty miles in the rain, dodging drunk spring-breakers."

"I get it."

"Listen, the bottom line is they needed to know what this bird would do. I needed to know, for pilots like myself, whether it was combat ready. It needed to be pushed, so I did. It's not my fault it fell apart."

Gunner quickly dispatched his first beer and slid it toward his host. He reached into his pocket and tossed his debit card next to the glass so that Hart could begin running a tab.

The attentive bartender had already turned to pour another Hooter Brown and set it in front of Gunner. Then Hart pushed the debit card back toward him. "Not today, my friend. Never on this day."

Gunner took a big gulp of the beer, and a wash of sadness came over his face. He nodded his appreciation. "You remembered?"

"I'll never forget, Gunner. Never. I'm sor—"

Gunner raised his hand to cut him off. "Thanks, Sammy. I know."

Suddenly, the three young women began giggling, grabbing both men's attention. Gunner glanced over his shoulder and noticed one of them giving him the *come-hither* look. Seeing that he'd made eye contact, she sashayed over to the bar.

"Two more Corona Lights, please," she said, glancing through the liquor bottles mounted on glass shelving in the arched brick back wall in an attempt to catch sight of Gunner in the mirror. She was unsuccessful, thus missing Gunner's eye roll at her choice of beer.

Spring-breakers had no appreciation for a fine craft beer, such as Oyster City, which was brewed across the street. They bought into the corporate-created vision of the beach with swaying palm trees, turquoise blue waters, and the tanned pretty people drinking a Corona, the taste of which had to be obscured with the tartness of a lime just to make it palatable. And the salt. Don't forget the salt. Gunner often wondered why Corona drinkers didn't equate drinking their favorite beer with the downing of the harshest flavored liquor he'd ever tasted—tequila.

The young woman, who was attractive in a University of Alabama cheerleader sort of way, leaned over toward Gunner and asked, "Can I buy you a beer, sailor?"

Gunner ignored her, and Sammy quickly provided the requested Corona Lights and the obligatory limes. "He's Air Force, and today he needs some time alone. Is that cool?"

"But—" she began to protest as Sammy slid the beers closer to her.

"Anything else?" Sammy's tone of voice indicated his persistence.

"Um, no."

"I'll make sure that your server takes care of you from here on, okay?"

The girl shrugged and returned to her friends, who were having a playful argument over the vintage Atari *Asteroids* game that sat in the front corner of The Tap Room. The sound of them laughing and tapping on the console, destroying space saucers and asteroids in rapid succession, did little to distract Gunner from the weighty things on his mind.

CHAPTER 6

Monday, April 2
The Tap Room
Apalachicola, Florida

"Hey, Sammy, could you turn on the closed-captioning?" asked Gunner, pointing up to the television monitor. He was attempting to spin a cardboard coaster like a top on the bar, with little success.

"Sure. You want me to turn up the volume? I'd love to unplug *Asteroids*. Those three would complain, but their quota of Coronas is about there anyway."

"Nah, closed-captioning is fine." Gunner sipped on his third beer and focused on the news report. It was nearly noon and several more diners had entered The Tap Room. An older couple sat next to him at the bar and focused their attention on the television.

The older gentleman politely interrupted. "We wouldn't mind listening if that's okay. It's big news."

Gunner shrugged and Hart motioned to the server, instructing her to give the young ladies their last call. He slowly turned up the volume until the older man gave him a thumbs-up.

Thus far, Gunner hadn't paid that much attention to Comet Oort and its near-Earth approach. Sometimes, the hype in the media didn't match reality. It just gave them something to draw viewers, that in turn enabled them to sell more advertising time. If he needed to get straight talk on something like this, he had half a dozen people he could call at the Department of Defense or NASA.

The reporter stood in front of the Jet Propulsion Laboratory at CalTech in Pasadena. "*The night sky came alive last night as the world got its closest view to date of Comet Oort on its approach toward Earth. The comet first* came into view in February, but it has steadily brightened as the sun has illuminated its long tail. In two days, Comet Oort will make its closest approach to Earth and will be visible with the naked eye."

Late-morning CNN news anchor, Megyn Kelly, asked, "When you say closest approach, just how close will it come to us? I mean, are we in any danger?"

"Well, Megyn, to be sure, the prospect of a comet of this size coming directly for us is frightening. However, all of the trajectory projections show it passing half a million miles away. That's more than twice as far as it is from here to the Moon."

"What about the tail? The so-called debris field that scientists have discussed at great length. It is the longest on record. Is it possible that the tail could spin off meteors or anything like that?"

The reporter nodded his head, acknowledging the purpose of Kelly's question. "Megyn, this comet has come on quite a journey from the far reaches of our galaxy. As it rounded the Sun, Comet Oort and its debris field remained largely intact. The brightness, coupled with the direct approach, will make it visible, but does not make it a threat in any way."

The elderly coupled clinked their pints of beer. "Well, that certainly is good news. We've just started our vacation and it sure would be a shame to become extinct."

Hart laughed with his new customers. "The good news is that we have plenty of beer to last through the onslaught from the sky."

"Megyn, the Little Dipper is commonly looked upon as our brightest constellation, especially the handle. Comet Oort will easily surpass that level of intensity. Amateur astronomers have relished the opportunity to join their professional counterparts in following the path of this Great Comet, hosting parties around the Northern Hemisphere each night."

Kelly began to stack her notes on the desk in front of her and then asked another question. "I've tried to follow the comet using my husband's binoculars. I have to ask, why does it look so fuzzy and ghostly?"

"Comet Oort is about a mile across, with a core that is three-quarters of a mile wide. It's a little-known fact that comets, like our planet, have an atmosphere, commonly referred to as a coma. In the case of Comet Oort, its coma is bigger than Jupiter's. When its orbit took it around the Sun, the icy nature of *the comet necessarily resulted in some melting. That's what created the glowing green cloud."*

Kelly added, *"That also explains why it blocked out the rest of the night sky. It's as if the stars behind Comet Oort disappeared."*

The reporter shrugged. *"Yes, I suppose it does have a bit of a masking effect. Well, in any event, after it passes us in a few days, stargazers can begin to focus their attention on the rest of the universe after having experienced the celestial event of a lifetime."*

The report ended and CNN went to a commercial break. The elderly gentleman ordered another beer for himself and thanked Hart for turning up the television. The volume was lowered once again and he turned toward Gunner.

"What do you think about all of this, young man?" he asked.

Gunner finished off his beer and took a deep breath. Usually closed off, Gunner responded, "You know, it's kinda like a game of cosmic pinball. It's hard to fathom how large the universe is in comparison to our planet. Comets, asteroids, and meteors buzz by us all the time, and sometimes they hit. Fortunately, this one is likely to miss."

"So we've dodged a bullet?"

Gunner nodded and held his hand up to Hart, declining the offer of another beer. "Being struck by a comet or asteroid is what scientists call a *low-probability, high-consequence event.* That said, it's happened before and will likely happen again."

"And then what?" asked the man's wife.

Gunner chuckled and responded with a smile. "Well, ma'am, have you seen any dinosaurs roaming around?"

Hart joined the conversation. "You know what bothers me, especially with these meteors? They don't see 'em comin'. I mean, just the other day, there was an article about a meteor that whizzed by Earth, and they didn't discover it until the day before. What the heck are we supposed to do about that?"

"They can do a lot of damage, right?" asked the elderly man.

"Yes, they can," replied Gunner. "Technically speaking, they're meteorites if they strike Earth. Meteors enter the atmosphere and then burn up."

"They're smaller than an asteroid, right?" the woman asked. She'd ordered gator balls and dipped one into some cocktail sauce, but she kept her eyes focused on Gunner.

"Yes, ma'am. Asteroids are bigger than meteors and are made mostly of rock. Unlike the comet that's approaching Earth, which is made of chunks of ice and rock, followed by a tail, an asteroid just rocks along, pardon the pun, and remains unnoticed. They are the most difficult space object to track because they don't have the ice coma and tail. Well, most times, anyway."

The elderly man jutted out his lip and nodded his head. "You seem pretty knowledgeable about this stuff. Are you a scientist?"

Hart moved in and placed both palms on the bar. "Let me tell you about my friend."

"Oh no. Here we go," lamented Gunner as he sat back against the bar chair's back. He was in an unusually jovial mood, considering the circumstances. The beers, coupled with hanging out with his friend, took his mind off things.

"No, seriously. You won't brag on yourself, so somebody has to."

Gunner smiled and gestured for Hart to continue. At this point, two diners who'd been eavesdropping on the conversation picked up their drinks and sat at the bar to Gunner's right.

"Ladies and gentlemen," began Hart, adopting an announcer-like voice, "this here is Major Gunner Fox, United States Air Force and a genuine war hero. And he lives right here in our very own Franklin County."

"A war hero?" asked one of the late arrivals to the conversation.

"You betcha," replied Hart. "Gunner has flown military missions all over the world for our great nation. He's been shot down in combat more times than I can count. But not because he's a bad pilot. It's because it took three or four chasing his tail before they got him. Am I right, Gunner?"

"Maybe, but that's classified," he replied, having just enough beer in him to decide to play along on an otherwise solemn day. Gunner hadn't slept well the night before. His body was weak from the incessant vomiting. And, well, it was not a day to crack jokes. His favorite bartender, Sammy Hart, who had a better understanding of Gunner's psyche than any psychologist, had a way of dragging him out of the doldrums.

"Well, here's what's not classified," added Hart. "In addition to being ridiculously handsome, in a chiseled, taller-than-Tom-Cruise sort of way, as you can see, he's smart as a whip. He is, in fact, a scientist."

"An Earth scientist," interjected Gunner.

"Exactly," continued Hart. "This guy shoots down bad guys with the most technologically advanced aircraft in the world by day, and at night, he can tell you everything you ever wanted to know about the center of the Earth to the stars in the sky."

"That's a pretty nice résumé, Major," said the older gentleman. "Our son is a Navy pilot. He trained at NAS Fallon in Nevada."

"The new TOPGUN," said Gunner. "Impressive." Despite Gunner's disdain for the Navy's attempts to oversee the design and build of fighter jets, he had the utmost respect for their pilots.

"Yes, sir," added the gentleman. "The Strike Fighter Tactics program has come a long way since the days of carousing and barhopping in San Diego portrayed in the movie."

"It has," said Gunner. "I've flown sorties with some of their aviators. I've admired their capabilities."

"Sir," interrupted the middle-aged woman to Gunner's left. "What do you think about the jet fighter crash yesterday? Did you see that on the news?"

Gunner made eye contact and laughed. He almost spoke when Hart answered her question first.

"Ma'am, he is the news."

CHAPTER 7

Monday, April 2
NASA Symposium on Planetary Defense
Johns Hopkins University
Baltimore, Maryland

"Hollywood has it all wrong!" shouted one of the scientists from Johns Hopkins who was part of a roundtable symposium on comets and asteroids that was hastily called due to the timing of Comet Oort's near-Earth approach. "Especially as is relates to asteroids. They are considerably tougher and require a much greater force of energy to destroy than any of us have calculated."

She and another scientist had been engaged in a lively debate, much to the delight of the audience of college students and academics. Comet Oort had raised public awareness about the threat of near-Earth objects and was being used by NASA and the Jet Propulsion Laboratory to increase their budgets with Congress.

The other scientist countered her argument. "All of our experiments and simulations have produced consistent results. The larger the object, the more easily it would be to break apart because they are more likely to have flaws and inherent structural weaknesses. This makes our proposed deflection and diversion protocols more than adequate."

"I'm telling you, it won't work, based upon the data received from the exploration of Asteroid Bennu. The results of the OSIRIS-REx mission proved my point. You simply cannot assassinate an asteroid. It would be a fruitless exercise. And, even if you were able to split it apart, the gravitational pull will take over and draw it into a clump of ejected shards of rock."

Another scientist chimed in, joining the argument. "Rebuild itself? Really. Now who has a Hollywood mindset?"

"Yes, rebuild itself, and it's not science fiction or part of a Hollywood script. Bennu proves my theory."

The sole female scientist on the panel, a late entry into the symposium from the Jet Propulsion Laboratory, was adamant in her position.

OSIRIS-REx—an acronym for origins, spectral interpretation, resource identification, security, and regolith explorer—was a spacecraft that reached Bennu in December 2018. Bennu was of particular interest to scientists because of its composition, size, and proximity to Earth. It was a rare type of asteroid, primitive and carbon rich, that had traveled over a million miles on its close approach to our planet.

The spacecraft performed months of experiments, and the success encouraged other nations, such as the Japanese, to target other asteroids in order to compare their findings. At a recent Lunar and Planetary Sciences Conference, representatives from several nations who studied the materials returned to Earth expressed surprise at the composition of the samples.

For one thing, the surfaces of asteroids are much rockier than expected, but devoid of large boulders. Bennu, for example, had little in the way of smooth surfaces, such as pebbles or loose soil. Not only did this make landing on the asteroid difficult for OSIRIS-REx, but it revealed why Bennu, which was as tall and wide as the height of the Empire State Building, was one of the darkest objects ever studied in the solar system—reflecting only four percent of sunlight.

"Blasting it will prove to be ineffectual. Painting is the better option."

Several members of the audience snickered at the suggestion. The female scientist noticed the giggles and guffaws and quickly explained her theory.

"Listen, I understand the headlines will make me out to be a crackpot, but hear me out. The Chinese are developing laser technology. Some of you supported the orbital slingshot method to alter trajectories. We have DART, the Double Asteroid Redirection Test. Naturally, the Russians are experimenting with a three-megaton nuke that is a few thousand times more powerful than the bomb dropped on Hiroshima. Three megatons! What I propose to do is alter the surface of a threatening near-Earth object. Give it a makeover, so to speak."

"Paint?" asked one of the scientists.

"Yes," she replied. "Consider this. Even just painting the surface a different color on one half of the surface would change the thermal properties and eventually alter its orbit. We have the technology, more advanced than OSIRIS-REx, I might add, to send a spacecraft to intercept the asteroid in time to paint its surface. Then we let the Sun do the work for us."

Another scientist came to her defense. "She might have a point here, and frankly, we missed an opportunity while OSIRIS-REx was on Bennu. As we all know, Bennu has a one in twenty-seven hundred chance of hitting our planet in 2135. Naturally, we're not talking extinction level here, but the damage could be catastrophic wherever it makes contact. We should have given Bennu a coat of paint ten years ago."

The female scientist was anxious to finish her thought before the panel got off onto other subjects. "The bottom line is this. The Sun pelts everything in our solar system with tiny particles that exert a little bit of pressure on every celestial body, from planets down to meteors. Obviously, these particles are of no consequence to Earth because our planet is massive, but for an object the size of an asteroid, which will be far more susceptible to the Sun's radiation, it could alter the path just enough to avoid contact."

The panel fell silent for a moment until a voice from the center of the audience grabbed everyone's attention. "I applaud you all for searching for a solution and commend you for your outside-the-box thinking. All of your theories and studies apply to these asteroids of fairly large size. They're not the ones we need to worry about. The ones we need to fear are those that aren't tracked by NASA. The ones that are undiscovered. The ones that are too close for your paint or your slingshots or your lasers. You need the equivalent of a quick-reaction force, or one day you'll find yourself face-to-face with a planet killer."

CHAPTER 8

Gunner looked forward to his ride back to Eglin that morning. He'd received half-a-dozen phone messages from his superior officer's aide alone, not to mention numerous calls from his psychologist's office. The calls were pleasant at first, portending to understand the difficult day he had yesterday, but by evening, requests became demands for his presence. Nonetheless, despite the anticipated psychoanalyzing followed up by a trip to the woodshed for a proper beatdown by the base vice commander, Gunner was excited for a trip up the coast.

Walking down the dock that morning, just as the tide reached its highest point, he paused to take in the sunrise. The waters of St. George Sound were like glass, with barely a ripple of bait fish causing any type of movement. He imagined he could make the one-hundred-forty-mile trip in two hours without pushing his ride.

He untied the dock lines attached to his blue and white Donzi 41GT sport boat and slid into the bucket seat behind the console. He immediately brought the three Mercury Verado 400 engines to life, enjoying the roar of the supercharged outboards that produced a whopping twelve hundred horsepower. They could easily bring the forty-one-foot *go-fast boat* to a seventy-mile-per-hour cruising speed on the warm waters of the Gulf of Mexico.

He eased through *The Cut*, the narrow pass separating Dog Island from St. George Island out of respect for the oystermen who were making their way out of Apalachicola Bay for the day. At speed, the Donzi had little drag, but it was enough to send the oyster boats into an early-morning, unwelcomed rocking.

Gunner got settled into the powerboat's cockpit, which resembled a miniature version of the F/A XX he'd dumped in the Gulf two days prior. He wiggled his fingers before he gripped the throttle and forced it forward, causing the bow to raise slightly as the powerful engines began to turn the three propellers through the water. By the time he reached the lighthouse at the center of St. George Island, he'd planed out and settled in for a smooth trip up the coast to Eglin.

With the digital display registering seventy-five, Gunner did a quick check of the other instruments. He hadn't been on the water in over two weeks. Between commitments related to the disastrous test flight and a mission he'd flown in Venezuela on behalf of the CIA, he'd been away from Dog Island more than he'd been home.

There were only a handful of pilots like Gunner in the Air Force. He'd followed in his father's and grandfather's footsteps and joined the Air Force after college. Because of his pedigree and his advanced education, he was chosen as a candidate to the USAF Special Operations Forces, which fell under AFSOC—Air Force Special Operations Command.

With his father's encouragement, he'd followed a career path with the Air Force that landed him in a special ops squadron. Initially assigned to the 4th Special Operations Squadron based at Hurlburt Field near Pensacola, Gunner trained on a variety of AC-130 aircraft—a Lockheed-designed C-130 cargo plane converted into a killing machine, a gunship complete with firing ports housing an array of cannons, howitzers, and Gatling guns.

Gunner proved himself and soon was recruited into the fighter jet training school before being assigned to Eglin to fly the next-generation F-35 Lightning stealth fighters.

War had changed considerably since Vietnam and even the two Gulf Wars. International politics and fear of escalation of hostilities inserted themselves into the decision-making process. To be sure, neither the Russians nor the Chinese nor the Americans were interested in World War III. However, all three nations had their own geopolitical agendas.

For the Chinese, it was to limit, if not completely eliminate, U.S. interference in the Far East.

For the Russians, it was to bring rogue nations like Iran, Venezuela, Cuba, and Syria under their wing and take advantage of the resources or strategic locations they offered.

The U.S. fought a never-ending battle to limit the influence of their rivals, while trying to appease their allies and pacify Americans who had become war-weary after the years of fighting in the Middle East.

Conventional warfare had taken a backseat to cyber warfare, but in some instances, good old-fashioned boots on the ground with appropriate air support was a necessity. In an age of proxy wars, typically Moscow took the position of one side, namely a dictator or communist regime, and Washington supported the opposite side, oftentimes unorganized rebels or those who were attempting to install democratic governments.

As a result, the number of disavowed combat missions was on the rise, and Gunner had become their go-to guy in many cases. Not only was he one of their best fighter pilots, but he could handle himself in covert operations on the ground as well.

He was looked upon by his superiors as calm, ready, and competent. Capable. Yet he had his flaws.

Hence, one of the reasons he found himself pulling up to the dock at The Bayview, Eglin's equivalent of an officers' club, was to see the resident shrink. Located on Choctawhatchee Bay, social occasions at The Bayview included high-level parties with members of Congress and the cabinet—holders of the purse strings.

As Gunner pulled into an available slip, two uniformed military police hustled to greet him. A young, pimple-faced airman arrived right behind them and hurriedly helped Gunner tie off his boat.

"Good morning, Major Fox," the young man greeted him.

"Mornin', um ..." Gunner hesitated as he squinted through the sun to see the young man's rank. "Sergeant."

Gunner slipped off his Nautica jacket, revealing a pair of Levi's jeans and an untucked white polo shirt. He stepped off the boat and pretended to hand the keys to one of the MPs, who stood at attention, ignoring the attempt.

"Are you guys not valets? Or am I under arrest?"

The two MPs ignored Gunner and awaited the sergeant's response.

"Major, um, my apologies for the MPs. Colonel Tompkins is a little, shall I say, put out. He's ordered me to greet you with an escort so that, um, you make it to all of your required appointments."

The young man studied Gunner's attire and then added inquisitively, "Sir, you are aware that you'll be meeting in the vice commander's suite with Colonel Bradfield?"

"Yeah, so?" Gunner removed his Ray-Ban sunglasses and tucked them into the V-neck of his shirt.

"Yes, sir, adjacent to Brigadier General Dickson's office?"

"Yeah, I remember where it is."

The young man stammered as he continued. "Well, with all due respect, sir, um, I think they might have expected you to be in, well, at least your fatigues."

"Well, I guess they're out of luck," said Gunner. "I suppose we should get going. Let's not keep the doc waiting."

The young sergeant scrambled to catch up as Gunner strutted up the ramp toward the MPs' vehicle.

"We're already an hour late, sir."

"All the more reason to chop-chop, wouldn't you agree?"

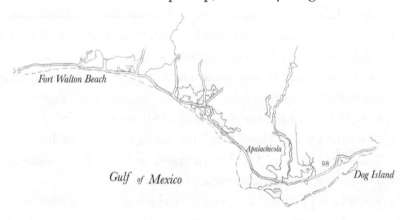

Fort Walton Beach

Apalachicola

Gulf of Mexico

Dog Island

CHAPTER 9

Tuesday, April 3
Director of Psychiatry's Office
Eglin Air Force Base

Gunner stared quietly out the rear passenger window as he was escorted by the base police to his meeting with Dr. Brian Dowling, the medical director of the Department of Psychiatry at Eglin. The day they retrieved Gunner from the Gulf, he had been medivacked to the 96th Medical Group Hospital for treatment.

The rough landing into the choppy waters didn't result in any broken bones, but he did ingest a lot of salt water while he floated haplessly awaiting rescue. His flight suit had a tracking beacon, as did his parachute. Despite the technology, it took Eglin's recovery team several hours to locate Gunner because he'd drifted so far east due to the stiff upper-level winds he'd endured during his descent from the troposphere.

Incredibly, he never blacked out during the entire ordeal, and as a result, he had been coherent when he was being examined in the small three-bed intensive care unit. This enabled him to speak briefly with Dr. Dowling, who cleared his release from the hospital under the condition that he travel to the base the next day. Of course, Gunner never showed up, drawing the ire of his superiors and Dr. Dowling.

Gunner entered the psychiatrist's office, something he'd done dozens of times in the past few years. The two were very familiar with one another. Gunner, who had become closed off, was the epitome of a man of few words when he was in the presence of Dr. Dowling. He didn't like to *share his feelings*. He didn't want to *talk about it.* He had no interest in *opening up* or *letting his walls down.* He just wanted the hour-long session to be over so that he could go about his business and be left alone. Today, he expected his tortoise-in-a-shell approach wouldn't be tolerated, so he prepared himself to *share.*

"Good morning, Major. Take a seat." Dr. Dowling's demeanor was standoffish. Gunner sensed the hostility immediately. His résumé was impressive and, frankly, exactly what Gunner needed, if he'd allow the man to do his job. The highly respected psychiatrist was a professor emeritus at Johns Hopkins and a past medical director of psychiatry at Walter Reed Medical Center. He'd been interviewed on television numerous times on the issue of post-traumatic stress.

He'd also conducted significant research on traumatic brain injuries, something applicable to Gunner due to the numerous concussions he'd suffered while in combat situations. Gunner once quipped that concussions were a way of life for someone who fell out of airplanes from time to time.

Gunner decided to take a different approach this morning, one that would confound and befuddle the good doctor, and quite possibly keep him from getting grounded. He decided to play *Chatty Cathy.*

"Good morning to you, Doc," he began with a smile, glancing down at the desk as Dr. Dowling turned on his desktop tape recorder, a common practice during their sessions and one of the reasons Gunner didn't *talk about it.* He took a seat across from the psychiatrist's desk, and instead of crossing his arms in his customary closed-off position, he leaned forward and rested his elbows on the man's desk. "I feel a whole lot better than when I saw you in the ER."

"I'm sure you do, Major," Dr. Dowling responded dryly as he wrote some notes in a journal. Without looking up, he asked, "What happened to you yesterday?"

"Yeah, about that. Listen, you know they shot me up with painkillers, and when I got home, I turned all the ringers on the phones to mute so I could get some rest. It was a long trip back to Earth for me and I was worn out. The good news is I slept all day. I really apologize for missing my appointment."

Dr. Dowling's glasses rested on the end of his nose, but his eyes peered over the top. Gunner had assessed the doctor's bullshit meter in the past and knew what he could get away with. Today he'd be pushing the boundaries of their relationship, but it was a game worth playing.

"Understandable, Major. Now, let's talk about what happened."

"Sure, let's. Doc, I admit that I went a little bit off the reservation Sunday. It was purely a misunderstanding on my part."

Gunner hesitated, as he wanted to be careful with his words. Dr. Dowling would most likely call the colonel as soon as his patient walked out the door and across the compound to the administration building. By the time he stepped into the colonel's office, she'd have a complete rundown on Gunner's story.

"Misunderstanding?" asked the doctor.

"Okay, let me be perfectly honest here," Gunner lied as he leaned forward some more. "I don't want to cast blame, but perhaps *miscommunication* is a better word for it. You know, the suits and pilots don't always speak the same language. Certain words to them, obviously made in jest, might mean something entirely different to a fighter pilot."

Gunner paused again and provided himself some kudos. He was pretty good at this Chatty Cathy game.

"For example?" asked Dr. Dowling, who'd suddenly assumed the role of the closed-off party in this *tête-à-tête*.

"Well, you see, Doc, the suits told me to push her. You know, see what she's got. That sort of thing. Now, I applied that type of directive to what I know of real-life combat scenarios, one, in fact, that I've been personally involved in. So, as instructed, I drew upon my own experiences and I pushed the F/A XX into the same scenario."

"A direct, vertical ascent into the stratosphere at Mach 3?"

"Yup."

"And you consider that real-life?"

"The Chinese can do it. And they did, right off the coast of the

Philippines. You see, Doc, I felt like the nice people at Boeing needed to know what their aircraft was, and was not, capable of. So I pushed her, just as instructed."

Dr. Dowling leaned back in his chair and removed his glasses. He scowled at Gunner and slowly began to clap. "Bravo, Major! That was an incredible performance. Did they teach you that crap in SERE school at Fairchild?" The US Air Force version of SERE school—an acronym for survival, evasion, resistance, and escape—was conducted at Fairchild Air Force Base near Spokane, Washington.

Gunner's face turned white as he was unable to keep up the façade. "No, seriously, Doc. That's how it happened. It was all a misunderstanding. I just did what I thought they—"

"Major," Dr. Dowling interrupted Gunner's stammering, "why did you turn off your comms before you performed this stunt?"

Damn. Forgot about that.

"Well, I didn't want to be distracted, you know, by a bunch of ground chatter. In a real-time sortie, you wouldn't have a bunch of people yelling in your ears while you're chasing a J-20 in the sky."

Dr. Dowling allowed a smile and leaned forward to turn off the recording device. "Major, once in a while, this old psych doctor has a brain fart and forgets to turn on this machine. Today happens to be one of those days. Do we understand one another?"

Gunner craned his neck to confirm that the recording had ended. He made eye contact with Dr. Dowling and nodded. "Understood."

"I like you, Gunner. You're probably one of the best fighter pilots in the Air Force. You are also highly educated and very astute. But we both know there are issues for you to overcome, and after all this time, today I intend to change the dynamic of our relationship."

"What do you mean?"

"Gunner, I think you need a friend. Someone you can talk to besides your father or Sammy Hart, your bartender, or—"

"You know Sammy?"

Dr. Dowling reached into a desk drawer to his right and pulled out a three-inch-thick file. He plopped it in front of Gunner. It was marked classified and had his name and current deployment stamped on the front cover.

"That's my file?"

"Yes, and you'll see that I've had an opportunity to speak with your bartender and several others in the Apalachicola community. Naturally, nobody knew who I was or why I was asking about you, but all the notes of my encounters are contained in this file."

"Why? Why would you go through all of that for me?"

Dr. Dowling took a deep breath and exhaled. He leaned back in his tufted leather chair and clasped his fingers together across his slightly protruding belly. "Gunner, you are a tremendous asset to the Air Force and our country. An asset, a human asset, that is worth saving and not discarding. I'll be honest, there are many who wanted to push you into retirement. *He can get a commercial airlines job*, they said. Or, *we'll get him placed with a defense contractor where his expertise can help us down the road.*"

"What?" Gunner was genuinely astonished and confused.

"Gunner, they thought you were done. Mentally unfit. Is that clear enough?"

Gunner was growing angry. "Hey, there's nothing wrong with my mind. I'm good to go. I always have been!"

"I'm telling you that there were folks in the Department of Defense who wanted you out, and I've made sure that you've stayed in. Our sessions, the ones where you clam up or refuse to let me help you, have been portrayed as making great progress. Even though what happened Sunday is beginning to make me wonder."

Gunner sat back in his chair and crossed his arms. The unconscious gesture lasted only a moment, when he realized what he'd done. He quickly sat up and rested his hands in his lap. "Look. I admit I've been through some tough times, but I've always responded to the call of duty. The people in Washington don't know what—"

"Gunner, don't worry about them for now," said Dr. Dowling as he checked his watch. "We'll save that for another day. For right now, we've got to get you prepared to meet with the colonel. I've gotta tell ya, she's got smoke coming out of her ears over this. Your no-show yesterday didn't help."

"Is she gonna ground me? Or worse?"

"Not if you're careful with your words. Gunner, I need a promise from you. A commitment."

"Go ahead."

"Let me help you through this. I swear you'll be glad you worked with me."

"Kinda like a pet project."

Dr. Dowling laughed. "Yeah, if you want to call it that. You've got to be open and honest with me. After what I've disclosed to you today, I believe I've earned your trust. Can you reciprocate?"

Gunner grimaced and then smiled. "Yes, Doc. I can. Thank you."

"Okay, good. Now, let me coach you through the ass-reaming you're about to get from Colonel Bradford."

CHAPTER 10

Tuesday, April 3
Colonel Joanne Bradford's Office
Base Administration Building
Eglin Air Force Base

Gunner slowly walked from the medical facility across the large grassy compound, with his two military policemen in tow. Base personnel, some in civilian dress and others in Air Force fatigues, shuffled about, delivering paperwork or going from one meeting to the next. One of the things that Gunner had learned about the military in his ten years in service was that there were far more administrative paper pushers and meeting-goers than there were soldiers. He understood there was a need for support personnel, but there was also a greater need for airmen, sailors, soldiers, and Marines.

Before Gunner left, Dr. Dowling reminded him that the Air Force was experiencing a shortage of pilots, and that was one of the safeguards protecting him from being forced into retirement at the young age of thirty-five.

A dire report was issued in 2021 that the Air Force needed to recruit and train over two thousand pilots. The requirements were high and the training was stringent. The Air Force Major Command told Congress it needed twenty thousand pilots between active duty, the Air National Guard, and reservists.

The biggest challenge for the Air Force and the DOD was that nearly thirty thousand civilian pilots were due to retire from the commercial airlines by 2030, leading to a talent grab between the industry and the military. The largely unionized civilian pilot pool offered salary opportunities that the military couldn't compete with.

Further, Air Force pilots didn't just spring up out of flight simulators. There was a process of undergraduate training, or UPT, followed by a more flight-oriented training process before being absorbed into operational, combat-ready squadrons. For years, the Air Force was only capable of graduating fourteen hundred pilots through UPT in a given year. That didn't keep up with their attrition rates due to retirement and lack of reenlistment as pilots sought greener pastures in commercial aviation.

The fighter pilots who remained in the Air Force did so because of their commitment and dedication to their service, coupled with love of country. In a word, they were *hard-core*, like Gunner.

"The colonel will see you now, sir," said an airman who exited Colonel Bradford's office. He stood to the side and gestured for Gunner to enter.

Gunner had a good relationship with his superior officer, one that dated back to his arrival at Eglin. Colonel Bradford had risen through the ranks, taking advantage of career advancement opportunities that presented themselves until she became the second in charge at Eglin behind Brigadier General Harrison James. With James nearing retirement in the near future, it was assumed that Colonel Bradford, who had been taking on more of his duties in recent months, would be the logical replacement. She stood to be the first female base commander at Eglin.

Gunner, despite being inappropriately dressed, a mistake he regretted following his conversation with Dr. Dowling, still offered his superior officer a snappy salute, which she returned.

Colonel Bradford was hard to read, a trait that suited someone at her level of command. Gunner, who was a major, was in line to become a colonel at some point, but his career path was not suited for administrative duties. He'd always be assigned a combat role or, as the last several years had shown, special operations missions that would always be considered *extraordinary*.

"Have a seat, Major."

As advised by Dr. Dowling, Gunner canned the *Chatty Cathy*

routine and stuck to what he knew best—keep his mouth shut and his opinions, and other forms of nonsense, to himself.

Gunner sat, but Colonel Bradford remained standing and immediately began wandering her office, ultimately stopping in front of a large window overlooking the entrance to the administration building.

"Where should I start?" she began with a hint of snark in her voice. "Your treatment of the Boeing civvies on the tarmac? The out-of-this-world climb that was completely outside of the project's protocols? Failing to show up for the mandatory postflight psych eval? Reporting to my office in blue jeans, an untucked golf shirt, and sneakers?" She spun around and glared at him, her glare demanding a response.

Gunner tried. He really tried to check himself. He'd heard the admonishments of Dr. Dowling. The honest advice that would most likely keep him in the game. But, somehow, the words came out without a filter.

"Well, Colonel, let's start with the fact that I'm still alive. That's a good thing, at least as far as I'm concerned. But, more importantly, do you wanna know what I think about the bird?"

Colonel Bradford looked toward the ceiling and then back to Gunner. She shook her head in disbelief. "Major, you can't charm your way out of this one. I don't do charm, and you know that."

"I'm not being charming, Colonel. The fact is that the F/A XX has great potential, but it still can't stack up with the J-20 and the Su-35S. If it can't make that climb, it won't be able to chase their bogies out of our airspace, and most importantly, our guys won't be able to outmaneuver them when we're in theirs."

"That's beside the point, Major. That stunt. And, make no mistake, it was a stunt. Everyone from the representatives at Boeing to Senator Gaetz, who ripped me a new one on the phone yesterday, wants to know why you destroyed their hundred-and-eleven-billion-dollar aircraft."

"Colonel, I didn't destroy that bird; it fell apart at the seams. It's got the kind of category 1 problems that plagued the F-35 variants years ago. Don't get me wrong. It performed as expected, until I asked it to do what our pilots need it to do. Otherwise, it's just another version of the F-35s we've been flying for decades, only with more whistles and bells and a fancy coat of paint." In military parlance, a *category* 1 flaw in a plane could prevent a pilot from accomplishing a mission.

Colonel Bradford sat down across from Gunner. She studied him intently for a moment and then asked, "Major, do you have a death wish? Look at me. No BS, Fox. Do you wanna die? Because you probably should have yesterday."

She opened a file folder that sat on her desk. Gunner's eyes quickly glanced at the letterhead from Dr. Dowling's office.

"No, ma'am, I do not want to die. Nor do I want a fellow fighter pilot to die because they think they can rely upon a newfangled jet that can't perform when they need it."

Colonel Bradford stuck out her chin and nodded. "I've always admired your capabilities, Major. I've been in your corner from the moment you volunteered to be a test pilot. I pushed for your expedited training at Maxwell. I made sure you were inserted into Test Pilot School ahead of other candidates. And, until now, the feedback you've given the Air Force and the defense contractors has been invaluable."

"Yes, ma'am, and I hope to continue."

She sighed and let go of the memo, allowing it to remain in plain view for Gunner to glance at. "I have to explain to Boeing, and Congress, why there are millions of dollars of scrap metal strewn across the Gulf of Mexico. They're looking for a scapegoat, as you can imagine."

Gunner remained silent. He wanted to know why they built an aircraft that almost got him killed, but he was following Dr. Dowling's orders to keep quiet, finally.

Colonel Bradford took a deep breath and rendered her judgment. "I'll deal with Senator Gaetz and Boeing. My concern is where do we go from here. For now, you're grounded."

"But, Colonel—" Gunner began to protest before she held her

hand up to stop him.

"Wait, Major, I'm not finished. By grounded, I mean no test flights until you go through FFD evals with Dr. Dowling." Fitness for duty evaluations were required in two basic situations in which it's determined that a soldier might be considered a danger to the well-being of himself or others, or if their actions were deemed detrimental to the efficiency or general atmosphere of their unit.

Sometimes, military personnel exhibit problematic behavioral conditions, including substance abuse, peculiar conduct, or suicidal tendencies. Other times, serious medical conditions arise that interfere with their duties. Either way, a psychiatrist or licensed psychologist conducts an extensive evaluation to determine if the individual was fit for duty.

Gunner feigned surprise and dismay at her conditions, but he'd actually been given a heads-up by Dr. Dowling that this would be required of him. It was part of the commitment that Gunner had made earlier.

"I understand, Colonel," said Gunner.

"Now, that said, you're to remain on the call list because, as you know, the world is a dangerous place and you have many talents of use to our nation. Be ready, Major Fox, because you never know when that call will come through."

Gunner took that as his cue to be dismissed. He stood at attention, snapped a salute, and thanked the colonel for being fair with him. Minutes later, he was walking across the compound, relieved to be without his military police escort, and still employed, but contemplating how he was going to get back to his boat.

CHAPTER 11

Wednesday, April 4
The News-Reporter
Serving Wilkes County since 1896
Washington, Georgia

TRAGEDY STRIKES WASHINGTON-WILKES

Tragedy has struck the Washington-Wilkes community as the bodies of four local teenagers were found pinned under the wreckage of a one-car accident in Reedy Creek. The Georgia Highway Patrol has confirmed that the driver and all three passengers, one male and two females, were killed in the accident that took place off a bridge overpass on Lundberg Road. Names of the victims are being withheld at this time pending identification of the bodies and notification of next of kin.

According to investigative reports and eyewitness statements, the group of teens were seen driving at a high rate of speed northbound on Lundberg Road in a late-model Dodge Challenger. One driver reported that the vehicle had been seen swerving in the dangerous, wet road conditions.

From police reports, a portion of guardrail was demolished and part of the concrete bridge railing was knocked down where it was struck by the vehicle. Then, according to the statement of one rescue worker, the vehicle severed the tops of several trees before crashing through branches that were unable to arrest their fall. When the vehicle landed on its roof at the bottom of the ravine, the victims either died from the impact or by drowning in the swift-moving waters of a swelled Reedy Creek due to the recent heavy rains. Reportedly, one of the teens had been decapitated.

Investigators are now attempting to retrace the whereabouts of the teenagers Sunday night in order to determine what caused this terrible tragedy. Alcohol was believed to be involved.

CHAPTER 12

Wednesday, April 4
Deerlick Astronomy Village
Crawfordville, Georgia

Jackie Holcomb couldn't stop sobbing when she heard the news. The investigators from the Georgia State Police had come around Tuesday morning after the vehicle was found and the tags showed it was owned by the parents of Nate Phillips. Nate's parents told the investigators that he was supposed to have gone to Deerlick that evening, but they hadn't been in touch with him until they became concerned about his whereabouts. His father had come by twice, checked their building on the property that contained Nate's telescope, and left. The third visit came from the police.

Jackie had received a call from Nate's mother earlier, who asked her to secure his telescope and other property until they could muster the will to pick it up. Jackie felt horrible for the Phillips family, having suffered a similar tragedy when her nephew died in a horrific car accident on Interstate 20 in nearby Thomson.

She entered the small cabin, which was nothing more than an uninsulated storage building that had been bought from a local Mennonite community and dropped into place off a flatbed trailer. It had a covered front porch, giving it a cabin-like appearance, and the roof had been modified to allow Nate's telescope to protrude through without allowing rain or other moisture to penetrate the roof.

A small desk in the middle of the room contained Nate's things, namely his Apple MacBook computer and several Air Force Airman's Journals bearing the logo that read *Aim High – Fly – Fight – Win.*

Jackie knew that Nate had had great things ahead of him, and his fascination with the stars would likely have landed him a career in the Air Force or with NASA. Now, that had all been wiped away in a single, horrific accident.

Jackie wiped the last of her tears from her eyes and exhaled. She felt like she was intruding, taking a peek into the young man's soul without permission. He was a good kid and didn't deserve to die.

After gathering herself, Jackie, a seasoned astronomer in her own right, studied Nate's equipment. She noticed the red light flashing on the astroimaging camera attached to the EDGEHD. This piqued her curiosity, so she touched the space bar on the MacBook, which had entered sleep mode. The display immediately responded and revealed the app Nate was using to record his view of the skies.

She studied the recording and then glanced through the eyepiece, which revealed a clear view of Comet Oort's enormous tail. She furrowed her brow and glanced at the footage. She contemplated stopping the recording, but then she queried why Nate would set up the recording in the first place. In a whisper, as if out of reverence for the dead, she spoke her thoughts aloud.

"If I can go back to the time the recording was first established, I might provide the investigators some insight as to when Nate and his friends were here last."

Jackie stopped the recording and settled into Nate's chair, pulling the MacBook close to the edge of the desk. The smell of stale beer caught her nostrils and she searched for the source. As she turned in her chair, her legs swung into two empty cans that were sent rolling around under the desk. Disgusted by the smell of the alcohol, and the fact that it had likely led to the kids' deaths, she angrily kicked the cans across the small space until they caromed off the plywood and two-by-four wall.

With a sigh, and a slight sense of relief from being able to work out a little frustration, Jackie turned back to Nate's computer. With her telescope rig, she employed the same application that he used, and was familiar with its processes. First, she saved the footage to the MacBook's hard drive. Then, in case there was a failure of the hard drive for some reason, she sent herself a copy via Apple's AirDrop, a service available to transfer files among Macintosh and iOS devices.

She started the video and made a mental note of the time stamp to provide to investigators. Naturally, she'd let them draw their own conclusions, but she presumed this was the approximate time that Nate and his friends had left the DAV.

The next several minutes changed Jackie Holcomb's life. She watched and her eyes grew in astonishment. She rewound the video countless times, frantically trying to control her fingers to make the proper keystrokes as she took raw screenshots with no additional markings, and then recreated the same screenshots, marking an area in the sky that caused her heart to leap out of her chest.

For an hour, she took more and more screenshots: some clean copies, others with circles and arrows and approximate lines of trajectory.

Periodically, she stood and walked around Nate's building, wiping sweat off her brow and messing with her hair. She would glance out the single window from time to time, wondering if anyone knew she was there.

She talked to herself, sometimes in silence, and when she assured herself that she was alone at the DAV for the moment, her words poured out in a burst of excitement.

"What am I supposed to do with this? My calculations are rough, nothing like what they'll do at the MPC."

Then her mind found its way back to Nate. *Had he seen what she'd discovered? Is that why he chose to record the event? But why would he leave? Was he too drunk to comprehend the magnitude of what he'd found?*

"My God," she muttered as she fell back into the chair, staring at the laptop one final time before she closed it up and fled the cabin. "What in the hell am I supposed to do now?"

CHAPTER 13

Wednesday, April 4
The News-Reporter
Washington, Georgia

Jackie Holcomb raced out of Nate's cabin with the deceased young man's MacBook tucked under her arm. She nervously surveyed the DAV to see if any residents were stirring at that early hour. The majority of the lots sold within the planned unit development were to researchers who lived throughout the southeast, but there were at least a dozen full-time residents living in cabins and RVs alike. For the most part, her fellow astronomers were late sleepers because they were night owls by nature.

Jackie was a longtime resident of nearby Washington, Georgia, where she grew up as a child before going to college at the University of Georgia in Athens, about an hour away. Like most kids in Wilkes County who didn't see any career opportunities in the area, Jackie had set out to find a better life in larger metropolitan areas like Atlanta and Charlotte. Eventually, however, the adventurous kids of Washington returned to their familiar, more laid-back stomping grounds.

One of Jackie's best friends growing up was Sparky Newsome, a fixture in Washington-Wilkes, a common way of referring to the residents of Washington and Wilkes County, whose population hovered around ten thousand. The Newsome family had owned the local newspaper—the *News-Reporter*—for over six decades.

Sparky had been born into the newspaper business and spent his days as a kid napping on the stacks of virgin newsprint that were delivered in sheets, not rolls. A good student as a child, he was destined to be a writer but fell in love with the mechanical side of the newspaper business. His parents encouraged him to publish articles, and in an attempt to please them, he obliged. But his real passion was bringing the stories to print.

The *News-Reporter*, now a weekly publication in both print and digital editions, had been founded in 1896. The longevity of the newspaper befitted a town where time stood still. Fortunate to be bypassed by Union General William Tecumseh Sherman's pillaging rampage across Georgia from Atlanta to Savannah, the Washington community boasted more antebellum homes still standing than any city of its size in the state.

As she drove up Lundberg Road, more tears came to her eyes as she followed the same fateful stretch of backcountry highway that Nate Phillips and his friends had driven until their deaths. The bridge across Reedy Creek had reopened, although the right side of the highway was clearly cordoned off with POLICE: DO NOT CROSS caution tape.

Her mind had wandered so much during the drive to Washington that when she came upon South Alexander Avenue, she could hardly remember driving from Deerlick. She drove slowly as she entered the historic district of Washington, never tiring of the beautiful architecture and the historic nature of the homes.

On her right was Holly Court, constructed in 1840, known as the last refuge of Varina Davis, the wife of Jefferson Davis, the president of the Confederacy. While President Davis met with members of his cabinet for the last time in the nearby Georgia State Bank Building during the final days of the Civil War, Mrs. Davis was kept safe from Union troops, who were searching for her husband.

Jackie turned by the post office and parked in front of Rider House, the home of Sparky Newsome and his wife, who operated the newspaper out of the rear portion of their home. The days of the printing press were long gone, and when the Newsomes moved the paper from the twelve-thousand-square-foot facility they'd occupied since the seventies, the computers made the trip and the antiquated printing equipment was dispersed elsewhere.

Sparky sat in a rocking chair on the front porch of their restored Victorian home beautifully adorned with period architecture and a white picket fence. He noticed Jackie's approach and bounded down the inlaid-brick entry steps to greet her.

The two were in frequent contact with one another, as Deerlick advertised in the paper and held events that Sparky was happy to promote. Despite that, Jackie couldn't hold back her emotions as she provided her old friend an emotional hug, coupled with a few more tears.

"Jackie, what's wrong?" Sparky began, pulling away slightly to study her. "Nate was a good kid. It's a shame, but—"

"It's not just about Nate," she interrupted, looking nervously about. There was little activity at the post office, and the fire department was devoid of activity. It was a typical, sleepy morning in Washington. "I've found, um, I mean, Nate may have stumbled upon …" Her voice trailed off.

"Come on, let's go inside and talk." Sparky put his arm around her and led her inside. His wife, Mary, had put on a pot of coffee and laid out a variety of pastries for them to munch on.

"Hi, Jackie," Mary greeted her and the two hugged. "You two look like you've got some serious stuff to talk about, and I need to make sure the print editions are ready to distribute. I'll be in the office if you need me, okay?"

Sparky kissed his wife and thanked her. He led Jackie to a settee that had been in the Newsome family for generations, having been reupholstered due to wear and tear. He took up a seat on a broken-in leather chair across from the spread of pastries served up by his wife.

"Sparky, I don't wanna rehash how I came upon this," she began, tapping the top of the MacBook. "It belongs to Nate and I found it in his cabin while making sure everything was locked up."

"Okay," said Sparky, allowing the word to draw out, as he was unsure where this conversation was going. A teenage boy's laptop could contain any number of things, some extremely embarrassing to the young man's family.

Jackie took a deep breath and regained her composure. She

reached for a scone and dipped it into a cup of coffee Sparky had poured for her. She took a bite of the biscuit-like cake, washed it down with the hot, black brew, and began.

"The night the kids died, they were at Nate's cabin at the DAV. He, like everyone else who cares about astronomy, was studying Comet Oort as it came into full view for the first time. I know this because his telescope was set toward the sky where the comet's tail was in full point of view, and he'd set his camera to record."

Sparky concentrated as Jackie found the words. He'd learned from a lifetime of being around the newspaper business that you should listen first, question later.

After catching her breath, she continued. "Anyway, I thought it would be helpful to the police to know when the recording started, as that might determine when he was at DAV last. Sparky, I watched the video. I'm about to show you something that to the untrained eye wouldn't be seen. Please bear with me as I go through this."

Jackie opened up the laptop and started the video file she'd created that played Nate's recording in real time, supplemented by slow-motion and screenshot images pointing out what she'd found.

"Do you see what I've circled here and then here?" asked Jackie, pointing to the screen.

Sparky pushed his glasses up on his nose and squinted. He leaned toward the MacBook's screen and nodded. "I do. Is that part of the comet's tail? I mean, did it break off or decide to go off on its own?"

Jackie leaned back against the settee. "No, it's not part of the comet. It's something else, and it's headed right for us."

CHAPTER 14

Wednesday, April 4
The News-Reporter
Washington, Georgia

"Jackie, I was never a stargazer. Can you help me out here?"

"Sparky, everyone's eyes have been focused on Comet Oort. It's one of the brightest comets in recorded history, and its tail is incredibly long. But here's what else it's done despite capturing the attention of the world. The comet, its halo, and the thirty-degree tail have obscured an asteroid, one that is large, fast, and sporting a tail of its own."

"Wait, I'm no expert, but I didn't think that asteroids had tails. I know it's been a tough couple of days, but are you——?"

Jackie shook her head violently. "No. No. This is not some emotional breakdown, Sparky. Give me a break. Look at these images. Here, like this enlarged one."

She ran her finger across the touchscreen on the MacBook and swiped through the video until a close-up view of the asteroid appeared.

"I see what you mean. How do you know it's big?"

"Based upon its distance from Earth, I wouldn't be able to see it if it was under three or four hundred feet across. And there's more. I've done the calculations, Sparky. It's on a trajectory that could hit Earth."

"Calculations? Jackie, you know me. I believe in Joseph Pulitzer's motto—accuracy, accuracy, accuracy, and thoroughness. If you want me to take this story to——"

"No, not yet. I mean, I'm not sure what the best thing to do is.

That's why I'm here. I need your advice as a friend, not just a journalist."

"Okay, talk to me."

"It's all calculated guesswork right now. There are certain protocols that astronomers are required to follow, namely reaching out to the IAU MPC at the Smithsonian Astrophysical Observatory."

"Good grief, what's with the letters?"

"Um, sorry. International Astronomical Union Minor Planet Center."

Sparky laughed. "That's a mouthful."

"Well, newsboy, now you see why I used the acronym. MPC is all you need to know for now. The MPC is responsible for the designation of minor bodies in the solar system, like comets, natural satellites, you know, moons, and of course, asteroids."

Sparky stood and wandered around his living room. He was trying to digest all of this in order to help his friend. "Jackie, why is this important? Just call them or whatever."

"Because, and this is gonna sound callous, selfish, and any other rude names you might wanna call me, but if Comet Oort is a once-in-a-lifetime celestial event, the arrival of this asteroid will be a once-in-a-sixty-million-year event. There's gonna be a lot of pressure within the scientific community to study this thing, and naturally, they're gonna attribute this discovery to someone. I have to decide if I give the credit to Nate or take it for myself."

Sparky stopped pacing and swung around to Jackie. "Listen, if what you say is true, isn't that kind of a minor issue at this point. I mean, if it's half a mile wide or more, it could destroy a city."

"No, Sparky. It could destroy more than that. It might destroy us all."

"Then you need to tell somebody. Or do you want me to reach out to my news resources?" Sparky paused and then adopted a sarcastic tone. "Obviously, this is too big to put in next Wednesday's online edition of the paper."

Jackie was still all business. "You're right. This needs to be brought to the attention of the MPC. It would be a fitting tribute to

Nate for it to be named after him, but, Sparky, I mean, there is a possibility for some financial gain for me and, you know."

"I get it, you wanna protect your ability to become famous while possibly making a few bucks. Listen, when I take this story to a bigger news source, I'll want to maintain some semblance of control over the information they disseminate. Like you, I want to keep a handle on things in the event there is some notoriety to be had, or financial gain for us."

Sparky paused and began to rub his temples with both hands as he tried to mentally process this discovery. He continued.

"But, Jackie, hours matter, am I right?"

Jackie nodded and quickly closed the MacBook. "I need to get home and analyze this again to be sure. As soon as I can, I'm going to email you everything I have, and I plan on summarizing the implications of all of this for you. First thing in the morning, I'll contact the MPC."

"Are you going to ask for it to be designated after you or Nate?"

"Normally, the IAU assigns a number and, if it is a near-Earth object like this one, oftentimes the name is chosen from mythology. It usually isn't awarded a name until it has been observed long enough to analyze its orbit with precision. Sometimes that takes years."

"Years? But you said—"

"I know. A few weeks, Sparky, at best."

CHAPTER 15

Wednesday, April 4
NASA Mission Control
Johnson Space Center
Houston, Texas

The U.S. Commander of the International Space Station checked in with Mission Control's director, Mark Foster. Foster had been at this post for nearly five years, shepherding the NASA astronauts during a strained but working relationship with the other occupants of the ISS, namely the Russian cosmonauts.

"Houston, we'll be taking some time as a crew to download the most recent VPS updates."

Foster, who'd been on the floor of the FCR-1 at the time of the tragedy aboard the space station three years ago, was intimately involved in the events and the communications protocols established afterwards. The U.S. commander hadn't initiated a VPS communiqué in over a year.

"Roger that, Commander."

As if to reiterate the importance of the commander's message to the team monitoring the ISS on the ground, Foster raced up and down the aisles created between the four rows of computer consoles, making a slicing motion across his neck indicating they should cut off any unnecessary chatter. Foster trusted no one and had his suspicions about the cyber warfare capabilities of Moscow.

To the Russians and any of the other international space agencies participating in the ISS project, VPS meant voice protocol systems, something that the Russians had initiated and the Americans copied after the extended communications blackout on that fateful day.

However, to the DOD and NASA, VPS meant *vix parvam stillam*, a Latin phrase meaning *whisper*. The DOD, in conjunction with advice from the Central Intelligence Agency, had created a communications system that could not be infiltrated by their Russian counterparts. It required vocal communications over a secured, encrypted communications system and could only be used in quick sixty-second increments to avoid being detected.

NASA's ISS personnel had been trained in the importance of keeping this technology away from the Russians in particular and were also schooled in when it was appropriate to utilize the VPS protocols, and how.

Director Foster raced to his office and settled in behind his desk. He immediately grabbed a pad of paper to begin taking notes. He nervously twirled his pen, awaiting the secured transceiver to buzz to life.

The commander's voice was urgent, yet robotic. "Urgent for NEOCam or PanSTARRS. Inbound. Ascension, declination, elongation, and delta to follow. Possible mile-wide asteroid with debris field. Repeat, asteroid with debris field."

The commander finished the communication with a series of numbers that represented various measurements provided in astronomical units. An AU is approximately equal to the distance from the Earth to the Sun, or ninety-three million miles. So a distance shown as 1 AU is ninety-three million miles from Earth, and 0.1 AU is a little over nine million miles away.

Director Foster wrote down the values provided by the commander, and then the final numbers he provided were the nominal distance and the velocity in miles per hour.

"Nominal distance is zero-point-three-one AU. Projected relative velocity is twenty-seven kilometers per second. Transmission terminated."

Although the commander still had fifteen seconds or more to spare, the information he provided was all Director Foster needed for the blood to rush out of his face.

He scribbled the notes down and then he began to do the math.

At first, he thought the commander had provided him the incorrect figure for nominal distance. Then he pulled up the Solar System Dynamics calculator on the NASA Jet Propulsion Laboratory website. Using all of the variables provided by the commander, he confirmed the nominal distance to be correct.

"Less than a third of the distance to the Sun," he muttered. Then he converted the speed to miles per hour in his head and wrote sixty thousand next to the nominal distance figure.

"My god. Oh, my god."

He wrote a number on his notepad and then circled it. As he did, the lead snapped off the end of the pencil.

"Three weeks, more or less."

PART TWO

ASTROMETRY

Identification Number: Unknown

Right Ascension: 21 hours 18 minutes 12.6 seconds

Declination: -30 degrees 42 minutes 17 seconds

Greatest Elongation: 73.0 degrees

Nominal Distance from Earth: 0.558 Astronomical Units

Relative Velocity: 28,309 meters per second

CHAPTER 16

The MPC was the primary location for receipt and distribution of positional measurements of minor planets; comets; satellites of major planets, such as moons; and asteroids. Located at the Harvard-Smithsonian Center for Astrophysics in Cambridge, the MPC maintains the master files containing all observations and orbit computations for these space objects, and once a final analysis had been made, they were solely authorized to announce the discovery to the rest of the world via electronic circulars or its website.

Madeline Hapwell, the MPC director, had been awakened early that morning by Colonel Robinson with the Department of Defense. He immediately created a conference call with Director Foster of Mission Control at NASA. Hapwell immediately went from sleepy-eyed to eyes wide open as Foster relayed the information he'd received on the secured communication from the ISS. She asked that he send it to her in email format, just to ensure its accuracy.

After dressing, Hapwell reached out to her associate director, who followed the protocols established for an unusually late discovery of a near-Earth object. On the MPC website, her team kept running tallies of the NEOs, comets, and minor planets discovered on a monthly and yearly basis. By that point in April, there had been nearly eight hundred near-Earth objects discovered, which included asteroids and meteors. Of those eight hundred, nearly three hundred were found within fourteen days of passing by Earth.

Hapwell, as a seasoned scientist with an impressive educational background, often said that Earth was constantly playing a high-stakes game of Russian roulette. One day, she'd said, our planet will be on the receiving end of a bullet.

As she pulled out of the parking garage of her flat on Beacon Street, she wondered if this was the bullet that found its mark. By the time Hapwell crossed the Charles River and made her way to the Cambridge facility, her team was fully immersed in their research and analysis of the data received from NASA.

The sun was rising, shining through the east-side windows facing the John Wolbach Library. Her arrival was only noticed by a few of the astronomers and mathematicians, who were working frantically on their computers. When Padma Argawal, her associate director, noticed her arrival, she called the team to attention.

"Good morning, everyone," Hapwell greeted them. "I thank all of you for scrambling together to address this newfound object. I realize this is highly unusual, but based upon the information provided from NASA, so far, unconfirmed, I found it necessary to meet this booger head-on."

She paused to accept a cup of coffee from one of the student-assistants. She continued. "I'm sure that Padma has covered some of this already, but I need to reiterate something to all of you. This matter is being investigated under the purview and supervision of the Department of Defense. It's in the process of being deemed classified and available to people at the highest levels of our government. That means, I've been told, that no one will be allowed to leave this room today without an escort. There can be no external communications with family or anyone else via email, text, or phone. Does everyone understand?"

Everyone either nodded or answered in the affirmative.

"Okay, we've war-gamed this scenario before as part of the drills we conducted with NASA, the DOD, and the White House. The first step is to get eyes on this NEO. Second, analyze its incoming trajectory. Finally, and based upon my mental calculations, this is important, as always, we need to determine the impact date.

"Now, with this additional sense of urgency I've placed on all of you, let me be clear. No mistakes. No shortcuts. No assumptions. I want definitive conclusions. A group consensus, if you will. One that you'd personally stand by if you had to stand in the Oval Office and tell the President of the United States the results as if your life depended upon it. Why? Because it probably does."

Her associate director was waving frantically to get her attention, so Hapwell thanked her team and excused herself.

Slightly annoyed, Hapwell asked, "What is it, Padma?"

"Ma'am, the switchboard has received a call from a woman in Georgia who has claimed to have spotted a close-approach asteroid. She won't provide any further details to our screening team and insists upon speaking to, as she put it, *a higher-up.*"

"Do you think she's a crackpot?" asked Hapwell, who suddenly envisioned a deluge of skywatchers inundating the MPC with sightings.

"Based on the cursory information relayed to me, she may have spotted our NEO."

Hapwell sighed and instructed Argawal to direct the call to her office. Once she was seated, she took the call and placed it on her speakerphone.

"This is Director Hapwell. How may I help you?"

"Um, yes, ma'am. My name is Jackie Holcomb and I live at the Deerlick Astronomy Village, um, south of Washington, Georgia. Ma'am, I believe I've, um, I mean, jeez, I'm sorry, ma'am. I'm very nervous and, well, excited, too."

"That's quite all right, Ms. Holcomb. Perhaps you'd like to gather your thoughts and call back. My team is perfectly capable of taking the information you have for—"

"No!" Jackie shouted into the phone. "This is too big, I mean, too important. This needs to be given to someone of importance, um, authority, like yourself."

"Okay. Okay, go ahead, then, I'm listening."

Argawal had entered the room and was greeted by a shrug and an eye roll from Hapwell. She slowly took a seat and crossed her legs, listening as Jackie continued.

"Here's the thing, I won't get into how I discovered this, but let's just say that I'm fairly certain that there's an asteroid coming directly for us and at a speed that gives it a potential impact within three weeks."

Hapwell sat up in her chair and immediately grabbed a notepad, which she shoved in front of Argawal. She whispered, "Take notes."

"All right, Ms. Holcomb, let's start from the top. I need to get some basic information from you so that we can open a file." Hapwell smiled and winked at her associate director.

Jackie gained her composure and the words flowed out of her. She began to tell the story, leaving out the part about how she'd discovered the asteroid on Nate's video feed, and the fact that she'd kept Sparky in the loop regarding her findings.

Several minutes later, Hapwell shooed Argawal out the door and into the war room to feed this data to their team. She also secured Jackie's commitment to email everything she had to Hapwell's personal email address at the Minor Planet Center. Finally, she told Jackie that it was very important that she stay at home, with her data, and near the telephone. It was important for her to be available, as the MPC would need to discuss her findings and gather insight into the processes she'd used to identify this near-Earth object.

Having calmed Jackie down, and securing her commitment to stay put, Hapwell put in a call to Colonel Maxwell at the DOD to notify him of the additional sighting. After their brief conversation, Hapwell took a moment to gather her thoughts.

By day's end, she'd be able to make a fairly precise determination of this NEO's trajectory and impact date. She swelled with pride as she thought of presenting this information to the president herself. After another minute of self-aggrandizement, Hapwell suddenly came to a realization—this might be a planet killer.

CHAPTER 17

Sparky Newsome had never genuinely feared for his life until today. Certainly, each day brought news stories to explore, but he mostly followed a set routine day after day, week after week. Washington was a quiet town, full of history dating back to the American Revolution. It was relatively crime-free and only on rare occasions was there something to report deemed newsworthy, at least by the standards of larger cities.

Jackie Holcomb's visit to his home changed all of that. His life would never be the same, and now he wondered how much longer it would last.

Thursday had begun pretty much the way Wednesday had left off—hand-wringing over what to do with Jackie's discovery. When they parted ways the afternoon before, and after several heated conversations by phone last night, their concerted opinion was to report this information to both the Minor Planet Center and the national news media as soon as possible.

Jackie had conducted additional calculations based upon Nate's recorded footage. She'd gone back to Deerlick in the early morning hours to access various telescopes that were on the property. She hoped to track the asteroid further, perhaps to ease her concerns, or to confirm what her gut was telling her. Unfortunately, the extreme brightness of Comet Oort, coupled with its extensive tail, obscured the trailing asteroid from view. She could only rely upon her initial calculations, which she'd checked and rechecked all night long.

When Sparky and Jackie last spoke earlier that morning, she was going to place the call to the MPC and he was going to reach out to his media contacts at CBS.

Many years ago, Sparky had established a relationship with Jeff Glor, the former *CBS Evening News* anchor and now a member of the *60 Minutes* team. When Glor had been with an independent news station in Boston, he'd traveled to Washington, Georgia, to cover a mayoral election that had garnered national attention because of its racial undertones. Sparky had become Glor's point of contact during the production of the story, and the two kept in contact via email for years.

Sparky believed this story was too big for the regional press, namely from Augusta, Georgia, the designated media market of which the Washington-Wilkes community was a part. He tried to contact Glor by phone; however, Sparky was told he was on assignment in Africa and couldn't be reached. He attempted to email Glor, several times in fact, with each email growing increasingly urgent.

There was no response.

Sparky became concerned about the time it was taking to get this information out to the public. Next, he considered reaching out to CNN by phone. He only had one contact there, a national correspondent named Jack Young, who had been a part of Atlanta's *Channel 2 Action News* team for years. He'd been to Washington on occasion during his early career and looked to Sparky to provide stories of local interest.

By midafternoon, Sparky was growing increasingly frustrated. He had the story of the century and nobody seemed to care. Glor was unavailable. Young had not returned his calls. Sparky considered going to his sources in the Augusta media market, but he wasn't sure that he could maintain control over the story. Above all, if Jackie's theory was correct, this asteroid had the potential to cause serious damage and loss of life. He was growing increasingly frustrated with the whole matter and found himself feeling trapped.

Plus, he was driving his wife crazy. He intentionally withheld much of Jackie's hypothesis until he didn't want to unduly worry Mary. Needing some fresh air and a change of scenery, his wife encouraged him to go down to the Square Cafe a block from their home to grab a couple of coffee drinks. Reluctantly, Sparky acquiesced and entered the square after a fresh spring rain gave the first seat of government in Georgia's history a wash.

He placed his order and wandered around the small café owned by a group of local entrepreneurs. He mindlessly perused the offerings in the café's lending library, studying the choices, noticing that half the shelves were filled with the novels of a local author and Mary's own illustrated children's books.

Sparky was jolted back into the moment, not by the barista announcing that his drinks were ready, but rather by the sound of vehicles roaring into the town's square. He separated the blinds and peered through them. Several black Chevy SUVs roared in front of the Georgia Realty Sales Office, past The Epigraph, and rounded the corner toward his home.

His eyes grew wide when their tires screeched to a halt, barely coming to a stop before men in dark suits jumped out and hurdled his white picket fence.

"Sparky, Sparky! Your drinks are ready." The barista tried to get his attention, oblivious to what was going on outside.

He ignored her and rushed out onto the sidewalk, his head on a swivel, trying to get a handle on what was happening. He quickly crossed through the parked cars, almost getting hit by a tourist searching for a space, He'd almost reached the statue of a confederate soldier that stood proudly over the square when he received a text message. It was from his wife.

run

Sparky took several steps toward the house, concerned for Mary's well-being, when several of the men-in-black emerged back onto the front porch, pressing their fingers to earpieces and scanning the small downtown area through dark sunglasses.

He trusted his wife, and Mary was a strong woman. So he followed her advice, but he didn't run. He tried to be nonchalant, casually strolling through the square until he was out of sight, and then he picked up the pace.

Run, but to where?

And why?

He made his way across historic Robert Toombs Avenue and walked briskly down Spring Street past the IGA grocery store. Sparky's mind raced as he left his beloved wife alone to deal with … with … whatever it was that had descended upon him.

Then his phone rang, startling him so bad that he almost spontaneously released his full bladder. He looked at the display, expecting to see his wife's name and number. Instead, it was Jackie's husband.

Sparky ducked between two cars parked at the small grocery store, and crouched down to hide. He connected the call but said nothing.

"Sparky, are you there? It's James. Hello?"

The voice was familiar, although he and James Holcomb rarely spoke on the phone.

Sparky mustered the courage to respond, "Yeah, um, hello."

"Hey, Sparky. I wonder if you could help me. Listen, I've just gotten back in from the road and found the house wide open. I don't know, I mean. Look, it's like a cyclone hit the place. The door was practically busted off the hinges. Our place has been ransacked. Jackie's astronomy equipment is missing, and her computers. And, um, Sparky, so is she."

Damn.

Sparky gulped. "James, have you talked to Jackie at all? You know, about what she and I have been working on?"

"No. I've been hauling a load from LA to Atlanta. I called to say goodnight and we only spoke for a minute. She seemed preoccupied or something. Say, what's going on? Why did somebody toss our house? Do I need to call—?"

Sparky didn't have answers for any of his questions, and he suspected his home would be suffering the same fate. He racked his brain, seeking to provide an answer to his friend's distraught husband, when he realized that James had been cut off.

"James? James? Are you there?"

He looked down at his iPhone's screen. It was blank. Not dark, as if the phone had lost its charge. No, this was different. It was a grayish color, as if …

Sparky dropped his phone as if it were a deadly parasite attempting to eat his flesh in a bad sci-fi movie. He attempted to kick it away from his feet, missing badly at first before finding the mark, sending the device through the IGA parking lot.

He looked in all directions, searching for what might've caused the device to fail. Panicked, Sparky broke out in a run, bolting in front of an oncoming car on East Liberty Street. Seconds later, he was inside Washington's city hall, looking for a familiar face.

The mayor's secretary, Veronica, occupied the first office on the right, and she was gently tapping away at her keyboard, most likely preparing for that afternoon's council meeting.

Out of breath, Sparky tried to regain his composure in an effort to avoid drawing attention to his predicament.

"Ah, hi, Veronica," he began, trying to contain his emotions.

"Hey, Parks," she replied. Veronica was one of the few people left in Washington who'd known Sparky since childhood and therefore used his given name.

"Hey. Listen, um, I lost my phone and I need to call home. Would you mind dialing Mary and let her know—"

Know what? What can Veronica say that won't give my location away?

Veronica grew impatient with his sudden pause. "Parks? Let her know what?"

"Um, we had a little fight, that's all. Please just give her a call and see how she's doin', okay?"

"You know, I have a council meeting in less than an hour. Can't this wait?"

"No, Veronica. It can't." Sparky was stern in his response, perhaps overly so, which drew an angry glare from Veronica.

Without saying another word, she lifted the receiver of her desk phone and began to dial. Flustered, Sparky slammed his hand down on the top of the phone to stop her.

"No, use your cell phone," he shouted, frightening Veronica. He looked outside into the hallway to see if his outburst drew any attention. He caught himself. "Jeez, I'm so sorry. Please, just call using your cell phone."

Veronica rolled her eyes and reached into her bag to retrieve her phone. As she did, Sparky saw one of the black Suburbans drive slowly in front of city hall, pausing only briefly at the intersection before continuing westbound on Liberty.

Sparky snapped to attention when he realized that Veronica had been connected to his home. "Um, wait, is this the Newsome residence? Where is Mary? What? Who is this?"

She glanced up at Sparky with a confused look on her face. She suddenly thrust the phone toward him. "Sparky, some man answered—"

Sparky jumped backwards, recoiling from the phone, and began waving his hands frantically. He mouthed the words *no, no, no!*

Veronica scowled and shrugged. She tried to force the phone toward him and it came close enough for him to hear the man's voice.

"Mr. Newsome, I know you're there. Come on back home. We just need to talk."

Yeah, sure. Like the way you're talking to Jackie?

Sparky ran down the hallway and raced out the rear fire exit of city hall, leaving Veronica with her mouth open and the cell phone quivering in her hand.

CHAPTER 18

Thursday, April 5
Gunner's Residence
Dog Island
Florida Panhandle

Gunner had spent the day at nearby Tyndall Air Force Base, training with Air Force Special Ops under the supervision of the 53rd Weapons Evaluation Group. The flight simulators at the 53rd were second to none, providing fighter pilots the closest thing to live combat available.

Today, a new weapons system was being introduced via the Air Force's air-to-ground weapons evaluation program known as Combat Hammer. What stuck with Gunner throughout the entire session was the fact that this new system could be made nuclear-capable should the situation dictate it.

After he pulled his four-wheeler through the pilings that supported the beach house, he shut off the engine and paused to reflect on his day. *Fighter jets delivering nuclear payloads. Will it ever come to that? And what will they think of next?*

Gunner shrugged off the thoughts of advanced nuclear weaponry, grabbed his rucksack out of the rear cargo hold, and headed through the ground level of his home toward the elevator. He glanced at the miniature Jeep Willys ATV that was parked on the other side of the elevator entryway. It had been gathering dust and sand for years. *Since the anniversary. The one that was never celebrated.*

With a sigh, he rode up to the main level of his home, anxious to grab a beer, flop on the sofa, and maybe catch a baseball game. It was opening day for most teams, and he looked forward to something brainless to take his mind off *things*.

When the doors opened, his visions of solitude quickly evaporated into a mirage, as two Air Force duffle bags had been tossed on the floor in front of him, and the sounds of laughter emanating from the kitchen filled the open floor plan.

Gunner shook his head in disbelief and dropped his rucksack near the duffels. He turned to the right, rounding the corner leading to the kitchen without being noticed by its noisy occupants. He managed a smile as he took in the view.

In front of the sink was his seventy-two-year-old father, Granville Fox, lovingly referred to by everyone as Pop. He was wearing a pair of Bermuda shorts, a white tee shirt and a yellow-and-white apron around his neck.

To his left was Gunner's childhood friend, and now a member of his quick-reaction force team, Cameron Mills. Cam, as she'd been called since they'd met in fourth grade, had joined the Air Force prior to Gunner. They'd attended USAF Special Operations School together at Hurlburt Field and were eventually paired on several missions.

Gunner took in the scene. The nine-foot-long kitchen table that doubled as an island was covered in wax paper, baking sheets, recipe books, and a myriad of ingredients ranging from flour to flavorings. Despite the hellacious mess the two had created, the aroma of fresh baked something-or-others filled the room and immediately reminded Gunner that he hadn't taken the time to eat that afternoon.

Pop and Cam were completely immersed in the task at hand, which, to the best of Gunner's poignant analysis, seemed to be baking for an Army, or a bake sale. Since his mom had died, Gunner's dad had found a variety of ways to cope, including learning the basics of running a household.

Mom had handled all of the chores from cooking to cleaning to making sure her boys were well taken care of. As a result, Pop was never allowed to participate in any of the day-to-day household functions and found himself at a loss when she suddenly died from cancer. Over time, he'd learned to fend for himself, and after a year or so of microwaveable dinners and takeout, he learned to cook. The final step, one that also involved stepping out into the social world, was joining the local bake club.

Yes, Apalachicola had a bake club that gathered once a month. The demographic was about what one would expect—older ladies, many of whom were widowed, and all of whom had the perfect recipe with just the right secret ingredient to make a pie or cake or muffin better than the rest.

The bake club had a secondary purpose—teaching newlywed young women the art of preparing baked goods and meals for their husbands, many of whom were stationed at nearby Tyndall Air Force Base. So there was a mix of grandmothers and twentysomethings who got together in one another's homes every month to discuss baking, cooking, plus the caring and nurturing of the men in their life.

And then along came Pop. As the twenty-first century was well underway, and despite the fact that society had made leaps and bounds in terms of social interaction, there were still some frontiers left unexplored. Until Pop arrived on the scene, the Apalachicola Bake Club had been one of those.

In a historic first, a story that even made the *Apalach Times*, Pop was welcomed into the previously ladies-only Apalachicola Bake Club. He was welcomed with open arms and made into a mascot of sorts.

Then he got serious. He studied and practiced, invading Gunner's kitchen from time to time because, as Pop chided, *somebody's got to use it*. Soon, when various social organizations and clubs held bake sales or fundraisers, his offerings became in high demand, eventually becoming more popular than the goodies prepared by even the oldest members of the bake club.

It didn't take long until a friendly rivalry between clubbers turned into a claws-out, fangs-bared, I'm-gonna-show-them-who-makes-the-best-pineapple-upside-down-cake competition. Pop continued to attend club functions, but he rarely introduced his best work, saving that for special events. Gunner's home had become Pop's test kitchen, and obviously, tonight, there was a lot of testing going on.

Gunner shook his head in disbelief and strolled to the refrigerator in search of a Hooter Brown Ale, which was now being brewed in twelve-ounce bottles. Oyster City Brewing had gone regional, much to the delight of Southerners, but adding to the perpetual headaches of the microbrewer's founders.

He glanced toward the sofa that faced the glass wall panels overlooking the Gulf of Mexico. He was surprised that Howard, his basset hound, hadn't come to greet him at the elevator. Gunner surmised that Howard was exhausted by all the activity, as he heard a faint snore coming from that direction.

Gunner opened the refrigerator and froze. There was no beer. There was no food. There was no nothing but mixing bowls of a variety of doughs, all covered with Saran wrap, and a couple of trays of cookies awaiting their turn in the oven.

He set his jaw and gritted his teeth. Then he took a deep breath and exhaled. Now these two had crossed a line. He decided to make his presence known.

"What the hell, you guys? Where's my beer?"

Pop was startled and jumped a little. Cam swung around with a wooden spatula as if she were going to make some type of ninja move on her assailant.

"Gunner!" she shouted. After tossing the spatula on the table and wiping her hands on the matching apron to Pop's, she approached her friend and partner to exchange a brief hug.

Their relationship was purely professional when in the presence of others, with Cam overcompensating for being a woman by working hard to be one of the guys. When she was alone with Gunner and Pop, she was more like a sister, a best pal, who'd grown up with Gunner through high school until they'd followed different career paths, eventually reuniting at Hurlburt Field.

"Hello, son," said Pop with a smile. "Um, Cam came to visit and I told her I was thinking about trying out a couple of recipes. Well, you know, one thing led to another and, um … hungry?"

Gunner laughed and reached down to pluck a cookie off an

oblong platter. White chocolate with macadamia nuts, coupled with a hint of nutmeg. Pretty good, Gunner thought to himself. He'd never been one for baked treats, but until Pop joined the how-to-cook-three-square-meals club, if there was such a thing, cookies would have to do.

"Hungry, yes. Thirsty, hell yeah. What did y'all do with my beer?"

"Don't panic, Gunner," replied Cam, shaking her head. "I brought the Yeti cooler from downstairs and filled it with ice and your beloved Hooter Brown. And, out of respect for the king of this fabulous castle, I didn't drink any until you came home."

"Wise move, Cam," he said with a chuckle. She pointed toward the kitchen pantry, which was tucked away behind a pocket door adjacent to the refrigerator. Gunner grabbed a beer, which was much colder than if it had been stored in the refrigerator. As he returned, he asked, "What did you guys do to Howard? It's not like him to sleep through my coming home."

"We filled his tummy with yummies," replied Pop.

"Cookies? Come on, Pop. He's too old for—"

"No, not cookies. I fixed him some rice and burger, topped with Nummy Tum-Tum pumpkin."

Gunner set his beer on the table and ran his fingers through his hair. This evening was straight out of an episode of *The Twilight Zone*. "Nummy what? Pumpkin?"

"Yeah, it'll be good for him, so I picked some up at Publix in Tallahassee. It's called Nummy Tum-Tum pumpkin."

"Is it for dogs? And what's so good about it?"

Pop paused and wandered toward the sofa as if to make sure Howard had, in fact, survived the meal. He rubbed the pup's considerable belly, causing Howard to stretch and let out a long fart. "Yes, son, it's good for him. It promotes digestive health, which will make him poop better."

Gunner rolled his eyes. "He poops just fine, Pop."

Cam tried to stifle a laugh, as this conversation was destined to devolve into something not befitting a baking session.

"Son, he's having difficulty. Haven't you heard him strain?"

"Good lord, Pop. Seriously? No, I haven't listened to whether Howard is straining as he takes a—"

"He's straining, and I can't give him Senokot, so Nummy Tum-Tum pumpkin is the solution."

Gunner wanted it to end, so he grabbed his beer and surrendered the argument. Pop – one. Gunner – zero.

He passed Pop in the kitchen and shook his head in disbelief. Just as he was about to take a seat, he heard the elevator get called to the ground floor.

"Now what?" he muttered to himself.

CHAPTER 19

Thursday, April 5
Dog Island
Florida Panhandle

The elevator doors opened and two heavy duffle bags were thrown out, joining Cam's and Gunner's gear with a thud. A voice boomed through the opening.

"Hi, honey. I'm home!"

Gunner closed his eyes and allowed his chin to drop to his chest. *Jesus, take the wheel.*

"Bear, what a surprise!" shouted Cam from the kitchen.

Gunner wished he were back in the F/A XX, flying into the heavens.

"Hey, am I too late for the samples?"

"Front and center, Sergeant," ordered Pop, a former USAF staff sergeant himself. "I've got something I think you'll like."

Staff Sergeant Bear King reported to duty, casually acknowledging Gunner as he passed. "Hey, Gunner."

Gunner raised his beer and tipped the top of the bottle in response. He loved Dog Island because there was no way to access it by car, making arrival very difficult. Somehow, these invaders had figured out a way to descend upon his home anyway.

"I think you'll like these," said Pop.

He presented the plate to Bear, who grabbed a handful of the cookies. He wasn't shy.

He passed the cookies under his nose and took a deep breath. "Oh, man. Snickerdoodles. My favorite. Are these Mom's recipe?" When Bear first met Gunner, it had been at Mom and Pop's house.

The team had been deployed, and Bear had swung by with Cam in tow on the way to Eglin. Mom insisted that Gunner's new partner try her snickerdoodle cookies. Bear immediately fell in love with the chewy centers covered with cinnamon sugar.

"They are," replied Pop. "There's a slight improvement, however. They're gluten-free."

"Huh?" asked a puzzled Bear. "What's wrong with gluten?"

"It can lead to a number of problems, Sergeant, from nerve damage to osteoporosis to infertility."

"Really? This gluten stuff can keep me from, you know—" Bear's voice trailed off as he raised his muscular right arm and flexed his bicep. He slapped the palm of his left hand over his bicep and then flexed his forearm, a gesture that, in his mind, emulated a showing of his sexual prowess.

Cam immediately picked up on what the man-child was referring to. "No, you idiot. Infertility has nothing to do with your ability to make your manhood perform."

"Whew, that's a relief," said Bear, and he crammed an entire cookie into his mouth all at once. While he munched it down, he approached his attractive, single partner. "Since I've had one, maybe I should make sure your theory is correct."

Cam started laughing and slowly backed away from Bear, but continued teasing him to induce his approach. She leaned back toward the kitchen counter as Bear came closer, and when he was a few feet away, she slid her hands behind her and opened the kitchen drawer. In a flash, she produced two ten-inch kitchen knives and presented them to her assailant.

"Let's not, okay?" she said with a grin.

Bear, who stood six feet four and weighed two hundred forty pounds, stopped in his tracks. Gunner, who'd been watching the interaction between the two, knew that Cam had a plan to exploit the big man's greatest weakness—the opposite sex.

"Sure, Cam. Jeez. I was just teasin'." Bear devoured another cookie and then he turned his attention to Gunner, who'd just finished his beer.

"Say, Gunner, can I get you a beer?"

"Yeah, brother. Grab one for yourself and Cam, too." Gunner smiled, as he knew that was what Bear wanted to begin with.

"Roger that."

Cam playfully shoved Bear and then gave him a big hug. The two joked with one another, but when on mission, they'd saved each other's lives on more than one occasion. The trio shared a close-knit relationship, one that was all business when it needed to be, but fun and games when they were alone. As a unit, their interaction wasn't complicated by jealousy, judgments, or sexual interests. It was if they'd been molded into a single cohesive fighting force, with the combination of their talents rolled into one machine.

Staff Sergeant Barrett King had been an all-American football standout at the Air Force Academy, where he was also an Academic all-American. Born in Texas, Bear often played the dumb-Southern-country-boy routine to throw his adversaries off guard. In fact, he had a keen sense of awareness and an innate ability to read people. He was rarely caught off guard, except when Cam took advantage of his sole weakness—women.

Gunner had to ask the question, but he already knew what the most likely answer was. "So, Bear, it's good to see you. I couldn't help but notice you brought two large duffels with you."

"Um, yeah, about those," Bear began, shyly stammering his words. "You see, um—"

Gunner let out a hearty laugh. "She kicked you out again, didn't she?"

Bear grimaced and shook his head from side to side, a motion totally inapposite to the answer. "Yeah, man. I mean, I told her she was kinda overreacting and that a text message doesn't mean anything. But, um—"

"What kind of text message?" asked Gunner.

"Well, I met this girl in a bar, you know, spring-break type. Well, she sent me this picture of her. And that was it."

"No, Bear, there's more," said Gunner, who knew his friend well.

"Well, she didn't have any clothes on, but, hey, that wasn't my fault!"

Cam started laughing and then said in an accusatory tone, "You were sexting!"

"No, I wasn't!" Bear shot back.

"Did you send her a snap of that thing? You know, put the slinky on her?"

Bear flopped on the sofa, causing Howard to rise into the air slightly on the other end. Somehow the basset hound managed to maintain his slumber.

"All right, maybe I did. I stopped by Shalimar Cheers on Eglin Parkway last night after training at the range. You know, I was with the younger guys, and they eat up the attention they get from the girls who are down on spring break. Anyway, there was this one girl, cute, you know. Well, we had too many beers and she asked me if I wanted to see what she had under the hood."

Pop's interest was now piqued. "She said *under the hood?*"

"Yeah, Pop. I mean, this chick was stacked, so, you know, I'm a guy. I was just kinda curious. Anyway, she asked for my phone number and said she'd text me a picture. She sent it to me and I was totally impressed, you follow?"

"Yeah, I follow," said Cam, who was truly enjoying the whole exchange. "So, let me guess, moron, you snuck off to the men's room, whipped it out, and showed her what you've got under your hood. Am I right?"

Bear blushed as much as a black man was capable of blushing. He sheepishly nodded his head.

"Wait! Wait!" Cam was a little too enthusiastic, but funny nonetheless. "You gotta let me finish the story. So you two played *show-and-don't-tell*, right? Then you get home late, smelling like a brewery. You hustle off to the shower to wash away your sins, and guess who sneaks a peek at your cell phone."

The whole time that Cam was summarizing the events as they occurred, Bear grimaced and nodded his head in agreement.

"My old lady saw the texts and threw my ass out of the house," the man-child groaned.

Gunner kicked off his shoes and slumped in his chair. He made eye contact with the trio of misfits who stood before him and then directed his attention back to Bear. "So, let me guess. Now your problem is my problem."

"No, man. It's not like that. I won't be a problem. I swear. You'll hardly know I'm here. I can slum it on the couch. Or take the guest room upstairs."

Gunner quickly responded, "There's no bed up there. It's a weight room, remember?"

"Plus, I claimed the couch already," insisted Cam, drawing a look from Gunner. She hadn't explained what she was doing there yet.

Bear frowned, trying to think up more options. "How about the hammock in the back? Seriously, just let me crash a few days until my old lady comes back to her senses."

Pop, the fatherly figure to these three, stepped in. "Bear, it seems to me that she has come to her senses. First of all, you've been having sleepovers at her place for years and you haven't even thought about putting a ring on her finger. Then, let's recap, shall we? This isn't the first time you've been kicked out of her place for chasin' tail, is it?"

"Nah, Pop. You know how it is. A strong, chiseled, good-lookin' black man, who's smart too, is in high demand. I feel a sense of duty to womankind to make sure everybody gets a piece of this." Bear raised his arms and flexed both of his massive biceps at once.

Cam rolled her eyes and threw a kitchen towel at him. "Dude, you're so full of yourself. If you were my boyfriend, I would've shot you."

Bear fought back. "Oh, who are you to judge? How many boyfriends have you been through? A dozen in the last year?"

"That's not true, and you know it," Cam defended. "Dates are not boyfriends, technically."

"Oh, okay. Booty calls."

Cam stuck out her jaw and came after Bear. He curled up on the sofa and tried to pull a cushion over his head to protect himself from the onslaught of fists pounding his arms and back.

Gunner pleaded with his team to calm down. "Come on, you guys. Howard's gonna get pissed, start bellowing, and you know the saying, when Howard ain't happy, ain't nobody happy."

CHAPTER 20

Thursday, April 5
Dog Island
Florida Panhandle

Eventually the raucous exchange died down. Pop finished up his baking and filled the tummies of his three hungry taste-testers. He loaded up all of his baked goods in large Tupperware containers and made the twenty-minute drive back to the east end of Dog Island, where he had a one-story bungalow facing the mainland.

Cam and Bear helped Gunner clean up the kitchen, and eventually the trio was ready to relax on the upstairs deck with the Yeti cooler and another dozen beers on ice.

Four Adirondack chairs were spread across the deck, separated by short wooden tables. Between Gunner and Bear, a cigar ashtray was set out as the guys fired up a pair of Macanudos.

They exchanged small talk, and eventually, as the skies grew pitch black, the stars emerged in their full glory, together with the spectacle that had captured the world's attention—Comet Oort.

"What do you y'all think of this comet?" asked Bear as he let out a puff of smoke that momentarily obscured their view of the comet's tail.

The smoke dissipated and Gunner focused his eyes on the brightly lit comet. "It's the brightest comet in recorded history. Theoretically, no comet can be brighter than magnitude minus twelve. The lower the magnitude, the brighter the star. From what I've heard on the news, Oort is emitting enough energy to send it closer to a magnitude minus ten."

Cam mustered the courage to ask, "Have you thought about pulling out her telescope? The Celestron might be a few years old, but you could get a better look."

The group fell silent for a moment, and then Gunner finished off his beer and set it on the deck with a thud. "No. If I wanna look into space, I'll either watch it on television or go there myself."

Cam tilted up her bottle for another swig, then glanced over at her best friend. Gunner's face was only illuminated by the cherry of his cigar. At Dog Island, the few residents who lived there respected the sea turtles who nested along the white sands. The turtles frequently got confused by artificial light coming from the homes. As the saying went, dark sky at night, turtle's delight. Gunner had not installed any lights on the exterior of the home and typically dimmed the interior lights as darkness set in.

She pressed Gunner about the other day. "Is that what the plan was on Sunday? Fly until you couldn't fly anymore?"

Gunner shrugged and twirled another beer through his fingertips before screwing off the top. "Are you here to lecture me, Cam?" He tilted his head in her direction and made eye contact.

"Nope, no lectures from me. Just genuine concern from a friend."

Gunner grimaced and nodded. "Thanks. I'm fine."

"Keep it real, bud," said Bear, whose bullshit meter just went into the red zone.

"Okay, fine. I'll admit that I kinda lost it there for a moment."

"What about your comms?" asked Bear. He and Cam were now tag-teaming Gunner in this interrogation.

Gunner's head snapped toward Bear. "How'd you know about that?"

"Man, people talk. You know that. Why'd you shut off the comms?"

Gunner took another drag on his cigar. "I didn't want anybody to stop me. I knew that bird was capable of taking me well into the stratosphere, and I wanted to see what it was like for myself."

"You could've been killed," said Cam, a hint of emotion in her voice.

"I'm sorry, Cam. Really, I am. I mean, I regret this for many reasons. Dying was part of it. Here's what I learned from my joyride."

Gunner paused and stood to stroll around the deck. He leaned against the deck's railing to face his team as he continued. "Guys, I don't want to die. I know that now. I do have something to live for. Many things, in fact. There's Pop and Howard. Those two need me. And then there's you guys. I had a lot of time to think as I was falling back to Earth, um, well, after the main chute opened, anyway. You two are my family, and I'd be lettin' you down if I screwed around and killed myself."

"Yes, you would have," said Cam, who'd recently received an elevation in rank to major. "If you die, they would most likely put me in charge of our little unit. That means I've got to deal with Bear on my own."

"Oh, lawd!" the Texan groaned.

"That would never work, would it?" said Gunner with a laugh. He truly enjoyed his friends and trusted them with his life. "Here's the good news. I'm grounded for a while, but for flight combat missions only. I'm still in the game for special ops stuff."

Cam sat up on the edge of her chair. "The shrink cleared you?"

"Well, sort of," Gunner explained. "He and I have a pretty good understanding of what he expects from me, and in exchange, he coached me through my dressing-down by the colonel."

Cam smiled, stood, and gave Gunner a hug. Bear lifted his hefty frame out of the Adirondack chair and offered his beer to toast. The three clinked their bottles.

Bear started by saying, *"Day by day."*

Followed by Cam. *"Minute by minute."*

Then Gunner joined in. *"Ride or die."*

Lastly, they put the exclamation on their small unit's motto.

"We stick together."

CHAPTER 21

Five Years Prior
Dog Island
Florida Panhandle

"Come on, Gunner! Check this out!" Heather Fox ran down a well-worn path onto the beach with an excitement befitting a young child. She and Gunner had made numerous trips to their newly purchased seven-acre tract that ran from the beach to the bay. The barrier island stretched parallel to the shoreline, roughly four miles from where Highway 98 ran along the coast. They were scheduled to start construction on their new home the next day when they realized they'd never spent any time on their beach at night. On a whim, the two sped along the backroads to Tallahassee's Walmart and bought a tent, a sleeping bag large enough for them and Howard, together with some miscellaneous camping gear.

Earlier, Gunner had barely brought their Hummer H1 to a stop at the ferry landing, which carried residents from Carrabelle to Dog Island. He had been focused on unloading the truck when Heather raced toward the water taxi launch.

"Wait up!" he'd shouted after her, knowing full well that his plea would be ignored. Heather loved Dog Island. She saw it as a place of refuge where the two of them could shut out the busy world that ordinarily surrounded them.

Gunner had stumbled down the dock, carrying the gear and a cooler by himself. Heather, realizing that she'd abandoned her husband, trotted back and helped relieve some of the load.

Because Dog Island wasn't connected to the mainland by road, residents generally opted to use the water taxis to get back and forth.

As part of his agreement to move to the barrier island, he'd negotiated with Heather to buy a boat, one that could be used to travel into Eglin. The two shook hands on the arrangement and later closed on the property.

After the thirty-minute ride across the bay, they were dropped off at the dock on Dog Island, and borrowed a golf cart, the primary means of transportation to travel from the airport on the east end of the island to the state park on the west end overlooking St. George Island.

Gunner pulled onto their property and Heather was off to the races. "Come on!" she enthusiastically shouted to him.

After securing Howard with a leash, the two of them stumbling slightly in the soft white sand, Gunner finally reached the dunes and made his way through the tall grasses that provided the shoreline protection from storm surges. Heather, her long hair flowing in the Gulf breezes, stood still, gazing across the eerily still waters, admiring the reflection of a full moon.

"Just look at this, Gunner." She paused and took in the scene. It was if the two of them had walked into a still photograph of the famous nature photographer Simone Bramante.

Gunner wrapped his arms around his wife's waist and nuzzled into her neck, causing her to shiver. He was deeply in love with Heather and admired her zest for life.

"I love you," he whispered in his wife's ear as his eyes took in the beauty of their surroundings.

"I love you back."

He took her by the hand and they began to stroll along the water's edge, which was beginning to chill as fall set in. It was completely silent except for the gentle lapping of waves along the shore. The breezes caused the sawgrass to whisper, voices of nature acting as the couple's tour guide.

Heather stopped and pointed toward the moon. With no ambient light that ordinarily pollutes the sky, every star shined bright, and the sun's reflection off the moon was almost blinding.

Gunner took it in, speaking in a low whisper in reverence for the moment. "It's incredible, isn't it? I mean, you know, up there."

Heather squeezed his hand. "Despite all I know, and what I've experienced, the universe never ceases to amaze me. Think about it, stars, planets, and moons—they're always where they should be. Night after night, same place. They do this complex dance around one another, performing flawlessly in a rendition of Sir Isaac Newton's theory of gravity."

His wife shuddered as a cool wind washed over them, and Gunner hurried to wrap his arms around her. She hadn't been feeling well, and he was concerned this outing in the cool night air might be a little much for her. Yet she insisted on spending the night at the beach.

Heather continued to soak it in, allowing her thoughts to randomly pour out of her. "Sometimes, the universe gets out of whack. Like Mercury. Its orbit varies a little bit every year but not enough to impact the other planets. Newton noticed it, but it was Einstein who explained how the Sun's incredible gravity pulls and tugs on the tiny oblong planet.

"And then there are the parts of the heavens that go rogue. The comets and asteroids—aimless wanderers, nomads really, that don't have a home. They don't have a partner to dance with, so they search until they find one.

"They get dislodged from the asteroid belt, or they come from the far reaches of our solar system, drawn to the center by the Sun and then thrown back out by a slingshot effect. Astronomers are transfixed on what lies beyond our solar system. We should be studying these celestial nomads that are nearby, lurking in the vast darkness around us."

Gunner hugged his wife, once again pressing his face into her neck. He wanted to build this home for her. So she could stare at the sky. So she could wonder about what's up there. So they could grow old together with their toes in the sand.

CHAPTER 22

Thursday, April 5
Minor Planet Center
Cambridge, Massachusetts

It had been an extraordinarily long day at the MPC. Director Hapwell had consumed a pot of caffeine-rich coffee, although her adrenaline did plenty to keep her moving. As the day wore on and the data was analyzed, there was no mistaking the conclusion—the modern world was facing a threat like no other.

Hapwell had spent years studying the skies and the historical record on how Earth had been pummeled in the past. *Impact events*, the terminology used by scientists to define collisions between celestial objects, regularly occur throughout the solar system. The most frequent impact events were between asteroids, comets, and meteoroids, with negligible effects. Larger planets have an atmosphere that help defend themselves from these random attacks of astronomical objects.

Throughout Earth's history, impact events have been tied to the formation of the Earth-Moon system, commonly referred to as the Big Splash. This *giant-impact hypothesis* suggests that the Moon was formed out of the debris left over from a collision between Earth and another large planet, most likely Mars, some four and a half billion years ago.

Other impact events are attributed to bringing water to our planet, establishing life on Earth, and destroying it as well, in the form of several mass extinctions. The most widely known impact at Chicxulub, sixty-six million years ago, was believed to be the cause of the extinction of the dinosaurs.

In modern history, the extensively studied Tunguska event was a large explosion that occurred in the forests of central Siberia, Russia. The event, believed to be an air burst of a meteor, created an explosion equivalent to thirty megatons of TNT. Eight hundred square miles of Siberian forest was flattened in seconds.

Studies found that the meteoroid that exploded above the forest was between two and six hundred feet wide. Hapwell thumbed through the most recent calculations provided to her by the MPC team. This incoming asteroid measured more than a mile wide. The energy upon impact, at its projected sixty-thousand-mile-per-hour speed, would be beyond any nuclear weapon created by man, times several hundred.

Hapwell knew the consequences of a direct hit of this magnitude, but she had to put that out of her mind for the moment. *One thing at a time.*

She was concerned about this information being made public. When the woman had phoned in earlier in the day, the first thing that Hapwell thought about was how this would be treated in the media and how the public would react.

She studied the raw footage and calculations sent to her by the Georgia woman via email. Three members of her team huddled in a small conference room and debated the accuracy of the information, but after further analysis, they marveled at how an amateur astronomer could be lucky enough to catch a glimpse of this newly discovered near-Earth object and then extrapolate some fairly accurate data from what she had to work with.

Hapwell wondered if anyone else out there had caught a glimpse of the NEO and naturally confused it with the tail of Comet Oort. The comet had provided the perfect camouflage for the asteroid, making an already difficult task of identifying these threats even more so.

The solar system was full of unconfirmed near-Earth objects. At any given time, the MPC and related entities were tracking eighteen to twenty thousand NEOs. Beginning in 1998, Congress mandated that NEOs of a kilometer or larger be tracked, but after recognizing the threat that even small objects posed, the requirement was modified in 2005 to include objects as small as five hundred feet.

Hapwell, who had been making her way through the ranks of NASA during those years, applauded the increased observation in the skies. In 2005, the budget for asteroid research was twelve million dollars. Decades later, the budget was less than the original twelve million despite a large increase to one hundred fifty million dollars in 2018.

Systematic budget cuts came a few years ago, and as a result, staff salaries were frozen, causing mass defections to private entities like SpaceX, owned by Elon Musk, and the Blue Origin project by Jeff Bezos. The private sector partnerships with two of the wealthiest people in the world had culminated in an outpost being established on the Moon.

The task of monitoring near-Earth threats remained with the government, and the need for early warning systems resulted in the continued development of Pan-STARRS, the Panoramic Survey Telescope and Rapid Response System, in Hawaii. Supported by NASA's Planetary Defense Coordination Office, Pan-STARRS led the way in discovering and tracking near-Earth objects.

Upon the discovery of an asteroid, telescopes around the world were designed to perform ground-based observations in various wavelengths, including near-infrared, radar, and those visible to the naked eye. All of these worldwide agencies made initial and follow-up observations, attempted to define the NEO's precise orbit, and then coordinated their findings, generally through Director Hapwell and the MPC.

Through technological advances and some of the brightest minds on the planet watching the skies, both professional and amateur, the MPC boasted a ninety percent success rate in identifying these threats to Earth. Overall, the odds of an asteroid impact event was considered small—about one in twelve hundred, or about the odds of drawing four-of-a-kind in a poker hand.

To be sure, by any standard of measure, a ninety percent discovery rate could be seen as wildly successful. However, Hapwell, an occasional online poker player, knew it only took one planet-killing impact event to result in the end of the world as we know it.

"Director Hapwell." Padma Argawal interrupted her thoughts. Hapwell rubbed her eyes with the palms of her hands and glanced up at the clock on her wall. It was five minutes until midnight. Her mind immediately wondered if the Doomsday Clock would strike twelve when the news of this asteroid hit the media. "I believe we've reached a consensus."

"Sit down," said Hapwell, who stretched her arm across the desk to receive her copy of the report.

"Ma'am, we utilized the ZTF at Palomar to survey the sky just beyond the last known coordinates provided by the lady in Georgia. We've got eyes on it, ma'am."

The Zwicky Transient Facility at the Palomar Observatory in California was designed to pan the skies for objects that rapidly changed in brightness, like gamma ray bursts and supernovae. In this case, the MPC used it to cut through the light noise generated by Comet Oort to isolate the asteroid and its unusual tail.

"Smart thinking, Padma. Tell me what you've found."

"I'll skip the orbital elements and other parameters and bottom-line it for you. Size is irregular with a maximum width of one-point-two miles. The Earth MOID can only be measured in days, as the AU value is miniscule."

The Earth MOID, or minimum orbit intersection distance, was usually calculated in astronomical units because the discovery of large asteroids was typically years in advance.

"Four, twenty-seven," mumbled Hapwell. "Location?"

"Northern Hemisphere, precise location to be determined."

"Padma, it won't matter."

CHAPTER 23

Thursday, April 5
Mary Willis Library
Washington, Georgia

Paranoid, and with good reason, Sparky quickly moved behind the parked vehicles at city hall and found his way into a stand of newly leafed trees that marked the coming of spring in North Georgia. He considered his options and ruled out getting anyone else in town involved in his drama. His primary concern was his wife's safety, but she was tough and resilient, perfectly capable of staring down anyone. He dashed along some overgrown azalea bushes until he came to nearby South Jefferson, where he paused to view the traffic.

Except for the occasional local vehicle passing by, he didn't encounter any of his pursuers. Sparky glanced at his watch. He studied the parking lot of the Mary Willis Library, the oldest free library in the State of Georgia. It was nearing five o'clock and they would be closing soon.

Sparky knew the layout of the building well. Founded in 1888, the library originally encompassed twenty-six hundred square feet, but then subsequent annexes had added an additional ten thousand square feet in 1977 and 1991.

There were plenty of places for Sparky to hide. He looked up and down Jefferson and he dashed across the front lawn of the home at the back of the library. Sparky wasn't an athlete and he hardly considered himself to be fleet afoot, but somehow, adrenaline turned his aging body into a bona fide sprinter.

He ran up the steps to the rear entrance and immediately turned right toward the small meeting room that was used for monthly presentations and special events. He hadn't been noticed and began to feel comfortable as he crawled behind a stack of folding tables in the corner of the room. Sparky pulled his knees close to his chest, wrapped his arms around them to emulate a cannonball, and waited, trying to control his breathing in order to avoid discovery.

He continuously tapped the Mickey Mouse display on his Apple watch, urging Mickey's arm to move farther around the dial. *Why haven't they left already? Of all days to work late!*

Sparky closed his eyes and tried to calm his nerves. He focused his senses on the sounds emanating from the main library.

Then he heard them—muffled voices and the customary goodbyes as the last two remaining members of the library staff approached the rear exit to the building. They paused to enter the code into the keypad of the library's alarm system.

The push bar on the exit door made a loud clank, and as the door opened, light from the setting sun reflected off plate glass and shiny appointments on the library's wall, causing odd flashes of sparkle to appear above his head. But when the door slammed shut and Sparky was enveloped in silence, he knew he was safe, for now.

A sense of relief washed over his body. The Mary Willis Library had had a state-of-the-art security system installed ten years ago, but the one thing they couldn't afford to do on their limited budget was install interior cameras.

Sparky, as the town's newspaper publisher and sole reporter, knew the system well, as it had been a newsworthy item when it was installed. He'd discussed the lack of interior security measures with the librarian, who responded jokingly that the only way for someone to get in was using some kind of *Tom Cruise, Mission Impossible, fall from the ceiling like a spider* stunt. Frankly, she'd said, there wasn't anything worth stealing in the library that would warrant that maneuver.

He waited a few minutes and then he slid on his butt until he could extricate himself from his hidey-hole. Sparky exhaled, adjusted his shorts and shirt to look more presentable, and made a beeline for the men's room. Throughout the entire ordeal, he'd realized how badly he needed to pee.

After he relieved himself and washed his hands, Sparky looked in the mirror. "What have you gotten yourself into, pal? You're seriously too old for this."

Sparky used a wet paper towel to wipe the salty sweat off his face and then made his way to the librarians' desk and their offices behind it. There were numerous telephones at his disposal as well as computers. He assumed the bank of computers in the offices were password protected. The computers in the library accessible to the public were as well, unless you were part of the Friends of Mary Willis Library, a nonprofit organization that raised money to promote reading in the community, among other things. Sparky and his wife were part of the Friends, and therefore he had a log-in to use the public computers at any time.

Before he did, he walked around the library, careful to steer clear of the doors to avoid triggering any alarms. He wanted to give the streets a final look to check the level of activity. The original structure featured stained glass, making it difficult to see outside, but there were other windows installed that allowed clear views onto Liberty and Jefferson Streets.

Sparky rolled his eyes and sighed when he saw that the Georgia State Patrol had joined the hunt. In the five minutes that he viewed the library's surroundings, he counted five different law enforcement vehicles. *What did the feds tell them? That I'm a fugitive? A murderer? Seriously?*

He was afraid to use the telephone system for fear that all of the calls in and out of Washington were being monitored by some spy agency or something. Sometimes, paranoia causes one's mind to race to the absurd, but he just didn't know for sure.

He considered using his email, but immediately assumed that someone was watching his activity there as well. Then he remembered the email account he and his wife used for online purchases. They'd become increasingly annoyed with the amount of spam email they'd receive after making an online purchase, so they established one account to handle all of that.

Sparky settled in behind one of the public computers and powered it on. Seconds later, he'd logged in and was navigating his way to the Hotmail account. He rubbed his fingers against the palms of his hands and flexed them as if he were about to perform a piano concerto.

Then it dawned on him. He was all dressed up with no place to go, as they say. *Who, exactly, can I trust?*

He decided to reach out to Jack Young at CNN again. He calmed his nerves as he racked his brain to remember Young's email address. He closed his eyes and tried to remember the last time they'd corresponded with one another. He tried to visualize typing the keystrokes, and then he remembered.

He began the email with a plea.

Jack, I desperately need your help. I'm not exaggerating when I say that it is a matter of life or death not only for me, but for all of us as well. Please email me back as soon as you see this.

Thanks, Sparky Newsome.

Now, he waited. He suddenly found himself parched, so he worked his way through the darkened library illuminated only by the setting sun through the incredible stained-glass windows on the west side of the building. The light cast a series of colorful hues across the interior of the building, periodically capturing the makeshift planets that hung from the ceiling in the children's reading room. Ironically, that summer's theme was titled *Universe of Stories.*

A small refrigerator in the librarians' offices yielded some bottled water, a few brownies left over from their recent bake sale, and a Yoplait yogurt. The odd combination of yogurt and brownies didn't deter Sparky from mixing the two together to provide him some carb-fueled energy.

After downing a bottle of water and procuring another from the fridge, he went back to the computer terminal to check his emails.

Nothing except a spam email from Walmart.

He shrugged it off and decided to check the major news websites to see if there had been any reporting on the asteroid. He logged into his Associated Press portal and scanned through the real-time news feeds that he relied upon often.

The world had no idea what was headed toward it. Sparky began to wonder if Jackie was correct in her calculations. He started to have his doubts. And then the shrill high-pitched sounds of sirens racing by the library silenced those thoughts and scared Sparky out of his chair, and sent him scrambling under the table.

After the sirens passed, and the sounds of a SWAT team breaking through the doors didn't occur, Sparky took up his place behind the monitors again.

He navigated the cursor to the refresh button on the email program. He pressed it and waited.

One new message.

It was from Jack Young.

CHAPTER 24

Friday, April 6
Washington, Georgia

Sparky pounded away at the keyboard, not bothering to spellcheck as he typed. His mind was racing faster than his fingers could work, furiously pounding away until he'd told Young just enough to ensure that he'd help get Sparky out of this predicament. Sparky was just about to hit send when his eyes quickly glanced over the body of the email.

His sentences were disjointed, full of misspellings and grammatical errors. Not his best work and certainly not representative of a newspaper editor. Plus, Young might think that Sparky was drunk or something, and disregard the urgency of his request.

Sparky took a deep breath and steadied his nerves. He took another moment to polish the email and then sent it. This time, rather than wander away from the computer terminal, he sat there, repeatedly hitting refresh in the email program every minute or so, awaiting a response.

Fifteen minutes had passed and Young hadn't responded. Sparky grew nervous, the paranoia setting in once again. He'd purposefully withheld the meat of the story from Young in order to maintain some semblance of control over its dissemination and to get credit for breaking it.

Should I have told him more? Jack knows I'm withholding the details. Will he insist upon more information before he drives all the way to Washington? Is he calling the feds?

Sweat broke out across Sparky's brow as he stared at the monitor, hopeful that Young hadn't double-crossed him.

One new message.

The words on the screen sent a jolt of excitement through his body.

Sparky hurriedly attempted to open the email message, almost deleting it by mistake in the process. He pulled his hand away from the mouse, shaking it violently as if he were scolding it for bad behavior.

He opened Young's email.

Sparky, sorry for the delay.

I had to get approval from my boss. I hope that was okay. Anyway, I'll be on my way shortly with one of the CNN producers. My boss insisted.

Jack.

"Hallelujah!" Sparky spontaneously shouted to the ghosts of the Mary Willis Library. Fortunately for him on that night, they didn't respond. His nervous system couldn't have handled it.

He left his post at the computer in search of another bottle of water and a bathroom break. On the way, he raided a jar of change donated to the library for a fund-raiser, vowing to pay it back when this ordeal was over. He had a sudden hankering for a Hershey's bar, which he purchased with the borrowed money on the way back from another trip to the restroom.

Sparky plopped in front of the monitor again and checked his emails in case Young wanted to communicate further. There was nothing, so Sparky navigated to Google Maps, where he calculated the distance and route Young would take from CNN World Headquarters in Atlanta. It was just over a hundred miles.

"One hour and fifty-one minutes," Sparky muttered.

He tapped on Mickey Mouse to hear the time. The squeaky voice of Disney's greatest character quickly responded in a high-pitched mouselike voice. "It's 9:57. Good evening!"

Sparky did the math and determined that he'd be on his way out of Washington by midnight. He thought about what lay ahead for him. Conversations with CNN's muckety-mucks. There would be possible nondisclosure agreements and, hopefully, a payment arrangement for bringing them the story of the millennium.

He was sure an on-air interview would be in the cards, a thought that sent him scampering back to the restroom to fix his disheveled hair. Then he had a thought. He hesitated and then entered the women's restroom. He was sure he was breaking all kinds of laws by doing so, but then again, he was also breaking the *stowaway-in-the-library* law that was surely on the books as well. He rummaged through the vanity and found what he was looking for.

Sparky adjusted his hair and then gave it a generous dousing of hair spray to keep it all in place. He rinsed his face with water again to freshen up. He didn't want to look like he'd been sleeping in a gutter during his interview, which would be viewed by millions, if not more.

He wandered the library, constantly checking the windows and his email account. He thought about his wife, whom he felt certain was okay. She had to be. The information he possessed, and that Jackie had been abducted over, had to be revealed to someone. He knew Mary would understand.

Minutes turned to hours and Sparky was beginning to break out into a nervous sweat. On three different occasions as Thursday night rolled into Friday morning, Sparky returned to the computer to reconfirm the distance from CNN studios to the library. The result of his search was the same every time.

Panicked, he double-checked the last email communication from Young, thinking he'd gotten the time wrong. Nope, that wasn't it. The fact of the matter was that Young was almost an hour past Sparky's estimated, albeit best-case scenario, arrival time.

It had been three agonizing hours. He paced the stacks in the library, running his fingers along the spines of the titles offered to readers. He couldn't keep up with how many times he'd calculated the distance, plugged in a variety of average speeds, and then stared down at his watch, wondering why Jack Young wasn't there yet.

Did he change his mind? Was he unexpectedly detained? Or worse, had he turned on Sparky and snitched him out to the feds?

All of this ran through his mind as he made a constant vigil from window to window, scanning the library's surroundings for activity.

It was nearly two in the morning when he heard the sound of car doors slamming. "Jack!" he exclaimed as he ran past the audiobooks section of the library and made his way to the double glass doors separating the rear exit from the rest of the building. What he saw froze him in his tracks.

Two men were approaching the rear exits, and both were dressed in dark suits. Sparky squinted his eyes, trying his best in the low light to determine if one of the men was Young. *Would he be dressed in a dark suit this late at night? And what about his producer?* Usually field producers wore jeans and a polo shirt because sometimes they had to tote a heavy camera on their shoulders.

Sparky's eyes grew wide and he slumped behind the doorjamb when he saw one of the men reach for his coat lapel and speak into it. He couldn't discern what was being said, but he knew one thing—Jack Young didn't speak into coat lapels unless he was on camera.

His heart sank at the thought of being discovered, either by his use of the computer or as a result of Young contacting his pursuers. Either way, he now hoped that his only salvation, the CNN newsman, was running behind so these two guys didn't intercept them.

The two men walked away from the door, and Sparky took a chance and attempted to follow where they went. One by one, he quickly moved from one window overlooking the library's grounds to another, following the progress of the two men as they circled the property. He scurried about, tripping over the corners of the bookcases from time to time. His head was covered in sweat once again, a combination of stress and adrenaline ruining the look he'd tried to achieve in the women's restroom.

He lost sight of them for a moment and scampered back to the rear exit to catch a glimpse of their car. Sparky breathed for the first time when he saw them get into the black sedan and pull out of the parking lot. He leaned against the wall and allowed his head to fall backwards, hitting the one-hundred-thirty-year-old plaster with a thud. He closed his eyes for a moment, allowing his mind to wander as he considered whether it was safe to continue waiting in the library.

That was when he heard it. The gentle rapping at the rear exit. The sound of a single knuckle tapping away. It wasn't the pounding of law enforcement—the unmistakable *thump-thump-thump-open-up-or-we'll-bust-it-down* sound. No, this was more polite. Almost stealth-like. It had to be …

"Sparky? Are you in there?" Jack Young's Midwestern American perfect announcer's voice was familiar to Sparky.

Sparky rushed toward the double glass doors and greeted Young with tears in his eyes. He spoke to his rescuers through the glass. "Jack! Thank you so much. I was getting worried. Um, listen. Stay right here."

Sparky turned and ran back into the library. He shut down the computer and double-checked that he hadn't left a trace that he'd been there. Then he did something he wasn't proud of, but felt it was necessary to cover what happened next.

He approached the vending machine in the back hallway, stood back, and raised his leg to kick the glass. After three attempts, he was successful in breaking into the machine. He frantically began to throw crackers, cookies, and candies all over the floor, except for a couple more Hershey chocolate bars. You know, just to make it look like a break-in. Then he turned his attention to an astonished Jack Young.

He addressed his rescuer through the glass door. "Jack, get the car ready. When I come through this door, all kinds of alarms are going to sound within half a minute. Okay?"

"Okay, Sparky," replied Young, who led his producer back to the unmarked white panel van with a small antenna mounted on the roof.

The engine started and Sparky made his move. He burst through the door, hitting the panic bar with far more force than necessary, and ran down the stairs, stumbling on the last step until he landed chest first on the concrete sidewalk. He skinned both knees and hands as he attempted to break his fall.

So much for looking spiffy for my big interview, he thought to himself as he scrambled to the awaiting van.

CHAPTER 25

Friday, April 6
The Situation Room
Ground Floor, The West Wing
The White House
Washington, DC

A steady rain added to the dour mood that had overcome Director Hapwell as she was escorted onto the grounds of the White House. What should have been a momentous occasion for her, meeting the President of the United States and leading a briefing before his most important advisors, was dwarfed by the overwhelming feeling of dread due to the discovery of 2029 IM86.

Ordinarily, newly discovered space objects were provided a temporary designation until they were studied and then given a more formal name, typically associated with the individual or astronomy facility that made the discovery.

The next numbered designation in line, IM86, was poetic in a way. The use of the number eighty-six was often associated with the restaurant business. Many years ago, there was a neighborhood bar in Greenwich Village, New York called Chumley's. Located at 86 Bedford Street, the building was devoid of modern conveniences like air-conditioning. When the heat of the afternoon set upon the bar, patrons were known to *eighty-six* themselves from, or leave, Chumley's. In modern times, restaurants used the term eighty-six when something was to be canceled or removed from the menu. If a restaurant ran out of a menu item, servers were instructed to eighty-six the dish from the day's offerings.

The driver slowed as he maneuvered the car through the

protective barricades on West Executive Drive that crossed the White House grounds. Hapwell considered the term *eighty-six* and how the meaning could be applied to cancelling, or eliminating, life on Earth. It dogged her since her team proposed the use, but the designation 2029 IM86 could not be changed.

Hapwell waited as a uniformed officer opened the door for her. She stepped under the umbrella he provided, allowing the misty rain to refresh her spirits. She had to be unemotional during her briefing this morning. People with a whole lot more responsibility than she had would have to make several decisions. She anticipated arguments and counterarguments. She even anticipated naysayers who would question the MPC's findings. Hapwell was up for the challenge.

She entered through the double doors that led into a desolate hallway on the bottom floor of the West Wing. A smattering of staffers wandered about at this early hour, stopping by the cafeteria for coffee and pastries.

She'd only been in the White House on one other occasion, a social event in which the new director of NASA was being appointed, and Director Hapwell had unexpectedly found her name on the guest list. Security was always tight, especially since the assassination attempt on the president following the 2020 election. Fresh on the minds of the Secret Service, additional safeguards had been put into place, and Hapwell was being run through the process as she waited in the ground-floor lobby.

After several minutes, she was cleared and led to the Situation Room, which had the audio-visual equipment necessary for her to brief the attendees. Outside the door, the watch officer greeted her, standing next to the black-and-gold plaque that read *White House Situation Room – Restricted Access.*

The five-thousand-square-foot complex of rooms that occupied a large corner of the West Wing was commonly referred to as the *Woodshed.* Once a bowling alley until the sixties, when President Kennedy ordered it destroyed following the Bay of Pigs crisis in Cuba, the Situation Room had technologically evolved into a command center utilized by the president, his military leaders and intelligence advisors, and the cabinet in times when the nation's security was in peril.

After another brief identification check, the watch officer spoke into a collar microphone. The lock on the door buzzed and a loud click preceded the door becoming slightly ajar. Hapwell was one of the first to arrive, by design. She'd emailed her report to the Watch Team at midnight, who then performed their daily function of preparing the Morning Book.

Each day, several agencies, including the State Department, the Director of National Intelligence, and FEMA, provided staffers within the Situation Room's Watch Team daily reports of matters of national security. Once the Morning Book was compiled, it accompanied the driver who picked up the national security advisor every morning. She in turn provided it to the president, the vice president, and various senior staffers for review.

An aide to the Watch Team handed a copy of findings relevant to the MPC's report to Hapwell as she entered the room and showed the director to her seat. She was then introduced to a staffer who offered to assist her with the visual aspects of her presentation, and who, thanks to her calming demeanor, would serve to reduce Hapwell's nervousness.

While Hapwell prepared her notes and coordinated the visual material with the Watch Team's aide, the president's closest advisors filed into the room. She was surprised at their calm demeanor considering the magnitude of the primary topic of discussion. After studying the expressions on their faces, she decided to ask the aide if this was normal.

"Miss, do you think they've read my report? I mean, it's all here."

The aide laughed. "Truthfully, many have not. To be blunt, most of the people in attendance this morning like to focus on their own shit, if you know what I mean. If it doesn't affect their agency or department, then it's not their—"

"Yeah, I get it." Hapwell understood.

"Exactly."

Hapwell rolled her eyes and shrugged. After she was finished laying out the threat the world faced, she'd expect that all of these individuals who held the most powerful positions in the United States government would either realize that what she had to say was, in fact, *their shit*, or they might actually shit themselves instead.

All of the seats were taken when the president's chief of staff made her first appearance. "Good morning," she said, sliding into her seat at the head of the table without looking up.

"Good morning," several attendees responded.

"Let's get started with the mundane before I bring in the president," she began, flipping open the Morning Book.

Maggie Fielding, the president's chief of staff, ran a tight ship, using her former naval command experience to keep a clamp on staff leaks and to make sure the president's time was used wisely. To the president's credit, he resisted the urge to micromanage the White House, as so many presidents before him had tried to do. Governing the United States of America was difficult enough without trying to concern himself with the inner workings of the White House and its interaction with agency heads.

Fielding continued. "All events on the president's schedule for the day have been cancelled."

"Maggie, just a moment," interrupted the Secretary of State. "We've been putting off the Saudi prince for months and have assured him that he could be seen with the president today. I mean, have a meeting with—"

"I know exactly what you mean," Fielding shot back. "You've been promising the newly crowned prince an audience so he could get his photo op and stick it up the ass of the Iranians. It'll have to happen another day. This matter is far too important, and therefore politically volatile, for the president to be seen schmoozing with the *prince-slayer*."

"With all due respect, Maggie, we shouldn't use that kind of language to discuss the new head of state of the richest—"

"Crown Prince Mohammed bin Salman had been a friend to this administration, and the U.S., since his rise to power. The president is not overly excited about being seen with the new crown prince, hence the reason this meet and greet was postponed until way after the inauguration. Now, let's move along."

The chief of staff went through various matters that were customarily addressed during the morning briefing. She touched on the geopolitical hot zones around the world, including a series of tornadoes that had struck Dixie Alley overnight, before turning her attention to Hapwell, who patiently waited her turn.

Although Fielding rarely spent more than a few moments on any one topic, Hapwell became intrigued by the process, which helped take her mind off the magnitude of IM86's discovery.

The president's chief of staff stood from her chair and slid the Morning Book in front of an empty chair to her right. She thumbed through the tabs until she reached the center of the binder that contained the MPC's report.

"Director Hapwell, the rest of the briefing is devoted to you. Take a moment to gather your thoughts while I send for the president."

CHAPTER 26

Friday, April 6
The Situation Room
The White House
Washington, DC

President Mack Watson was less than one hundred days into his new presidency when he was challenged with a catastrophe like no other in modern history. He was already under intense scrutiny by the media and the American public following a contentious presidential campaign that had been marred by allegations of voter fraud from one side and voter suppression from the other. After a Supreme Court hearing in which the outcomes of three key states were determined, Watson took the oath of office and began the task of governing.

The Watson administration relied heavily upon longtime Washington insiders and military leaders with proven track records in dealing with international security matters. The nation found itself embroiled in hot wars in both the Middle East and South America. Just as troublesome were the cold war conditions with China over the South China Sea, and Russia over its continued incursions into Eastern Europe as the Moscow government continued its quest to reconstitute the old Soviet Union.

The politically astute president knew that very little could bring the world's leaders together, but an extinction-level threat like this asteroid must, for the sake of humanity.

The president arrived, exchanged some pleasantries, and then settled into the chair at the head of the table, awaiting Hapwell's briefing.

She took a deep breath and began. "Mr. President, my team at the Minor Planet Center has worked around the clock analyzing the data provided to us by one of our astronauts aboard the International Space Station as well as information provided by an amateur astronomer in a remote area of Georgia."

The president interrupted her and turned to his national security advisor. "What about that?"

"Contained, Mr. President," he quickly responded.

"The reporter?"

"The Atlanta field office of the FBI has descended upon the gentleman's hometown and are conducting door-to-door searches. I've been assured that he'll be taken into custody by day's end."

The president paused and looked around the room. "Maggie has done a tremendous job of clamping down on the leaks that have plagued prior administrations. I have to say that this information must be kept out of the public eye until we can make a decision on how to deal with this threat, and how to control the release of information. Let me also say this, if prior administrations were genuinely concerned about how the population would react to the revelations that extraterrestrials have visited our planet, they'd lose their minds if they thought we were about to go the way of the dinosaurs. It's very important that our release of this threat be coupled with a cohesive, solid plan for protecting the planet from the impact."

The president paused, made eye contact with several members of his national security team, and then turned his attention back to Hapwell. With a slight nod, he encouraged her to continue.

"Mr. President, if I may expand on your thought, this situation is far different from the Chelyabinsk event in Russia sixteen years ago. It was just sheer luck that the meteoroid exploded over the Bering Sea, largely unnoticed. Within a matter of days, or less, amateur astronomers in the Northern Hemisphere will be able to pick up IM86's approach as Comet Oort continues out of view. The trajectories of the two near-Earth objects intersected, but follow wholly different paths."

"Director, um—" the president glanced down at the Morning Book "—Director Hapwell, we need to deal with absolutes. If I'm to declare a national emergency, then I need to know exactly what we're dealing with here."

"Mr. President, I completely understand. As we get closer to the impact date, the variables are lessened and accuracy can be assured."

The president's national security advisor interrupted Hapwell. "Isn't it true that IM86 could bypass Earth altogether, albeit a close shave?"

"Yes, sir, that is true. Our initial calculations show that it is on a collision course with the planet, especially due to the gravitational pull of the Earth. NEOs have been known to alter their trajectory as the Earth draws them in, so to speak."

The Secretary of Energy cleared her throat and raised her hand slightly. The president nodded and acknowledged her. "Madam Secretary, would you like to weigh in on this?"

"Mr. President, with your permission, I've brought with me the Undersecretary of Science, Paul Ashford. He was a former director of the Minor Planet Center as well as the former deputy administrator at NASA."

"Please," said the president, who leaned back in his chair. "I'd like to hear all perspectives on this matter."

"Thank you, Mr. President," began Ashford. He looked over at Hapwell and smiled. "Mr. President, I am familiar with Director Hapwell's work and have admired her efforts at the MPC following my tenure there. I need to briefly relay to everyone our nation's experience with a similar near-Earth object, 1997 XF11.

"XF11 was discovered and then immediately considered our next planet killer. Orbit calculations indicated that it would make an unprecedented close approach to Earth with a miss distance of less than one-quarter of a lunar distance. The ESA, the European Space Agency, placed it at even less than that.

"XF11 was slightly larger than our newly discovered IM86, at more than a kilometer across. The news of this behemoth spread and it wasn't long before the media generated a panic. At the time, we didn't have the technology to study, much less divert, an asteroid. As it turned out, both NASA and the ESA were overstating the close approach, and XF11 passed our planet at nearly a million and a half miles away.

"My point is this, Mr. President. Before we decide to embark on a diversion or destruction strategy, we might also want to consider the extraordinary opportunity that is presented to us for study, including mining the asteroid."

The room erupted in whispered chatter, causing the chief of staff to tap the end of her pen on the conference table to grab everyone's attention. She addressed Ashford's suggestion. "From the report prepared by the MPC, Mr. Undersecretary, I don't think we should run the risk of trying to study something that could kill us all."

The attendees began speaking to one another.

The president raised his hand to calm his advisors. "Listen up, everyone. I'm known to consider all sides of an issue and make an educated decision, one that includes a cost-benefit analysis, if you will. Mr. Undersecretary, knowing the potential risk this asteroid poses, what possible benefit could we attain from its study or, as you suggest, mining it?"

Ashford gathered his thoughts and responded, "Mr. President, there are certain obvious benefits of mining an asteroid, especially one this close to us. The logistical difficulties of delivering personnel and payload is eased considerably because of the close proximity of the asteroid.

"Sir, the concept of space mining is in its infancy, and exploring is very costly. Attempts to study and mine an asteroid at a greater distance would cost in the neighborhood of a billion dollars just to bring home ten pounds of material.

"With the close approach, we could obtain, return, and study many times that amount of material at a fraction of the cost. This could potentially add trillions of dollars to the global GDP and completely redefine our understanding of natural resources."

The Energy Secretary added, "Mr. President, studies have shown that an asteroid of one hundred feet wide could yield fifty billion dollars of platinum and possibly other resources that have never been found on our own planet. These undiscovered resources could have a myriad of uses."

"How do you propose to put together this so-called mining operation on a short timetable? If I understand Ms. Hapwell, we only have a couple of weeks to take action."

Ashford responded, "Sir, investors such as Google's Eric Schmidt and Larry Page, filmmaker James Cameron, and software mogul Charles Simonyi have already developed the technology and capability to mine a near-Earth asteroid. With the use of SpaceX rockets, they could be ready in days to intercept IM86, but certainly by April 20, the date I've calculated as our last best opportunity for diversion."

President Watson made some notes, leaned into his chief of staff and whispered, then returned his attention to Hapwell. "Director Hapwell, what do you think of this idea?"

"It's nuts, Mr. President."

CHAPTER 27

Friday, April 5
Dog Island
Florida Panhandle

Gunner had taken a more casual ride back from Eglin that early afternoon, allowing himself the opportunity to consider his short session with Dr. Dowling, as well as his briefing with the colonel. His normal wide-open-throttle crushing of the waves was replaced with a fifty-mile-an-hour cruise, still fast by most boats' standards.

Dr. Dowling had started the session by confirming with Gunner that he was ready to put all the cards on the table, as he'd promised. Gunner was completely honest in his answer. He believed that discussing the past was unnecessary, as all it did was open up old wounds that needed to heal.

The renowned psychologist agreed that ordinarily, the passage of time does alleviate the pain and scars of emotional wounds in most of his patients, but he then reeled off a list of behaviors Gunner had exhibited that indicated he had a lot of work to do. In Gunner's case, he masked his pain and suffering by avoiding it, but he manifested his inner feelings by taking unnecessary risks.

All in all, Gunner thought it was a good start to their new understanding of what Dr. Dowling was there to do, and he actually found himself looking forward to their next session in a month. Meanwhile, it was back to work, something Gunner considered to be the best therapy.

He was briefed by Colonel Bradford on his next mission, and Gunner was thrilled to be back in the saddle so quickly. There were a lot of holes in the information relayed to him by the colonel, but he was assured the mission leadership team at Fort Belvoir would give him a total picture upon his arrival.

Gunner pulled back on the throttle of the Donzi, allowing the bow to drop in the water and the stern to be pushed by the considerable wake the forty-one-foot-long boat left as it cut through the Gulf waters. A pod of dolphins had taken up residency along the shores of the barrier islands to St. George Sound and even found their way along the beach in front of his home.

He navigated through the gap between Dog Island and St. George Island, a space that had more than doubled in size thanks to Hurricane Michael in 2018, a devastating Category 5 storm that was the first to make landfall in the U.S. since Hurricane Andrew in 1992.

The dolphins, which had gathered in a pod of several dozen, had delighted beachgoers with their close proximity to shore. For Gunner, it was a treat to spot them gracefully dipping in and out of the surf. Dolphins were intelligent, social creatures that ran in pods to protect one another from danger and to care for injured individuals. These clusters sometimes ran across each other, crossing paths to temporarily create superpods of hundreds or even thousands.

Food was in high abundance for the dolphins in the sea-life-rich area where the Apalachicola River dumped into the Gulf of Mexico. In particular, the still waters of St. George Sound provided dolphins and seagulls ample opportunity to feed, which was all the more reason that Gunner was careful with his speed when approaching the entrance to the sound.

He picked up speed slightly as he entered The Cut and turned toward the right. In the distance, he heard the high-pitched whine of a single-engine plane approaching from his rear. As it got closer, Gunner smiled, knowing who was piloting the aircraft. He resisted the urge to turn and look, knowing the pilot would get a kick out of putting a scare into him.

Gunner held his breath and gripped the wheel of the Donzi, contemplating forcing the throttle down in a race to the finish line, but he caught a glimpse of several dolphins off his port side, and he didn't want to disturb them. So he decided to let Pop have his fun.

The Cessna drew closer, and then with a rush of wind, the seaplane's floats whizzed barely thirty feet above him. Gunner looked up as the plane whizzed by, and caught a glimpse of Bear's muscular black arm hanging out the window, giving him the middle finger.

Gunner let out a hearty laugh and returned the gesture. He truly loved his father, and his misfit, extended family. Each of them would take a bullet for the other and defend their team to the death. Even Pop, in his golden age of retirement, was a loyal soldier who'd go into the field of battle with his son and partners if called upon to do so.

Pop expertly maneuvered the Cessna 185 Skywagon to take advantage of the light wind conditions. He turned ever so slightly, allowing the seaplane to weathervane into the Gulf breeze until it gently touched down in the shallow waters off Dog Island. He brought the plane to a planing position and then used his rudder to taxi up to the dock that extended into the sound.

Pop's time in the Air Force as a noncommissioned air traffic controller had resulted in a twenty-year career culminating with a retirement as a chief master sergeant, the highest level of enlisted leadership in the Air Force. After Pop left the service, he had the opportunity to go to Oklahoma City at the behest of the Federal Aviation Administration. The FAA was actively recruiting military retirees to become civilian air traffic controllers, but Pop opted to lead a simple life and focus on raising his son.

On a whim, he went to Island Air Express near Panama City one day and discussed their flight training program. With Gunner's mother's reluctant approval, Pop learned to fly. He passed the flight simulator and classroom training with flying colors, and later aced the FAA practical flight test.

Once he was licensed, he turned his attention to flying seaplanes. The tourist industry around Apalachicola was booming, and Pop saw an opportunity to supplement his retirement income by carrying visitors above the beaches to provide them a different perspective of the turquoise blue waters and the sugary white sand beaches.

He then expanded his one-man operation to include taxi services between Carrabelle and Dog Island. Dog Island, which was once part of Camp Gordon Johnston, a World War II amphibious training center, was one of the few inhabited islands off Florida's coastlines that did not have bridge access. Several water taxi services and Pop's seaplane provided the residents a regular means of transportation back to civilization.

Gunner pulled the Donzi up to the side of the dock opposite where the seaplane was tied off. Bear helped Pop secure his lines to the cleats and position the large white buoys to protect the plane from bumping its sides.

"How did it go?" asked Cam as Gunner cut the engines. She grabbed his lines and helped him secure the boat, not always an easy task considering its length.

"All right," replied Gunner, who was typically a man of few words. He made eye contact with Cam and managed a smile. She was the closest thing to an empathetic human being in his life, second only to Sammy Hart, the bartender equivalent of a psychotherapist.

"Well, we've got a surprise for you," said Cam. She stretched out her hand and hoisted Gunner onto the dock.

"Yeah, and I've got one for you guys, too. You first."

Gunner glanced down the dock. Bear was carrying the large Yeti cooler, his triceps bulging like it contained gold.

Cam took Gunner by the arm and explained, "Pop flew us over to Cedar Key and we picked up some clams. How would you feel about a good old-fashioned clam bake tonight? You know, we'll cook 'em in a sand pit, throw in some red-skin potatoes, corn on the cob, and enjoy several brewskis."

Cedar Key was known for its clamming industries. The small community boasted that it harvested more clams than any other place in the U.S. Visitors came from all over the country to Cedar Key, took tours of the commercial clamming operations, and then partook of the many ways to serve them. Cedar Key was one of Pop's favorite places to visit. He'd always commented that the brownish water at the shoreline wasn't pretty to look at compared to Dog Island, but it was perfect for clams.

Gunner stopped and grimaced. The prospect of hanging on the

beach with his team sounded more than appealing, but he had to break the news to Cam. "Um, I don't think that's gonna happen."

Cam turned to face him. "Why?"

"We've been deployed," he began in response. He glanced down at his watch and shook his head from side to side. "In fact, the chopper is scheduled to pick us up in about three hours at our usual spot in Tate's Hell."

Tate's Hell State Forest comprised two hundred thousand acres to the north of Dog Island. Rugged trails traversed the landscape, a favorite of four-wheelers and Jeep outings alike. It also provided a desolate area near Gunner's home for military helicopters to pick him up to embark on missions without piquing the curiosity of the locals. In Gunner's line of work, situational awareness was tantamount. Loose lips sink ships, and could also get him killed.

Cam patted Gunner on the back and motioned for them to continue. "Bear and Pop will be disappointed. Those two cooked up this whole idea and they've been chattering about it ever since you pulled out this morning."

"We can postpone it. Without hiccups, we should be able to be back Sunday night."

Cam laughed, which caught the attention of the guys in front of them. "Sure, no hiccups. Okay, silky smooth, as always."

"Yeah, I know."

"So, Major Fox, where are we headed this time?"

"Russia."

CHAPTER 28

Earlier in the day, Gunner's briefing with the colonel had been just that—brief, which was not necessarily out of the ordinary in the special role Major Gunner Fox played within the military and intelligence apparatus of the United States government. There was a whole lot of need-to-know and classified aspects of his chain of command.

While Colonel Bradford was technically his superior officer since he was assigned, for all intents and purposes, to Eglin, the nature of Gunner's special ops missions found him under the command of a variety of government agencies. One thing was understood by every handler that had the privilege of working with Gunner, he only had one true commander, and that was himself.

And he had a team that was a mandatory requirement for everything he was tasked to do. The three of them were a package deal, and that was a given.

They were en route to the Defense Threat Reduction Agency at Fort Belvoir, Virginia. The secretive military facility, located on a peninsula extending into the Potomac River, was home to a variety of military units, including the Army Intelligence and Security Command.

Operating a central base of operations for many anti-terror operations, the DTRA added a combat option to the intelligence apparatus that worked night and day to protect Americans. When Colonel Bradford had informed Gunner that his team would be briefed and staged at Fort Belvoir, he was somewhat bewildered. Typically, the DTRA was known for acting upon events that were considered *right of boom*, terminology associated with the timeline of an attack or disaster. As part of the War on Terror, U.S. governmental agencies focused their efforts as much on the aftermath of a terror attack, referred to as *right of boom*, as they did on prevention. Valuable intelligence could be garnered from following up on leads related to the catastrophic event.

Gunner had quizzed the colonel and was satisfied she knew very little about his upcoming mission. This was frustrating to Bear and Cam, as they were hyped about being deployed, but they knew nothing except their destination would be Russia, not exactly friendly territory as the second Cold War ramped up.

The Coast Guard–operated MH-65E Dolphin helicopter was often employed to ferry Gunner to his deployments because it didn't raise the eyebrows of the locals, who were used to seeing the Guard patrol their waterways. The chopper delivered the trio to Tyndall, where they caught a newly operational Air Force Learjet 75, which landed at Fort Belvoir right around dark.

They departed the aircraft and were met by several Army officers wearing their fatigues. After their brief introductions, they were led inside to a small conference room, where Gunner saw a familiar face.

"Welcome to the DTRA, Major," the man announced formally, providing a snappy salute and a broad grin.

Gunner returned the salute and then chuckled. "Do these people realize who they let inside their gates?"

"Of course they do. I gave them a complete rundown on you, pal."

"No, I'm talking about you, Commander."

"Shhh, they have no idea who I am. Remember, Major, I'm a ghost."

The two military men laughed and exchanged a bro-hug, clenching one another's right hand and bumping their chests. Gunner slapped his old friend and former commander on the back with his left hand.

"Well, Commander Ghost, before we catch up, let me introduce you to my team. This is Major Cameron Mills and Staff Sergeant Barrett King." As the three exchanged salutes and handshakes, Gunner continued. "Cam, Bear, this is Colonel Gregory Smith, who once upon a time took me under his wing at AFSOC at Hurlburt Field. He left six months before you two arrived on the scene."

"I remember seeing your picture on the wall in the command center, sir," said Cameron. "I remember that you were missed by everyone."

Smith, who was dressed in civilian clothes, was in fact referred to as *Ghost*. He'd had a distinguished career with the USAF Special Operations Forces and became so invaluable to the Pentagon that he was pulled out of AFSOC to coordinate special assignments.

"Ghost," began Gunner, who despite the differences in rank and age, was on a first-name basis with his former base commander, "they joined me at Hurlburt Field after the Pentagon pulled you out to work with the three-letter agencies."

"Major Mills, if I'm not mistaken, you were an acquaintance of—" he began before catching himself.

"That's right, Colonel."

The room fell silent for a moment and then Gunner switched the topic of conversation. "Ghost, I can't help but notice you're dressed in civvies."

"There have been some changes since you and I worked together last. Technically, I've retired from the Air Force and taken on a new position within the government, one that allows me to dress like this." Ghost held his arms apart to present his khaki pants and pressed white cotton shirt.

"The look suits you," lied Gunner. The chiseled, broad-shouldered former operator didn't look comfortable in khakis and a white shirt at all. He either belonged in uniform or in a ghillie suit.

"Liar," responded Ghost with a laugh. "Let's take a seat, because I'm afraid this op is on a fast track, a decision that goes all the way to the top."

Gunner's team exchanged glances and followed their mission

leader's instructions. As he sat, he asked, "What's the operation?"

"You're not gonna like it, but, Gunner, I've insisted upon you handling this for a number of reasons, not to mention that I can be assured you'll be tight-lipped about what you learn in Russia."

"Ghost, this sounds vaguely like a surveillance mission. You know how—"

Ghost raised his hand and cut Gunner off. "I know. I know. You hate surveillance."

"Well, at least tell me that after the surveillance, we might get to blow some Russki shit up. I owe them for shooting me out of the sky over the Arctic Circle."

Ghost chuckled. "With all due respect, Major. You kinda had that coming. That MiG had barely tipped his wings into our airspace before you took him out. Then you decided to go chase the rest of them back into Siberia."

"Yeah, yeah. I remember. International incident. Violations of UN treaties. Precipice of World War III. Blah, blah, blah."

"Yes, Major, all of the above. But listen up, this is serious. You might notice that there's nobody else in the room with us. There's a reason for that. What I'm about to tell you is classified Level 6 Top Secret. There are only a handful of people on this planet aware of what you are about to do."

"Sir," interrupted Bear. He fired off the logical questions. "Are we under attack or in imminent danger of attack? From the Russians?"

"Not from the Russians, no," replied Ghost. "Frankly, Sergeant, that's all I know. I've never seen anything like this, and as a former operator, I didn't look forward to going on a mission without all the facts. Unfortunately, in this case, the security level is so high that we're talkin' president and Joint Chiefs type of stuff."

"We're listening," said Cam.

"A few days ago, NASA made a discovery," began Ghost. Cam shot a glance at Gunner, who gripped the arms of his swivel chair until his knuckles became white. The words hung in the air for a moment before Ghost continued. "Based upon the information received from the ISS and another undisclosed source, Washington needs to get eyes on the Russian equivalent of Cape Canaveral, a facility in eastern Russia known as the Vostochny Cosmodrome."

"Their spaceport?" asked Cam.

"That's correct," replied Ghost. "In recent days, they've taken extraordinary measures to mask their activities there from our eyes in the sky, including taking the astonishing steps of trying to crash one of their satellites into our reconnaissance satellite to cut off our view. Naturally, they profusely apologized for the near mishap, and our built-in computer defenses enabled the recon satellite to avert a disaster, but it's been taken offline for several days, leaving us blind."

"Ghost," began Gunner, who'd relaxed somewhat, "do we have intel that they might be preparing a nuclear launch from what is ordinarily a space-based facility?"

"I don't know. This is part of what bugs me about this operation. Our task is to get in, take a lot of pictures from as close in as you can without discovery or capture, and transmit them back to us here."

Gunner felt compelled to say what was on his mind. "You know I'm not a fan of NASA. Is this their operation or the agency's?" he asked, referring to the Central Intelligence Agency.

Ghost nodded, acknowledging where Gunner's question was coming from. "Certainly, NASA is involved, but at this stage, because of the national security implications we can presume from the level of secrecy, this is for the benefit of the CIA and ultimately the White House."

"Sir, I take it we're not going to fly commercial into Moscow and rent a car," said Cam.

"That's right, Major. Vostochny is located in the Amur Oblast, a federal district located in Russia's Far East. It adjoins the border with northernmost China, roughly three hundred fifty miles southwest of the Sea of Okhotsk."

"What do you have in mind for insertion?" asked Gunner.

Ghost turned to Bear. "Sergeant, I understand you're checked out on the AV-280 Valor."

"Yes, sir, I am. Are you talking a tilt-rotor drop? Three hundred fifty miles across some hostile soil is quite a haul."

"That's why I called in the best," replied Ghost. "Are you up for it?"

"Sir, we don't shy away from any mission," replied Gunner. "It's just that getting in and out in one round trip is doable. However, the Russians will have eyes wide open if we attempt to try it twice."

Ghost nodded his head and grimaced. "That's why we're only gonna do this once. You'll set her down, get the pictures, and then hightail it the hell out of there."

"Oh, sure, no problem," groaned Bear. "It's a shame we can't break all kinds of treaties like the Russians do. They park their nuclear subs all up and down our coastlines, ready to fry us with a press of the button, and we've gotta sneak in there, all stealth-like, just to see what their space cadets are up to."

"We've got this, Ghost, no worries," implored Gunner, trying to downplay Bear's whining and to assuage any concerns his former commander might have about his team's readiness.

Cam raised her hand. "Sir, what about comms? Are we gonna be in the dark other than access to a satellite feed to transmit images back home?"

"Actually, I'm glad you brought that up. There's one other member of this operation who will be your eyes and ears back here at the DTRA. You can lean on her for intel as much as you want."

Ghost stood from his chair and stuck his head out the door. He motioned to someone in the hallway and then stood to the side as a woman entered. Out of courtesy, Gunner's team stood and greeted the new addition to the briefing.

A short, unremarkable young woman entered the room with a laptop tucked under her arm. She shyly made eye contact with Gunner and pushed her thick eyeglasses higher up her nose as she glanced at the other two members of the team.

"This is Special Agent Theodora Cuccinelli. She's on loan from the bureau specifically for this project."

Gunner extended his hand to shake. "It's nice to meet you, Agent Cuccinelli."

The young woman was too shy to shake hands, opting instead to raise her right arm and provide the group a slight wave.

Cam tried to ease the tension and perceived nervousness oozing out of their communications specialist. "Theodora is an interesting name. I assume it's Italian, like a friend of my mother's. She used to go by the nickname Teddy."

"Um, my mom used to call me Teddy. I kind of outgrew that after I graduated from MIT."

"Whoa, MIT!" exclaimed Bear. "That's impressive, Theodora."

The young woman blushed, and then she made direct eye contact with Gunner. "Major Fox, I want you to know that your team can call on me for anything."

"She's right," interrupted Ghost. "In fact, there's a reason she's earned the nickname the Jackal."

"The Jackal?" Cam asked, as if she wasn't sure whether she'd heard Ghost correctly.

Bear couldn't contain his laughter. "You mean like Carlos the Jackal, the Venezuelan terrorist from back in the day."

"No, I'm a hunter, um, of information. I can find a way to access any database, any camera, or any nation's communications systems."

Ghost added, "The Jackal has been instrumental in bringing down terrorist cells and chasing the ill-gotten gains of Mexican drug cartels. She has the innate ability to process information quickly and access data at lightning-fast speeds."

"Here's the thing," began the Jackal, who was starting to overcome her shyness. "The internet, or databases, is only a useful tool if you know what question to ask or where to look. Usually, agents or operators, whatever the case may be, are very adept at catching or killing bad guys. In the process of any field mission, information is needed, and quickly. That's where I come in. There's nobody better at it in America than me."

Gunner grinned. He admired the young woman's spunk and confidence. "Well, Jackal, or, I mean, do we call you Special Agent Jackal or something else."

"You can call me the Jackal, or just Jackal. And, I hope, since we're working on this mission together, you'll allow me to address you more informally."

Bear laughed again and shook his head. He pointed to the team one by one. "Gunner, Cam, and I'm Bear. Barrett means bear power in German. Did you know that?" Bear puffed out his pectoral muscles and followed that with a flex of his biceps.

The Jackal provided him a blank stare in return.

Cam started laughing and put her arm around the Jackal. "Come on, let's sit down so I can tell you the kinds of things we'll be needing help with while we're in the backwoods of Mother Russia, the real bear."

CHAPTER 29

Director Hapwell's response to the president's question shocked the stoic members of his national security team and resulted in a jaw-dropping expression on Ashford, who was highly respected in the scientific community.

For a moment, the attendees didn't know how to react to Hapwell's out-of-hand dismissal of Ashford's suggestion to mine an asteroid, but then the president let out a hearty laugh.

"Well, Director Hapwell, tell us how you really feel."

Hapwell gulped and then commenced to do exactly that. "Mr. President, I don't mean any disrespect to Undersecretary Ashford, whom I have the highest regard for, nor do I mean to impugn this process. That said, I can't sit here and allow you to entertain the notion of mining an asteroid of this close proximity to the planet. Sure, there are scientific discoveries to be had or, as Mr. Ashford pointed out, trillions of dollars to be made, but the threat is too great."

"Mr. President," Ashford interrupted, "if I could be allowed to finish."

"Certainly," the president and former judge began in response. "But, Mr. Undersecretary, you'd better make a compelling argument because I'm inclined to agree with Director Hapwell. We can't risk American lives in the name of international commerce or scientific discovery."

"It's an opportunity for us to kill two birds with one stone." The words were out of his mouth before he realized the context in which they were said. Several attendees shook their head at Ashford's faux pas, and he quickly corrected the statement. "Okay, poor choice of words under these circumstances. Let me just begin."

The president nodded and smiled to encourage the oldest attendee in the room the opportunity to gather himself before he continued.

"Thank you, Mr. President. There are two options for processing an asteroid. One is to simply gather some raw asteroidal material and return it for scientific study. That's been done by the Japanese and, as we learned, the sample was much too small for comprehensive scientific study. Second, the preferred method, and the one that relates back to my inartful choice of words, is to process the material on-site, and during the process of establishing the mining operation, we can take steps to move the asteroid off its projected path toward Earth, assuming, of course, the trajectory is confirmed in the next few days."

The president stepped in. "I've campaigned in the coal country of Pennsylvania and West Virginia. Even with modern mining methods employed, and safety hazards accounted for, it can be a dangerous, complex process. Is that what we're talking about here?"

"And what about the cost?" asked Fielding.

"Well, the pricey part of asteroid mining isn't the up-front expense, as that has already been absorbed in the private sector. Nor is it the launch of the equipment and crew to actually achieve the goal. Again, both NASA and SpaceX are prepared, with some slight modifications, to make that happen.

"The really expensive aspect of the concept is getting the materials back to Earth. I would propose a joint public-private partnership between NASA and Planetary Resources, with SpaceX receiving a piece of the pie, so to speak, for delivering the payloads to and from IM86."

"What do you propose?" asked the president.

"Planetary Resources will turn over sample materials to us for study. In addition, they will help NASA take a team of scientists to the asteroid to initiate diversion protocols, protecting the planet from an impact event. In return, we will give them full exclusive rights to the mining permits, if deemed necessary, together with the profits from the valuable raw materials that might be found on the asteroid.

"We save the world from the asteroid while creating the opportunity to make scientific discoveries about our solar system, and possibly the origins of man, at the same time."

Fielding whispered to the president, who nodded as he spoke. The president shrugged and then addressed the room.

"There are legal complications to all of this that have never been discussed at the UN, to my knowledge. There's a treaty in place, if I recall, from the late sixties regarding outer space. Further, Congress signed the Space Act in 2015 that gave U.S.-based companies, like Planetary Resources, permission to own and sell the natural resources they mine in space. As we know, that had become a point of contention with the Russians and Chinese when it came to establishing the outpost on the Moon in recent years. Everyone tried to lay claim to the Moon, and we argued we were there first, so it was ours. The dispute almost erupted into World War III before my predecessors calmed the situation down."

Ashford continued. "Mr. President, I understand the need to maintain international relations, but let me be honest, the first country to mine an asteroid and discover its hidden resources, some of which may be unknown to us now and which may possess certain, um, characteristics of value militarily ..." His voice trailed off as the members of the Joint Chiefs of Staff who were in attendance perked up for the first time.

"Well, I understand where you're heading with this, Mr. Undersecretary, and I agree wholeheartedly. The fact of the matter is that if we are considering these options, once the Russians become aware of IM86, they will be having a conversation just like this one. It could be a matter of a race into space to see which country can plant its flag on this sucker first."

The president's chief of staff looked over her glasses toward the director of National Intelligence and asked, "Speaking of Moscow, I noticed in our briefing that there has been some activity at their Cosmodrome in Russia's Far East. What can you tell us?"

"We have a covert team preparing to deploy now. The Russians have taken extraordinary measures to conceal their activity at Vostochny, and in light of this report received by me last night, I immediately tasked the DTRA with getting eyes on the ground in Russia."

The president held both of his hands in front of him. "I've heard enough. Plausible deniability, you know."

"Yes, sir," replied the DNI.

The president turned to Director Hapwell. "You've been quiet during this discussion, yet I sense that you're chomping at the bit to weigh in, am I correct?"

Hapwell smiled and nodded. "Mr. President, I can't disagree with the proposed mining operation by Mr. Ashford, but just not in this instance. We don't have time for this. The margin of error is miniscule, as IM86 is approaching Earth at sixty thousand miles per hour. I must remind everyone that it is slated for impact three weeks from today."

"That is a tight schedule, Mr. President," interjected Ashford. "But I can guarantee that Planetary Resources and SpaceX will work round the clock to make it happen. I'd be willing to bet NASA can put together their A-team, as well."

"Let's talk about that," began Fielding. "Assuming that these private entities and the A-team, as you put it, can reach IM86 quickly, what then? How do you plan to divert the asteroid, and can you assure the president that such diversion tactics will work?"

"Naturally, there are variables and potential complications, but let me lay out the options."

CHAPTER 30

Friday, April 6
The Situation Room
The White House
Washington, DC

Director Hapwell casually glanced down at her watch as Ashford began to speak. It was intended to be a not-so-subtle reminder to the president and others that the clock was ticking on this planet killer's path toward Earth. Nonetheless, the president and his chief of staff allowed Ashford to continue to dominate the conversation with his proposed diversion and mining operation that, in Hapwell's opinion, was insufficient to protect the planet from potential destruction. Still, she sat respectfully to listen, hoping that the president would give her the final word.

"I'd like to start by preempting the most obvious argument regarding diverting IM86, which is to attack it with nuclear weapons. Without going into the mechanics of the DART mission and other proposed nuclear solutions, let me remind everyone that there are serious legal ramifications to using nuclear weapons in space."

Hapwell immediately recognized that Ashford was playing on the president's legal background to sway his opinion away from the destruction option.

Ashford continued. "All of the major space powers—the US, Europe, Russia, China, and the Japanese—have developed kinetic impactors, probes, if you will, designed to change the trajectory of a near-Earth object. These kinetic impactors are designed to strike the asteroid, break it into many parts, or simply alter its composition enough to divert it from its deadly path.

"The kinetic impactor approach came after years of debating the issue of nuclear weapons in space. Strong and nearly unanimous opposition to weaponization of space was expressed in the UN Conference on Disarmament years ago. China and Russia, as you know, proposed a treaty that we initially refused to discuss. Arguably, the treaties were one-sided and our intelligence agencies saw that some nations, like North Korea, would not be a party. It's been presumed that nuclear weapons have been deployed aboard North Korean and Iranian satellites for years, and therefore our government's position that removing nukes in defense of our nation was off the table, even if they were deployed in space.

"That leaves us the Outer Space Treaty of 1967 that the president mentioned earlier. There are five other treaties that arguably coexist and supplement the '67 accord, preventing space weaponization."

"Even if it was deemed necessary to save the world?" asked Fielding.

"I don't know of any exceptions carved into the treaties," replied Ashford.

Director Hapwell couldn't help herself. "Personally, I'd take my chances being called into the court of public opinion using my save-the-world-takes-priority defense over a sixty-year-old treaty."

The president chuckled at her remark.

Ashford scowled and continued. "Well, with the treaties in place, we do have viable alternatives that will allow us to advance our other goals, including building a space station on an asteroid in order to explore other parts of the solar system."

"A space station?" asked the president.

"Yes, sir," replied Ashford. "Mining an asteroid would necessarily have to be done from the inside out. Drilling in microgravity is hard because exerting downward force on the surface of the asteroid will push the equipment outward into space. Therefore, it would be necessary to build a space station inside the asteroid."

Hapwell interrupted. "Asteroids are made of solid rock and rotating at several times per minute. Size and makeup are significant variables in what you propose."

Ashford nodded, patiently allowing Hapwell to make her point. "Agreed. Metal-based asteroids are durable enough for us to land upon them and possibly penetrate with mining equipment. Carbon-rich rocks will most likely break up in space during the process. A stony body, which makes up the majority of all meteorites, falls somewhere in between. In my proposal, mining a stony or carbon-rich asteroid will break up its appearance and therefore alter its trajectory. If it's metal in nature, then we have some work to do before we can commence a mining operation."

"Like what?" asked the president.

"Well, we have the orbital slingshot method," began Ashford in his reply. "This was first developed when 99942 Apophis was discovered many years ago. When the God of Chaos, which is the translation for Apophis, comes within nine million miles of Earth in 2036, the Jet Propulsion Laboratory stands ready to deploy this unique method of capturing the asteroid and modifying its trajectory safely away from the planet."

"How do they propose to capture an asteroid?" asked the president. "And, once we do, what do we do with it?"

"Mr. President, I have to speak conceptually for now, as we don't have the precise trajectory defined and its relationship to the Moon, but let me lay out what I think is possible," replied Ashford. "The gravitational pull of planets, and even their orbiting satellites, like our Moon, can be used to our advantage in a situation like this one. If we can adjust the asteroid's orbit such that it makes a close approach to the Moon with a relatively low velocity, it creates a slingshot effect that can drop the asteroid into Earth's orbit. The Moon can slow the velocity of the approaching asteroid by ten percent, which yields two things. First, it could draw the NEO into our orbit, making mining much easier. Secondly, it will slow the path of IM86 so that it doesn't intersect with Earth's orbit, thus eliminating the threat."

Hapwell interrupted him. "The studies and theories that you're proposing are based upon a much smaller asteroid of only a metric ton or so. We're talking about a rock that's over a mile wide, fifty times larger than most of the studies imagine. As a result, the mission prep time and the fuel mass necessary to capture it are, well, astronomical."

"Of course, there are many variables to consider," stammered Ashford.

"Mr. Undersecretary, you mentioned another option that could divert the asteroid and still keep it intact for study," said the chief of staff.

"Yes, an odd proposal but one that certainly works on a theoretical basis," he replied. "We'd paint the asteroid a different color that would use the Sun's radiation to change the thermal properties and alter its trajectory. It only takes a little pressure from the Sun, in the form of radiation, to make a difference. Remember, we only need to move it slightly in order to avoid the two orbits intersecting."

The president turned to Hapwell. "What about this, Director?"

"The problems, sir, are time and the fact that we're dealing with an unproven theory. Now, let me say this. The painting option can certainly work if the Sun has sufficient time to modify the asteroid's composition via melting of ice or liquefying of gases. We do not know how long it takes for an asteroid to be affected by the Sun's radiation. Again, not to be the constant reminder of impending doom, but at sixty thousand miles per hour, IM86 will be upon us in just three weeks. Is anyone in this room comfortable with painting a space rock and then sitting back to see if it has the desired effect?"

The room fell deathly silent.

CHAPTER 31

Friday, April 6
The Situation Room
The White House
Washington, DC

The president's tone of voice changed as he appeared to be nearing a conclusion. "Okay, Mr. Undersecretary, I'd like you to bottom-line your proposal for me, one that if you had to stand before the American people, you could make with confidence knowing all of their lives are at stake."

"Sir, the opportunity to study, mine, and possibly establish a space station on IM86 is too great an opportunity to pass up," relied Ashford. "The scientific advances to be gained could change the course of history. The economic boom to our country would change the lives of every American. And my proposal also solves the task at hand, which is to divert the asteroid from Earth's path."

"So you want to send up a team of scientists and asteroid miners, land on this beast, and then what? Capture it or paint it?"

"Sir, I believe painting the asteroid can be done quickly and effectively. Because of its size, the capture or slingshot method may be hampered by time constraints. I believe NASA is capable of doing both with the proper equipment and a team of at least ten astronauts."

The president smiled. "Thank you, Mr. Undersecretary. I'd like you to prepare a detailed proposal for my review by tomorrow morning. In fact, you need to coordinate this with my chief of staff, who will make this an interagency project. I want America to see a level of cooperation in Washington that was unimaginable after decades of political rancor."

"Thank you, Mr. President. I'll make sure it's thorough."

"Good. Now, Director Hapwell, again, thank you for your patience in allowing me to gather information about Undersecretary Ashford's concept. I've gathered that you're convinced there's a better course of action."

"Yes, sir, in a word—nuke it. Okay, that's two words. But under these circumstances, there is simply no better option."

"Okay, Director, I understand where you're coming from. Are we talking a Bruce Willis, *Armageddon*-style drilling operation where a nuclear device is inserted into the core?"

Hapwell chuckled. While scriptwriters had done a good job of creating an interesting story, the science behind their destruction was completely wrong.

She explained, "To be honest, Mr. President, dropping a nuclear weapon in a hole won't be enough. Asteroids are harder to break up than we previously thought. A Johns Hopkins study used a new computer modeling method and, as a result of their analysis, our understanding of space rock fracturing has changed.

"For decades, we believed the larger the object, the more easily it would break. Larger asteroids are more likely to have flaws in their structure, providing weaknesses that can be attacked. The study revealed the composition of many asteroids, as was indicated earlier, is metal. The amount of energy required to shatter or even fracture an asteroid into pieces is much greater. In addition, the point of impact, that precise location upon the asteroid's surface, has been deemed far more important than our prior theories. In other words, you can't just broadside the asteroid with a nuke and expect to make a difference. We have to be much more precise."

"Obviously, it's still possible or you wouldn't be suggesting it," interjected Fielding.

"That's correct. Because we don't have time to send an unmanned probe to survey the surface and obtain a more precise analysis of IM86's composition, it will have to be done by an orbiting spacecraft that is also capable of delivering precise nuclear payloads at pressure points identified by the team."

"You said pressure points, as in plural, am I correct?" asked the president.

"Yes, sir. At a mile and a half wide, to ensure success, multiple detonations would be necessary to force the asteroid off trajectory and fracture it sufficiently to keep its gravitational pull from drawing the debris back together."

"What?" asked Fielding. "Are you saying we could blow it up only to have it reconstitute and stay on course?"

"Based upon the size and gravitational strength of the asteroid's core, any fragments would either become part of IM86's tail, a phenomenon in and of itself, or it could reform, albeit loosely."

"Then what?" asked the president.

"Well, sir, the remains of the asteroid should modify its trajectory, slow its approach, or be sufficiently obliterated that most of the debris will burn up in the Earth's atmosphere upon entry."

"Therein lies the rub, to quote *Hamlet*," interjected Ashford. "Director Hapwell's approach, while the preferred option of the Chinese and Russians, as well as those at NASA who've spent countless millions of dollars creating the DART mission, has inherent flaws. For example, if insufficient energy in the form of nuclear payloads is used, then there will be little effect other than to create a debris field that will spread far and wide across the Northern Hemisphere. I'd liken it to trying to dodge a shotgun blast of #10 bird shot that contains eight hundred or so pellets versus a single bullet."

"Yes, pellets that should burn up in our atmosphere for the most part," countered Hapwell.

"And destroy half the satellites in low-Earth orbit in the process," argued Ashford.

Hapwell took a deep breath and exhaled. "Mr. President, our planet has been hit by space rocks throughout its existence. Smaller impacts, bird shot, to use Mr. Ashford's analogy, didn't destroy the dinosaurs. The proverbial big one, the planet killer, did. I'd submit that we can pick up the pieces after an asteroid scatters throughout the Northern Hemisphere, but we might not be alive to rebuild after IM86 hits us in its present form."

The president paused for a moment and studied the faces of the attendees. Everyone understood the magnitude of his decision. He took a deep breath and then addressed Hapwell.

"Let me ask one more thing regarding the nuclear approach," began the president, who suddenly stopped to think before continuing. He took a deep breath and then spoke. "As to this bird shot that the Undersecretary refers to, this large amount of debris, is it possible to calculate the moment of attack on this asteroid to ensure the remnants of IM86, if any, struck Earth to minimize the effect on the United States?"

The president stared at Hapwell, and she could feel the eyes of the other attendees darting around the room to one another before becoming singularly focused on her response. His question was subtle in its meaning, but the ramifications of her answer certainly portended doom for some parts of the world. She chose a simple answer without elaboration, hoping that what he was suggesting never came to pass.

"Yes, sir, it is possible."

PART THREE

ASTROMETRY

Identification Number: 2029 IM86

Right Ascension: 19 hours 25 minutes 52.6 seconds

Declination: -26 degrees 25 minutes 55 seconds

Greatest Elongation: 69.6 degrees

Nominal Distance from Earth: 0.558 Astronomical Units

Relative Velocity: 28,309 meters per second

CHAPTER 32

Saturday, April 7
Sea of Japan

Flying around the world wasn't easy on the human body. While Bear and Cam slept through most of the trips, which included stops at Lackland Air Force Base near San Antonio, and then Joint Base Pearl Harbor-Hickam, Gunner thought back on his career and some of the operations he'd led.

Most Americans were familiar with Navy SEALs and Delta Force, largely because of their portrayal in movies and television shows. The Air Force special tactics units were different in that they incorporated an element of air combat into their operations. Because the airmen who were chosen to be part of the Air Force special operations required specialized training, their career path was quite different than Delta and the SEAL teams.

Gunner, in particular, was an anomaly in the U.S. armed forces. With an advanced degree in Earth science, he could've been hired in either the private sector with a large oil company, or in the aviation industry, or the public sector with agencies such as NASA or the Defense Department.

He'd opted to follow his family's chosen career—the Air Force. Initially, the Air Force tried to fit Gunner into the box that made sense for them. The Special Tactics squads at Hurlburt Field trained in everything from free-fall parachuting procedures to deep-sea diving as part of the combat divers' school in Key West.

Gunner, who was always a quick learner, suddenly found himself on a fast track within the USAF's ranks. Colonel Smith, as Gunner's commander, recognized his prize recruit's drive and capabilities. He pushed him to learn all aspects of Air Force Special Tactics, including combat skills. Ghost, as he'd been referred to around Hurlburt Field, even went to his superiors at the Pentagon to request that Gunner be exempt from the normal timetables for his training. The military had always been regimented, by design, but the courses were developed for the average airmen. Gunner was anything but average.

The decades of the eighties and nineties in the prior century had changed the direction of war. Battles were increasingly fought in cyber space, and the days of ground combat were numbered. With the dawn of the new millennia, a new breed of soldier was required by the nation's military. They were required to be more cerebral, many with college educations. The battles were fought with computers and drones. The days of the infantry grunt were numbered.

With this change in warfare toward the end of the twentieth century, U.S. government agencies became increasingly reliant upon seasoned veterans to join special operations units to be inserted into specific hot spots around the world.

Political assassinations, disabling critical infrastructure, or generally disrupting a government's operations to create instability became just as important as tank warfare. Also, air combat became increasingly relied upon to gain advantage over an adversary. Capable fighter pilots were sought after by all branches of the service, especially the Air Force.

When Gunner had entered the gates at Hurlburt Field, Ghost immediately saw an opportunity to create an invaluable weapon, a human asset, that his nation could rely upon to perform when called upon. Gunner was that weapon, and he'd been used often.

Gunner let his head rock back and forth as it rested on the cargo plane's fuselage. He glanced over at Cam and Bear, recalling how the three of them had come together at Hurlburt Field and ultimately formed a cohesive unit. He recalled how his new commander had steered the three together, placing them on missions and then quizzing them on their interaction during debriefings.

At first, base command hesitated to place Gunner and Cam in the same unit because of their longtime friendship dating back to childhood. But then Gunner had an opportunity to lead a mission with them into Ukraine and they impressed their superiors at how well they worked as a team. Bear was the perfect complement to the fearless, tactical Gunner and the stealthier, crafty Cam. He was a brute with advanced combat skills, both with weapons and his hands. Every special ops unit needs a guy to have their back. Bear was their man.

So, this team of three was formed and now they'd worked together for five years. One of the things that they only discussed among themselves was how they enjoyed the hunt. When on a mission, they knew their lives were at stake. They were determined to survive, which meant killing any threat that surfaced. Like other special operators, they balanced the risks and the rewards, and despite death being the risk, they went into every operation *balls to the wall.*

Their camaraderie was unparalleled, and their thrill of danger was borderline psychotic. They'd never turned down a mission and they'd never failed. They'd deterred military coups, and helped initiate them. They'd protected dignitaries from assassinations, and carried out orders to kill.

Ride or die.

*****

At some point, Gunner must have dozed off, only to be violently shaken back to life by the transport touching down at Andersen Air Force Base in Guam. After a brief opportunity to eat and take a shower, the team was back in the air, this time soaring across the Pacific Ocean in the latest variant of the famed Bell-Boeing Osprey.

The older V-22s had given way to the new V-26 aircraft that had a ferry range of twenty-five hundred nautical miles, more than enough to fly Gunner and his team to link up with Carrier Strike Group 5, led by its flagship, the USS *Ronald Reagan.*

CSG 5, its abbreviated designation, was on patrol in the Sea of Japan, as it had been for years since hostilities between the free world and North Korea continued. Attempts to reach a denuclearization treaty with Kim Jong-un had failed. Both the Chinese and Russians had openly pledged military support for the Kim regime in the event it was attacked, effectively shutting off any military options on the table to tackle the problem.

As a result, the CSG 5 patrols—consisting of the *Reagan*, the Ticonderoga-class guided-missile cruisers USS *Chancellorsville* and USS *Shiloh*, together with a variety of destroyers—maintained vigil in the Sea of Japan, ready to retaliate against any unprovoked attack initiated by the Hermit Kingdom.

The V-26 Osprey made a slow, drooping turn onto the designated landing area aboard the *Reagan* amidst a grouping of EA-18G Growlers that had incorporated the improvements from the newly commissioned F/A 18 Advanced Super Hornets. The tilt-rotor aircraft was hovering over the *Reagan*'s deck, its rotor wash throwing sea spray and particles of sand in all directions. The crew of the *Reagan* expertly guided the Osprey's pilot downward, and within seconds, they were back on a solid surface.

Bear had his nose pressed against the window of the Osprey, admiring the toys below. He pointed toward the stern of the carrier. "There's our ride."

Inspired by the Osprey, the Bell AV-280 Valor utilized tilt-rotor technology as part of the military's vertical-lift program. Tested and modified extensively since its inaugural flight in 2017, the AV-280 had proven to be an invaluable means of inserting special operations teams deep into hostile territory without the need for parachute drops and complicated extractions.

Easily capable of a cruise speed of over three hundred knots, approaching four hundred miles per hour, the AV-280 enjoyed the agility and operations of an airplane, but the landing capability of a helicopter due to its tilt-rotor design.

What sealed the deal for the Pentagon was its ability to carry heavy cargo while still maintaining two-hundred-mile-per-hour speeds. It was known to transport ten-thousand-pound Howitzers deep into a hot zone in addition to being used as a fighting machine. The AV-

152

280 variant was equipped with rocket launchers and missiles, providing a valuable tool in forward operations and battle planning.

Gunner stepped out onto the flight deck of the *Reagan* and immediately marveled at its size. It measured over a thousand feet, nearly as long as the Empire State Building was high. It had two runways together with dozens of aircraft on board.

A naval lieutenant greeted Gunner and led them inside toward a passenger elevator. The high-speed elevators nearby could support two fighter jets to be raised from the below-deck hangar to the flight deck in an instant. The *Reagan*, manned by over five thousand sailors and aviators, was designed to rule the seas, both on the water and in the air.

"Major Fox, please wait here while I let Command Master Chief Pollard know that you've arrived," the lieutenant said as the trio was shown into a conference room. As he exited, he closed the door behind him, leaving the group alone to talk.

"Listen, before we meet our hosts, is there anything we need from them in the way of intel that we don't have already?" asked Gunner.

"I've gotta say, the materials provided by the DTRA were far more detailed than what we usually have to work with," replied Cam.

"I agree," added Bear. "We've got recon photos, security layouts, and a pretty good idea of our LZ. As I see it, this op is all about how to get in and out undetected."

Gunner mindlessly spun one of the conference room chairs before he added, "I have to agree. I will have one question for the master chief when he arrives." The words were barely out of his mouth when a bald head entered the room first as the six-foot-seven master chief arrived.

"Welcome to the USS *Ronald Reagan*. I'm Command Master Chief Pollard and these are my aides. We have the latest satellite images of the Russian coastline along the Sea of Okhotsk to our north. Also, we've been asked to supply you with imagery of the Amur Oblast region."

Gunner was taken aback slightly by the gruff demeanor and all-business approach of the master chief. Then again, he wasn't interested in small talk either, nor did he care about the satellite intel. They were going in come hell or high water.

"Master Chief, I'm Major Gunner Fox. Will we have operational or combat support from the CSG 5 in case we have to come out hot?"

"No, Major, you will not. Any other questions?"

Gunner scowled as he stared at Bear, who seemed ready to go toe-to-toe with the master chief. Bear knew the look, as he'd received it before. It was the functional equivalent of *don't even think about it.*

"No, Master Chief, we're good to go. Thank you."

CHAPTER 33

Saturday, April 8
CNN Studios
Atlanta, Georgia

Jack Young was a multi-award-winning journalist for CNN who'd risen up the ranks after making a name for himself at a local Atlanta news station. For the past two decades, he'd traveled the world, reporting from more than thirty foreign countries, seeing firsthand the devastation caused by some of the world's biggest natural disasters, ranging from earthquakes and tsunamis to volcanic eruptions and pandemics.

From time to time, Young anchored the news desk for CNN International although most of his time was spent reporting from the field. It was unusual that he happened to be in Atlanta at the time Sparky reached out to him. Ordinarily, pursuing a lead for an ostensibly worldwide story came to Young's attention from the senior research team at CNN. This was rare for him to be contacted directly, and from someone who lived barely a hundred miles away.

Young had interviewed presidential hopefuls and Grammy winners, dignitaries and sports stars, but mostly, he reported on ordinary people who did extraordinary things.

Sparky had rambled continuously since they'd picked him up in Washington. His excited state rubbed off on Young's producer, who found himself driving ninety miles an hour on Interstate 20 into Atlanta. At that hour, traffic was minimal, and except for the occasional Friday night drunk driver wandering into their path, the return to the CNN studios was uneventful.

Sparky's story, however, was not. As the backstory was relayed to

155

Young, his mind tried to focus. There were so many factors to consider in dealing with this situation, including the safety of his source. If what Sparky assumed was true, the woman who discovered the video was stashed away in the dark recesses of a safe house maintained by the three-letter agencies of the U.S. government. She'd be released, of course, unharmed, once the administration was prepared to inform the public of the news.

Her abduction would be another story to cover although, in Young's experience, he'd learned that the carrot-and-stick tactics utilized by the feds generally worked in keeping someone like Jackie Holcomb in line.

After they arrived at the studios in Atlanta, Young tucked Sparky away in his office together with a production assistant, who was instructed to remain with him at all times, even on bathroom breaks. If Sparky wanted something to eat or drink, the PA was told to have someone else get it. And under no circumstances was Sparky allowed to use the phone or access the internet. CNN was masterful at keeping the lid on big stories until the timing of the network's release suited them.

Plus, as Young suspected, there were national security concerns in play. If the Holcomb woman had disclosed what she knew, or if it was discerned from her computer or cell phone, then the administration was well aware of the threat and was most likely in crisis mode.

The crisis, as Young and the CNN leadership team saw it, was twofold. First, if the calculations were correct, the planet faced an unprecedented threat from above. Second, once the news story broke, as Young had reported on in the past, society's reaction to the threat would be the subhead.

Young had covered the regime change in Venezuela and relayed the horrific living conditions the people suffered through. As desperation set in and the government clamped down on dissent, violence and lawlessness ruled the day. He often debated with his peers whether Americans would react in a similar manner should they face a profound crisis like the total collapse of the U.S. economy, as

Venezuelans had experienced, or in this case, an incoming asteroid.

There were those who firmly believed a spirit of cooperation would come over the nation's people as both government and the governed worked together to overcome the crisis. Young disagreed and pointed to several examples of societal collapse over the past hundred years, including in Venezuela, Africa, and the Middle East.

Young was a pessimist in this regard, but he was also a student of history. He would point out to his colleagues that most civilizations were responsible for their own demise, but on occasion, their destruction was assisted by others. Failing economies, war, and naturally occurring disasters all contributed to the collapse of the great empires, and, he pointed out, they all did.

Collapse, that is. There had never been a great empire in the history of mankind that had not collapsed, either at the hand of a more powerful conquering nation, or because they spent themselves into extinction.

He'd put off seeing Sparky as long as he could. It was now approaching noon, and his assistant told him that his guest had finally stretched out on the sofa at daybreak to sleep. When Sparky had awoken a few minutes ago, he was agitated and demanded to speak with Young.

Young took a deep breath and entered his office, where Sparky was pacing the floor. The production assistant sat in a chair near the door and yawned as Young arrived. Young patted the young man on the shoulder and told him he could leave.

"Jack, what's happening? I mean, do they not realize how big a story this is, not to mention the threat our planet faces?"

"They do, Sparky," replied Young. "Listen, take a seat so I can explain where we are with all of this."

Sparky hesitated and then finally did as instructed. He gently massaged his banged-up legs, which were covered with bandages. "I'm sorry, Jack. It's just, um, I've barely had any sleep and I'm worried about Mary. I wish there was—"

Young cut him off. "There's not, Sparky, as I will explain. But let me tell you what we've done to help in that regard."

"Okay, thanks."

"I want to tell you this is the most important news event that has been presented to us in my tenure at CNN, and possibly the biggest one in our lifetimes. The White House has put an unprecedented clampdown on any information. Our most trusted, loose-lipped sources within the administration know nothing, but they all have admitted that something big is happening in the West Wing."

"I told you! What happened to Jackie, and their pursuit of me, probably goes all the way to the top."

"Yes, you're right, but that has hamstrung us somewhat, but I'll get to that. Let me explain what we've done to help your wife."

"Yes, please," said Sparky, who scooted up on the edge of the couch.

"We had to be careful not to disclose that you were in our studios, much less contacted us directly. They'd be here with emergency-issued warrants in a heartbeat."

"So what did you do?"

"Our team placed several anonymous calls to the Wilkes County Sheriff's Department and the Georgia Bureau of Investigation, reporting that you were missing. There were also reports of unusual activity at your home initiated via anonymous calls from our production team. Now, we know that all of these law enforcements are searching for you, but by filing a missing persons report, coupled with the strange activity, we've brought the feds' activity into the light of day."

"What does that mean?"

"Well, acting on yet another anonymous tip, the CBS affiliate in Augusta has sent a news crew to Washington, to your home, which I imagine will stir the curiosity of everyone in town. That puts more eyes on the feds who are holding your wife and will minimize the possibility that she'll be moved. Basically, we've set the wheels in motion to protect you and force their hand to allow us to go public with the story."

Sparky had a puzzled look on his face. "What do you mean by *allow*?"

"Just before I came in to see you, Jeff Zucker, who, by the way, has taken complete control over all decision-making on this story, received a phone call from the president's chief of staff. She'd been informed that we were pressing all of our sources within the administration for information on something big. Of course, she denied that there was anything, but then she asked, no, actually, she begged us to lay off in exchange for an exclusive breaking-news opportunity."

"Do you believe her?" asked Sparky.

"Mr. Zucker does and that's all that matters. So, for now, we're standing down."

Sparky shot up off the sofa and began to pace the floor again. "You can't do that! Somebody will scoop us. Jack, you know how this works. Whoever gets the story out there first will benefit, you know ..." Sparky's voice trailed off as he became somewhat emotional. The events of the last seventy-two hours were clearly taking their toll on the old-school newsman.

"Sparky, please sit down," said Young, who reached out for his old acquaintance and led him back to the couch. "I know exactly where you're coming from, and let me assure you, this will be handled in a way that will please you both professionally and financially. I promise."

Sparky managed a smile and nodded. He fell back against the sofa and sighed. "So what do we do now?"

"Well, several things. First, we need to get you cleaned up and into some new clothes. Second, you and I are going to do several taped interviews that will become part of an extensive news story to be aired on *60 Minutes* tomorrow night."

"Really?"

"That's right. Anderson Cooper will actually present the piece, but I'll take the interviewer role, and with your help, we'll fill in the blanks on what happened from the night the young man discovered the asteroid up until today. How's that sound?"

"Well, um, what about Jackie? She actually discovered the asteroid. I mean, the young man must've seen it first because he set his camera to record it, but it was Jackie who pored through the video."

"That's true, and we'll mention that, but it makes for a better story that the last thing this teenage boy did before he died was discover the greatest threat to modern mankind in history."

Sparky frowned, but nodded his head in agreement.

CHAPTER 34

Sunday, April 8
Amur Oblast
Russian Far East

The AV-280 Valor screamed across the Sea of Okhotsk as Bear guided it through the Tatar Strait, the northernmost reaches of the Sea of Japan. He banked hard left as the advanced avionics responded on command, leading them just above an evening sea fog that customarily surrounded the Shantar Islands off the coast of the Russian Far East.

"Hey, at least the weatherman was spot on," said Bear cheerily as he picked up speed. He hadn't flown the AV-280 in about a year and had forgotten about its incredible handling capability. "This baby's half-plane, half-chopper. I want one!"

"Kinda like you," grumbled Cam as she checked her gear. "Half-man, half-child, half-beast."

Bear chortled. "Hey, that's three halves!"

"Yeah, well, in case you haven't looked in the mirror, you look like three halves," Cam shot back. When Bear turned to flip her off, she shouted, "Eyes on the road, big guy. I see trees."

The landscape quickly changed from a rocky beach with a gradual slope inland to stands of Siberian pine trees and cavernous valleys that split the jagged mountains. Bear dropped his airspeed to three hundred miles per hour as he settled into a river-filled gorge surrounded on two sides by rocky, partially snow-covered peaks. This part of Russia was beautiful and resembled the Western Canadian province of British Columbia.

"I see gold," he joked as he tipped the wings slightly to turn in a more westerly direction. Their intelligence briefing had discussed how the Amur Oblast was known to have the largest reserves of gold in Russia, with an estimated value of four hundred billion dollars.

Most of the region was desolate, especially around the newly expanded Cosmodrome. Sparsely populated with very little military activity, according to the National Reconnaissance Office, it was more likely that visual contact with the AV-280 would be made, although its stealth technology would effectively mask their approach from Russian radar.

To aid in their approach to the Cosmodrome under darkened conditions, the AV-280 was equipped with an integrated aperture system that allowed the aircrew a three-hundred-sixty-degree view through the skin of the aircraft. This multifunctional sensor system would assist Bear in finding a suitable place to touch down, while providing Gunner and Cam the ability to make a threat assessment before exiting the aircraft.

Bear checked his global positioning system. They were less than thirty minutes from their landing zone. Again, the recon images provided by the NatRecon Office were spot-on, taking the guesswork out of their approach.

"So far, so good," muttered Bear into the in-flight communications system.

"Yeah, this was the easy part," replied Gunner, not intending to dampen the team's spirits, but simply reminding them that getting the heck out of dodge might not be so smooth. He turned to Cam. "Do a final check with Fort Belvoir. What's her name? Lucy?"

Cam rolled her eyes and chuckled. "No, maybe it's Teddy, but she wants to be called the Jackal."

"Come on, Cam. Don't you think that's a little, you know, off?"

"She can call herself whatever she wants as long as she's there for us when we need her," Cam replied. "If she can hack into things as she claims, then we stand a better chance of knowing if we've been discovered or if our ride outta here has been compromised."

Gunner gave her a thumbs-up and turned his attention back to Bear. "Okay, big guy, find us a spot, then drop her down nice and easy. Cam and I'll monitor this fancy visual system, but to be honest, I want to clear the LZ the old-fashioned way."

"Roger that, Major," said Bear, who was preparing his mindset for battle. "We don't have a quarrel with the locals, but we certainly don't need them scurrying off to report us to the FSB." The Federal Security Service, or FSB, was the successor to the famed KGB. The Police of Russia, which was responsible for day-to-day law enforcement actions, was known to be filled with drunks and officers on the take of local Russian criminal organizations. If someone had a genuine threat to report, they'd go to the FSB, who had a direct pipeline to the Kremlin.

Cam and the Jackal performed their radio checks. The Jackal was monitoring a bank of satellite feeds from all the U.S. intelligence agencies with eyes in the sky. Thus far, there was no unusual activity that would suggest the team had been discovered.

"Five minutes to drop!" Bear announced over the comms.

Gunner adjusted his tactical throat microphone, a hands-free device that allowed the team to communicate on the fly. "Acknowledged." He checked his watch. It was three in the morning local time. They would have just over three hours to hike through the Russian forest and make their way to the Vostochny Cosmodrome.

He wasn't sure what they were looking for, as there had been no specific directives by the briefing team at Fort Belvoir. It was supposed to be a simple recon mission. Take some photos, record their findings, and transmit them back to the Jackal in real time.

Simple, Gunner thought to himself as Bear made a perfect landing in a small clearing surrounded by a rocky cliff on one side and dense forest on the others. *Nothing's ever simple in this business.*

Cam exited the AV-280 first, leading the way with her newly upgraded version of the M4, except it was chambered with 6.8 mm rounds. The round fell between the old M4 standard 5.56 mm round, and the more powerful 7.62 mm round used in the military-issue Mk 14 battle rifles. The new bullet had been designed from collaborative research at Colt and FN America, the Columbia, South Carolina, manufacturer of the M249 SAW, a mainstay within law enforcement and military ranks for decades.

The 6.8 mm round was created as an answer to improved body armor worn by the enemy, giving soldiers and law enforcement better barrier penetration as near-peer encounters escalated. The new round had superior accuracy and lethality to the M4 rounds, while providing similar ranges to the M16.

Gunner followed her out and surveyed the heavily wooded area through his night-vision goggles. Cam had already circled around the AV-280 and, within thirty seconds, declared her side of the aircraft to be clear.

"Clear," Gunner added, allowing himself to exhale for the first time. With their major challenges lying ahead of them, his heightened state of awareness would not relax until he was back on American soil.

Bear emerged from the AV-280, wearing his full kit and carrying the camera gear. He slammed the door shut and approached Gunner. "Um, do you think I should lock her up? I'd hate for someone to steal my new ride."

Gunner laughed and slapped his friend on the back. "Let's go, Bear. And you can't keep the Valor."

Cam, who could hear the conversation through her comms, added some brevity in the form of a cheesy joke. "Yeah, then it would be *stolen valor*. Get it?"

"Hardee-har-har," bellowed Bear. "Aren't you the funny one today?"

Cam joined them as they started through the Siberian forest, with Bear leading the way. "I'm always the funny one."

They walked for another half minute, and then the sheepish voice of the Jackal came through the comms. "You know, I can hear everything you say, and actually, none of you are funny."

"Really?" moaned Bear. "You're listening to every word?"

"I am," she responded. "I would like to mention that you guys are going in the wrong direction. You need to veer left or you'll be in the middle of a coal-mining operation."

"Gold?" asked Bear.

"No, you dope, coal!" admonished Cam. She then directed her remarks to the Jackal. "Jackal, why don't you guide us so Bear doesn't get us lost?"

"With pleasure," she replied. "It's ten klicks to the overlook. It's gonna be over the river and through the woods, and there's no grandmother's house at the end of the hike." The Jackal could be heard laughing through the comms.

"Everybody's a comedian," moaned Gunner.

CHAPTER 35

Sunday, April 8
The Vostochny Cosmodrome
Amur Oblast
Russian Far East

"It looks like the kind of shiny new gadget a gal could pick up at the local adult toy store," Cam observed dryly. "Whadya think, Jackal?"

"I wouldn't know, ma'am," she replied, her voice sounding somewhat hollow, as if she were in a barrel.

Cam persisted. "Oh, come on, Jackal. You mean you've never picked up something like this, you know, for a little—"

The Jackal cut her off. "No, Major! I have not."

Gunner interrupted the discussion. "Let's keep the chatter to a minimum. Don't forget where we are."

Cam couldn't resist. "You will, Jackal. Trust me, there will come a day when—"

Gunner, who was positioned above and slightly behind Cam, tossed a pine cone and bounced it off her shoulder. "Seriously, enough, you two."

"She started it, sir," said the Jackal.

Gunner shook his head. He stared down the cliff overlooking the new spaceport developed by the Russians in the last decade. Vladimir Putin's dream of having a new launch site in this remote area of Russia had been realized. There were only a few locations on the planet where space-bound rockets lifted off from, and the Vostochny Cosmodrome was one of them. With its first launch of a Soyuz rocket a dozen year ago, Moscow had sent a message to the world that it would have complete control over its space program, dropping its reliance on the US and the French.

The early morning sun cast shadows across the facility, which was still covered by a light snow from several days earlier. The spaceport had become Putin's pet project, much like the Winter Olympics in Sochi. No expense was spared as he funneled millions of dollars in oil profits into Vostochny.

When it was completed, a new town had sprung up in the Amur Oblast, including a railway station, a ground control complex, and a variety of other support facilities. It wasn't quite on par with Cape Canaveral in Florida, but it was far better than the Russian's former launchpad they'd leased from Kazakhstan.

Through the high-powered lens of his still camera, Gunner focused on the movements of the Cosmodrome's personnel. Cam continued to provide Fort Belvoir with live feeds, only switching batteries one time in the first three hours of filming.

"Gunner, this is Ghost."

"Go ahead."

"The images you've transmitted have been very helpful, but unfortunately, we don't have the requisite angle to view inside the

Mobile Service Tower, the larger structure in the center of the complex."

Gunner rose from his equivalent of a sniper hide to get a better look. "We'll have to abandon the high ground, sir. We'll need an hour to approach the western fence to get a look inside. From this angle, I can see that the doors appear to be open."

"Good, there's one more thing. Beneath the Soyuz-2 rocket, there's an assembly and processing structure. Based upon our analysis of the images, we believe the Soyuz-2 in plain view is a decoy. It doesn't appear to have its equivalent of the 14D15 first stage and accompanying boosters."

Gunner nodded. "No power. It's just for show."

"Roger."

"One hour. Out," said Gunner as he terminated the conversation.

Cam stowed her camera and Bear scanned the mountainside, hoping to find a trail.

"Whadya think?" asked Cam.

"I don't see an easy way, but that's not necessarily a bad thing," replied Bear. "A path or walking trail means patrols. I don't doubt that we could take them out, but it will definitely ring alarm bells in somebody's toasty-warm office down there."

"I agree," said Gunner. "It's no different from the six-mile hike earlier, other than the fact that we'll be exposed at some point as the forest ends."

"We've got good lenses," said Cam. "We may not need to break cover."

"Let's go," said Bear as he began to traverse the terrain, keeping natural rock formations and trees between the group and the security forces below.

It only took half an hour and the group arrived at the edge of the clearing. The sparsely wooded area made Gunner glad that they were outfitted in snow camouflage. The combination of white, brown tones, and the occasional hint of red leaves enabled them to blend into the landscape.

"Down!" whispered Bear. "Patrol."

Each of them dropped to the ground and crawled behind a leafless tree. Birch trees were the norm at the bottom of the ridge, with the majority of the pines having been cleared out. A Russian-made UAZ-3163 light utility vehicle that resembled a cross between a Ford Explorer and a Land Rover drove by. The driver and passenger had both rolled their windows down and could be heard speaking loudly and laughing. Cigarette smoke poured out of the windows as they drove by without a glance in the team's direction.

"That's the first roving patrol outside the walls that I've seen," observed Bear.

Gunner moved his sleeve and looked at his watch. "It's the top of the hour. These guys are just getting their day started."

"We're below grade here," said Cam. "We can't get a camera shot of the tower or the assembly room below the rocket because the wall obscures our view."

Gunner assessed the situation. The wall appeared to be ten feet or greater. One of them could get hoisted on top and take some quick pictures and maybe thirty seconds of film without being noticed, but he wasn't sure. Plus, the mere act of covering the hundred yards to the wall across open ground might get them discovered.

Bear was the first to hear the sounds of heavy, plodding footsteps behind them. He swung his rifle around and trained it on the narrow path they'd just followed down the side of the ridge.

Using hand signals, Gunner indicated he was going to flank the trail, and he pointed toward Cam to do the same on the other side. Their footprints in the light snow were sure to give away their position, so they had to eliminate the patrol that was stalking them.

Gunner got into position and focused his hearing on the rustling sound in the trees. It was a familiar sound, one not unlike what he heard in Tate's Hell near Dog Island from time to time.

He took a chance. He shouldered his rifle and pulled out his Morakniv Garberg fixed blade. The blade was not as long as needed for what he had in mind, but durable enough to get the job done. Further, Gunner liked the black carbon coating, adding to its stealth qualities.

On this occasion, he'd have to be careful. His target would most likely be alerted by Gunner's most surreptitious movements. After all, this was his homeland, not the trespassing American's.

Gunner readied himself by taking a deep breath and focusing on his movements. It was time. He was upon the interloper in a flash, using catlike reflexes to temporarily surprise his prey. Before the Russian boar could turn and run, Gunner embedded his knife in the animal's back, weakening its resolve. Before the animal could regain its will to fight, Gunner flipped the nearly two-hundred-pound animal on its back and delivered the death blow to his abdomen.

The Garberg knife was certainly not designed to be a pig-sticker, but several well-placed thrusts based upon Gunner's years of hunting wild hogs in the Florida Panhandle finally killed the animal.

Cam heard the commotion, as did Bear, and the two of them arrived almost simultaneously at the kill site.

"What did you do that for?" she asked. Cam always had a soft spot for animals.

"Dinner," Bear replied on Gunner's behalf, albeit incorrectly.

"We need a distraction," said Gunner as he replaced his knife in its leg sheath. "Help me, Bear. Let's drag this thing to the edge of the woods. After the patrol makes its next pass, I wanna place the boar just off the side of the road near that fallen tree's root ball. I'm sure they'll see it."

"Then what?" asked Cam.

"Well, we can't see over the wall and it's too risky to climb on top to take pictures. I'm thinking their truck and maybe even their uniforms might give us a way inside."

"You're nuts," said Cam.

Gunner grinned and grabbed the boar carcass by the hind legs. He nodded to Bear to pick up the front.

"That's what they tell me," Gunner growled in return.

CHAPTER 36

Sunday, April 8
CBS Broadcast Studios
New York

For sixty years, *60 Minutes* on CBS made a regular appearance on viewers' television sets, from the early days of Harry Reasoner, Dan Rather, and Morley Safer, to the present group of hosts, which included CNN correspondent Anderson Cooper and former morning show host Norah O'Donnell.

With the crossover talent of Cooper, CBS and CNN began to work together to produce the weekly news magazine, sharing correspondents, video feeds, and breaking news stories. On this day, both teams associated with the production of *60 Minutes*, in CBS's New York studios and at CNN Atlanta, were scrambling to produce the live broadcast slated for 7:00 p.m.

Executive producers were nervously pacing the control room, watching the monitors as the final round of the Masters was being broadcast from Augusta, Georgia. Forecasted thunderstorms and torrential downpours had forced the tournament officials to modify their final round format.

Ordinarily, the last few pairings were slated to tee off in the early afternoon, resulting in the final holes being played after seven that evening. This would delay the start of *60 Minutes*, similar to what happened on Sundays during the NFL broadcasts in the fall.

A delay meant their blockbuster revelation would have to be cut short, as the president had asked for network time to address the nation at eight o'clock eastern time. CNN and CBS had every intention of breaking the news prior to the president's Oval Office address.

The second headache for the production team was keeping the story under wraps. Both networks were taking extraordinary precautions to keep staffers from leaking the stories to other news sources, or even their families. Additional security was brought in to clear the production facilities on that Sunday. Employees were forced to turn over their cell phones, and their computers were locked down, preventing the use of email accounts.

Interviews with experts, and Sparky Newsome, were conducted against a blue-screen background with only the interviewer, in this case Jack Young, and two camera operators being present. All of the video was reviewed and edited by executive producers for later insertion into the live broadcast.

The heads of both CBS News and CNN had wrestled with their approach to breaking this story. They were sure to anger the White House, naturally, but also, they were concerned about the psychological impact on viewers.

They made their decision partially because of the notoriety and accolades the two networks would receive, but also because the White House communications office had turned their backs on them. Despite the fact that the head of CBS News made a personal plea to the White House communications director for an exclusive interview with the president in exchange for keeping the story under wraps, his request had been ignored. To make matters worse, the network had been threatened with violating several statutes. That, coupled with veiled threats of retribution from the Federal Communications Commission, later resulted in the decision to move forward.

Nonstop, around the clock, producers reached out to the brightest astrophysicists and scientists familiar with near-Earth objects. They were quizzed about the process of discovery, diversion, and destruction. Then they were asked about the ramifications of failure—a sobering moment for the production team.

Late Saturday night, a decision was made to transfer Sparky Newsome to New York. The FBI had appeared at the Atlanta studios unannounced around six p.m. and began to make inquiries of CNN personnel regarding Sparky's presence. Because he had been escorted into the building in the middle of the night before, only a few people knew he was there.

Concerned that their source was about to be snatched away to join the fate of his friend, Young made arrangements for him and Sparky to fly by private jet into New Jersey across from the Hudson River, and drive by car into CBS around four o'clock that morning.

Sparky had slept on the plane and caught another few hours on the couch of one of the executive producers before being awakened to prepare for his interview with Young. To help ease the tension and calm Sparky's nerves, he was taken on a brief tour of the famed *60 Minutes* broadcast studios by Young.

"Sparky, you might not know this, but the CBS News Broadcast Center was built on the site of an old dairy plant. It takes up an entire city block, which, as you can imagine, is high-dollar real estate in Manhattan."

Young paused in the studio to introduce Sparky to some of the members of the production team who were familiar with the big story. "This is Deborah, who runs the control room, and our camera operator, Jonas. He's the guy that doesn't know which way is up."

The production team laughed at the inside joke. Sparky was confused, so Jonas explained. "This relic, a true behemoth of days gone by, is our studio camera. Everything is opposite of what is seen by the viewer, or you guys, when being interviewed. Up is down. Down is up. Left is right, and so on."

Young drew Sparky's attention to the teleprompter. "I know this is gonna be difficult for you to do because its human nature to want to follow along, but you can't. Think about sitting in the church pew on Sunday. Everyone reads the program, following along as the hour passes, wanting to know what's next and when it's their turn to sing a hymn or recite something. The teleprompter will distract you from the task at hand. It's for me, and anything you see on it might just throw you off balance. Okay?"

Sparky smiled and replied, "Listen, Jack. I've got enough trouble with making sure I don't wet my pants during this interview. The last thing I need to do is try to do your job, too."

Young smiled and put his arm around Sparky's shoulders. "Now, let's cover a couple of things. Another potential distraction is the blue screen and the bright lights. It might be difficult at first, but you have to pretend you're sitting in a living room with a roaring fire behind you. That's what the viewers will see. You know, a casual conversation between two friends, that sort of thing."

"Okay," said Sparky, who instinctively wiped a few beads of sweat off his forehead.

Young immediately motioned for a member of the makeup team to join them, and then he shouted at a production assistant to increase the air-conditioning.

"Come on, people, we can't have our special guest sweating!"

Sparky wiped again just as the young woman arrived with a tray attached to her left hand that resembled an artist's palette, and a large brush in the other. As Young continued to speak, she touched up Sparky's face with the light skin-tone powder designed to dry up the moisture and keep his face from looking shiny.

"What about the interview process?" asked Sparky. "I mean, I've been interviewed by the local Augusta news stations in the past, but usually it's for fun events like the July Fourth fireworks show or a Christmas gathering in Washington's square."

"Well, here's the good news, you can just simply stick to the facts. You and I have gone over the events repeatedly, and my assistant has formulated questions that will fit our script for the airing this evening."

"Will we be live tonight?"

Young shook his head. "No, in fact, we'll start recording the interview right here in a few minutes. Now, just because this is taped to be aired this evening, we really try to avoid do-overs. Astute viewers will be able to see right through multiple takes. You may not even realize that you're doing it, but invariably your posture changes, as do your expressions and tone of voice. All of these things break up the continuity of the interview and, at times, draw criticism that the

Q and A was scripted."

"Okay."

"Here's another thing. We don't have a script, but we do have what you personally know or experienced. Avoid trying to explain anything scientific or what Jackie may have relayed to you. We have experts for that. No matter what, you have to be comfortable and knowledgeable about what you discuss. That way you'll avoid *ums* and *uhs*."

"Got it."

"Also, do you have any nervous tics? You know, hand gestures, foot tapping, eye blinking, etcetera?"

"Um, no," replied Sparky, who laughed at himself for using *um* to answer the question. He looked around the room and noticed Young's assistant was standing nearby with a notepad. He pointed toward her and asked, "Are those the questions? Can I take a look before we get started?"

"I'm sorry, Sparky, but no. These are all questions I've asked you before, or that we've formulated from what you relayed to us. This is not a gotcha interview, and I promise you there are no questions that you can't or don't want to discuss. If you're not prepped on the questions, your answers will come across as more authentic."

Sparky stretched his shoulders backwards and rolled his head around his neck to relieve the tension. "May I use the restroom first, and, um, have a bottled water or something?"

Young signaled to his assistant, who turned over the questions to him and led Sparky out of the studio. As he walked out, Young yelled after him, "Sparky, you're gonna do great. Just act like you've been here before. This will be the first of many opportunities to appear on camera. Let's make the best of it!"

CHAPTER 37

Sunday, April 8
CBS Broadcast Studios
New York

It was a quarter to seven that evening when a production assistant retrieved Sparky from one of three green rooms that were scattered about the massive CBS facility. He'd been isolated from the rest of the production crew as they prepared for the upcoming *60 Minutes* broadcast. They'd brought him a meal from the full-service on-site cafeteria and snacks from the convenience shop.

The television monitors were tuned to the Masters golf tournament, which was being held just fifty miles east of Washington. The close connection between the tourney and his hometown caused him to miss his wife even more. He'd never asked for any of this and at times resented Jackie for dragging him into it. Then again, he was excited to see himself on a broadcast that would be viewed by many millions of people around the world.

The production assistant escorted him down the long hallway overlooking West Forty-Seventh Street to Studio 41, the largest of the five studios on the floor. At the CBS Broadcast Center, programs like *Inside Edition, CBS Sunday Morning,* and *CBS News* were broadcast, as well as seasonal sporting events like *March Madness* coverage and NFL football coverage.

Today, Studio 41 had been transformed into a massive viewing stage complete with multiple enormous television monitors and seating for four or five dozen guests.

As Sparky entered the room, he scanned the faces, looking for Young, but could not find him. He did, however, recognized several others. The PA led him to the front row, past Gayle King of the morning program, longtime newsman Scott Pelley, and retired correspondent Bill Whitaker.

Sparky leaned into his escort and asked about Young. She told him that because he was most familiar with the events leading up to the discovery of the asteroid, he would remain in the production control room during the entire broadcast in case they needed to modify the live airing of the program on the fly.

Sparky had barely been seated when a flood of people entered Studio 41 from the hallway and scurried to take up seats in the rear. Sparky glanced at a wall clock and saw that it was only minutes before seven. Then a tall well-dressed man emerged from behind a curtain, followed by two aides carrying computer tablets and equipped with earpieces. The man chatted with both of them as he made his way to the center of the stage.

A hush came across the room as he nodded and thanked his assistants for their help. Then he addressed the attendees.

"Ladies and gentlemen, I need to be brief," he began, and then paused to address the others in the front row next to Sparky. "For those of you who've assisted us in the content for this extraordinary broadcast of *60 Minutes*, I want to introduce myself. I am Douglas Edwards III, grandson of a pioneer at CBS Television News who anchored our broadcasts back in 1948.

"As the president and senior executive producer of CBS News, I've been honored to work with the finest journalists in the world. As the offspring of newspeople dating back to the nineteenth century, I feel I have the news business in my blood.

"In my lifetime, I have never seen a story as big as this one. To be sure, in modern times, we've witnessed the flight of man, both for the first time and to the Moon. We've witnessed a world war started by a surprise attack on Pearl Harbor, and the same war being ended via nuclear devastation. We've seen the creation of computers and the advent of the internet.

"However, this is the first time in the history of modern man that a threat to our very existence is upon us. And thanks to the hard work of our journalistic teams at both CNN and CBS and the courage of a local newspaper publisher in a small town of four thousand, we will bring the story to the world that dwarfs any other."

Spontaneous applause broke out that Edwards immediately moved to tamp down. He paused and looked along the front row, eventually making eye contact with Sparky. "To all of you, our heartfelt gratitude goes out for your efforts in bringing this special edition of *60 Minutes* to fruition. For everyone else in attendance, we thought it was appropriate to reward you for all that you've done for the CBS News organization over the years and for being here, in Studio 41, as we bring the news to the world. Thank you."

Edwards walked off the stage and the lights in Studio 41 dimmed. Then the massive television monitors sprang to life and the familiar ticking clock indicating that the *60 Minutes* broadcast was about to begin filled the room.

Chills ran across Sparky's body as the familiar faces of the hosts and correspondents appeared one by one, culminating with Anderson Cooper, who would be the lead on this broadcast.

The program dove right into the threat the planet faced. Sparky imagined that the CBS News executives were concerned about leaks, so they wanted to preempt any other news source from co-opting the story. He was intrigued by the chatter and occasional gasps coming from the audience, which included seasoned news veterans from both in front of and behind the cameras. Most were unaware of the subject matter of the program and had most likely been exposed to the type of hype that Edward had provided at the beginning. In this case, the buildup was appropriate.

When the show turned to Sparky's interview, he cringed at times. When you see yourself on television, your voice sounds weird, your appearance isn't just so, and your mannerisms are all wrong. Yet you are always your own biggest critic.

The program broke for its first commercial break after fifteen minutes. The room erupted into conversation as they were astonished at the revelations concerning the asteroid and its trajectory. Several people sitting around Sparky leaned over the back of the seat and introduced themselves and offered him congratulations. One even handed him a business card with his agent's name on it and said, "Here, you're gonna need this guy."

It was the next segment that Sparky was most interested in. He understood the ramifications of Nate and Jackie's discovery and the appropriate steps he had taken to report the news to Jack Young at CNN.

What he wanted to know was now that the proverbial cat was out of the bag, what could be done about it?

CHAPTER 38

Sunday, April 8
CBS Broadcast Studios
New York

Anderson Cooper continued the program and turned immediately to the issue of how an asteroid of this size could sail through space, around the Sun, and directly for our planet without being observed by the multimillion-dollar early detection systems.

In the past couple of decades, one political party or another had used partial government shutdowns as a hammer to get its way on a variety of hot issues. Sometimes, the closing of national parks was used in the media to show the pain inflicted on the American people over the budget wrangling. Other times, kids' school lunches were eliminated. One way or the other, the politicians were skewered because they couldn't find a way to govern, resulting in the loss of services and, at times, the use of the furlough process to eliminate jobs.

NASA had experienced that pain every time the shutdowns occurred, including the present one that had continued into its ninth day. Cooper interviewed a spokesman for the Jet Propulsion Laboratory because NASA didn't provide anyone for an on-camera interview.

Cooper asked, "So, if I understand you correctly, you have no official comment on the newly discovered asteroid other than the fact that your agency has been notified of the threat thanks to this broadcast, am I correct?"

Sparky gulped, now understanding what gotcha journalism could do to a normally calm person's demeanor. The man being

180

interviewed looked like he wanted to turn and run away as fast as he could.

"Yes, Anderson. Like I said, this is news to us, and the JPL has procedures in place to deal with new inform—"

"But, sir," Cooper interrupted, "my question to you is why hasn't this been discovered already, and to what effect has the budget impasse in Washington contributed to this act of gross negligence by the very agencies charged with protecting us from space objects like asteroids?"

"Um, well, Anderson, the government shutdown had wide-reaching effects on all of NASA's operations, personnel shortages in particular. While we have the finest satellites in the world pointing up at the sky, constantly scanning for near-Earth objects that threaten us, the usual redundancies, you know, checks and balances, have suffered due to the manpower shortage."

Cooper was undeterred by the explanation. "Sir, it is a fact, is it not, that had this asteroid been discovered sooner, the administration's options would be broader?"

"Yes, that is true, but please, let me add this. We, and by that, I'm referring to NASA and the JPL, together with associated space agencies, are not the only eyes looking for newly discovered space rocks. The Europeans, Russians, and Chinese, to an extent, all have similar capabilities to ours. None of them have reported this object either."

Cooper pressed further. "But isn't it true that there is a lot to gain by being the first to land a manned spacecraft on a near-Earth object of this size? Therefore, the Russians, for example, would have much to gain by being the first?"

"That is true, but our experience is that geopolitical differences are—"

Cooper cut him off and turned to face the camera. "Clearly, the partial government shutdown and years of budget cuts have taken its toll on NASA, hampering its responsibility to protect our planet from asteroids such as this one. However, there is a larger issue at hand here. As you've seen from the interview in the first segment, the government and, by extension, the administration, has been aware of this threat and has done nothing to inform the American people, nor have we seen anything indicating action on NASA's part to intercept or destroy the incoming asteroid. For more on that, we'll turn to Norah O'Donnell, who interviewed Dr. Alma McClain."

O'Donnell, the former co-anchor of *CBS This Morning* until she was forced out, had been a mainstay on *60 Minutes* for the last decade. "Yes, Anderson. I had the opportunity to interview Dr. Alma McClain, who has been ill of late but who, I can assure you, is still full of knowledge. Let me say this for our viewers, our producers reached out to more than a dozen scientists at NASA, as well as the ESA, and none of them agreed to come on camera with us. Only time will tell as to whether they were aware of this asteroid, but in the meantime, Dr. McClain laid out what our planet faces."

The screen switched to Dr. McClain's home in Studio City, California, a modest one-story stucco home that she'd lived in since 2006. Dr. McClain, who was seventy-four, sat in her living room with her dog sitting in her lap as she answered O'Donnell's questions.

After praising the scientists and employees at America's space agencies, and taking a dig at the current administration and their secretive handling of this discovery, Dr. McClain explained how this late discovery most likely came about.

"Norah, the world's attention was captured by Comet Oort, or as we astronomers like to dub it, the next Great Comet. Comet Oort's characteristics in terms of brightness and the length of its tail are certainly worthy of attention, but these same characteristics are partly to blame for keeping this new asteroid from being seen. The heavens couldn't have provided a more efficient method of concealment, a disguise, to obscure our view of this new NEO.

"Frankly, it was just pure luck that the amateur astronomers in Georgia happened to record the object and be astute enough to know it was out of the ordinary. Kudos to them."

O'Donnell referred to her notes and then asked, "Dr. McClain, as you and I discussed off camera, there is so much that we don't know about this asteroid, such as size, speed, trajectory, and impact date.

You've seen the data provided to us by the newsman out of Washington, Georgia, what can you tell us about the date it might strike Earth?"

"Norah, I would estimate the impact date at being a little over two weeks. Naturally, NASA has probably already made these calculations, and I suspect the president will—or heck, he might not—disclose that to us in the next hour. I do know that all eyes will be searching for this asteroid, and by midnight, the actual impact date will be announced."

"Then what?" asked O'Donnell.

"Well, after the projected impact date is determined, the Torino scale will be applied and an impact rating will be established."

"Torino?"

"Yes, sorry. The Torino scale categorizes the impact hazard associated with NEOs in order to assess the likelihood of a collision and, based upon its kinetic energy, how much damage it will cause. For point of reference, the impact that contributed to the extinction of the dinosaurs was a 10 on the Torino scale, while in more modern times, the mile-wide Barringer Crater just west of Winslow, Arizona, was assigned an 8. There is another scale, the Palermo Technical Impact Hazard Scale, but it uses far more complex data points and information that will take days to discern. For now, the Torino scale is your best bet to provide your viewers a point of comparison."

"Dr. McClain, based upon what we know, do you have an opinion as to where this particular near-Earth object will fall on the Torino scale?"

"Most likely as a 9 or 10. For perspective, the largest hydrogen bomb ever exploded, the Tsar Bomba, was around fifty megatons. The 1883 eruption of the Krakatoa volcano was two hundred megatons. The Chicxulub impact, the dino-killer, was most likely a hundred million megatons."

"Are you saying that the impact could hit the planet with the force of thousands of hydrogen bombs?"

"Sadly, yes, Norah. This is what the human race faces."

Anderson Cooper came back onto the screen and glumly said, "*60*

Minutes will return in a moment, and when we do, we'll assess the options available to defend ourselves from this menacing object."

Unlike the commercial break between the first and second segments of the program, the room was deathly silent as the realities began to settle in. The excitement of the *big story*, the so-called *breaking news*, was crushed by the dread that the world was in serious danger.

For Sparky, he'd already come to that realization, and now he was waiting for this part of the ordeal to be over so he could get home to his wife. He slumped down in his chair and closed his eyes, allowing his sense of hearing to do the work for a while.

The program came back and several scientists were interviewed, providing the viewers of *60 Minutes* with the various options the governments of the world could choose from. By the end of the program, there was no agreement among the scientists, and speculation seemed to take over the program.

Sparky perked up as the program came to an end and the glum-looking President of the United States appeared on the screens. The man looked haggard and worn. Sparky grimaced.

He knew the feeling.

CHAPTER 39

Sunday, April 8
The Vostochny Cosmodrome
Amur Oblast
Russian Far East

Bear wedged himself behind the root ball, waiting for the sound of the truck to come around. Their surveillance of the sole vehicle's patrol allowed them fifteen minutes in which to place the boar in clear view of the road and hide Bear where he could assist in the ambush.

"Okay, team," said the Jackal into their comms. "The patrol car is rounding the turn now and should be in your view in four, three, two, now."

Gunner gripped his knife in his left hand and positioned his right hand near his silenced sidearm. He gave a slight wave to Bear, who was hidden behind the massive rotting root ball near the next corner. If the patrol behaved as expected, they'd see the dead animal just as they entered their next turn, allowing Gunner and Cam to sneak up from behind and strike.

As predicted, the dead boar caught the attention of the passenger, who motioned for the driver to pull off the gravel road toward the upended tree. The two uniformed soldiers stepped out of the utility vehicle, but did not draw their weapons. They slowly approached the bleeding hog and stared in wonderment.

Cam had a working knowledge of Russian, as well as several other languages, and tried to interpret for the team.

"They think the boar was wounded by a hunter and dragged itself out of the mountains to die. Now they're debating whether to throw it on the hood of the truck and take it back to their mess hall."

Cam paused for a moment. One of the men turned toward their position, forcing Gunner and Cam behind the trees. The two men began to talk loudly.

"What are they saying?" asked Gunner.

"The driver thinks he saw something."

The Russian soldier yelled, *"Ey, ty! Pokazhi, sebya!" Hey, you! Show yourself!*

Gunner immediately felt exposed and in danger. He felt for his sidearm but realized they were too far away to get an accurate shot. He had to rely on Bear.

"Bear?"

"No worries. I've got this."

Gunner allowed himself a better vantage point by sliding along the back side of the tree and crawling closer to Cam's position. They were able to catch a glimpse of what happened next through the leafless branches of the birch trees hiding their position.

Bear, who was only thirty feet away from the patrol guards, quickly emerged from behind the root ball and placed two well-placed rounds at the base of each man's skull. With his pistol drawn and pointed at the soldiers who'd landed facedown in the snow, he watched for movement. They didn't, but he plugged each in the back of the head to confirm their deaths.

"Got 'em," he announced as he holstered his silenced weapon. Then, with his muscular arms, he grabbed each heavyset man by an ankle and hurriedly dragged them backward behind the root ball.

Within seconds, Gunner and Cam had joined him, and they debated their next move. Gunner contacted the Jackal.

"We haven't laid eyes on the main gate. What is the security like?"

"That's a no-go, Major. Too much firepower and personnel."

Bear leaned over to Gunner. "I like the way she talks. It's kinda sexy."

"I heard that, Sergeant," the Jackal said calmly. Then she offered Gunner an alternative. "Major, there is a utility gate near a self-contained solid-waste depository."

"A what?" asked Bear.

"A dumpster," replied Cam. "Jackal, is it within the wall?"

"Partially. You can wedge the vehicle between the wall and the deposit—um, dumpster. You should be able to walk through the dumpster and enter the compound that way."

"Walk through the trash?" lamented Bear.

"Yes, you big baby," responded Cam. "This one's on me. You guys watch my back and, Bear, you point this thing out with the motor running, just in case."

With a plan in place, the three of them walked briskly, one at a time, to the patrol car and got settled in. Bear complained about the cramped driver's seat, but he eventually managed to slowly drive them around the corner of the complex, making sure to maintain a steady speed.

"I see the dumpster," said Bear.

"Any unusual activity?" asked Gunner.

"No, sir," replied the Jackal.

Gunner turned to Cam, who was readying herself in the backseat. "You got this? I'm already covered in pig blood. What's a little garbage stench to go with it, right?"

Bear disagreed. "Yeah, and you're gonna leave all that nasty shit on the ground when we pull out of here. You're not getting in my new AV-280 smelling like a dead animal."

Cam sat up in her seat as she pointed to where she had the best access to the dumpster. "It's got to be me. I know enough Russian to realize when I'm in trouble, and maybe I can convince them, if caught, that I'm a reporter or something."

Gunner stretched his fist into the backseat and she bumped it in return. She readied the video camera and waited for Bear to stop the vehicle.

"We've got your back," reassured Bear as Cam scampered out of the car and climbed into the dumpster.

Gunner took over the communications with the Jackal. "Jackal, you've got her on recon?"

"Yes, sir. She's in and walking casually between smallish buildings toward the west end of the complex."

"Recording," whispered Cam into her microphone.

"Well done, Major," said Ghost, who had been monitoring the entire operation, but rarely interrupted the team. "If you can, stop now and film the entire opening of the Mobile Service Tower."

Cam obliged and, crouching below a series of oil drums, she slowly panned up and down, filming another rocket housed inside. Except this one was far different from the easily recognizable Soyuz-2 out in the open.

"Major," said the Jackal, "I've got two vehicles headed in your direction. I don't see a sense of urgency on their part, but you might want to move on to task two."

"Roger that," said Cam.

She resumed her trek deeper into the compound until she was staring up at the Soyuz-2. As she walked past the umbilical mast, she filmed the base of the rocket until she heard Ghost's voice come across the communications system.

"As suspected. It's hollow. Continue, Major, it's another few hundred feet until you can see the rear of the assembly—"

"Major," began the Jackal in the closest thing she had to an urgent tone of voice, "those vehicles have suddenly picked up speed and are speeding in your direction. May I suggest you move very quickly?"

"Roger that. Gunner, meet me on the west side of the compound."

"How are you gonna scale the wall? I can create a diversion …" Gunner's voice trailed off as a sound resembling an air-raid siren pierced his ears.

"It's awwwn now," said Bear as he started the vehicle and drove toward the west, hugging the ten-foot security wall as best he could to avoid being seen from inside the compound.

"You've got to go faster, Major," the Jackal calmly instructed Cam.

"I need an exit," she replied.

"Understood. If you continue on a due west course, you'll see a stack of what appears to be railroad ties, or maybe short telephone poles. I can't—"

"I see them! Are you getting the footage?" Cam was running and recording back over her shoulder.

"We are, Major," replied Ghost. "You focus on extraction."

"Where should we position our—? Oh shit!" Bear slammed on the brakes just as Cam flew over the top of the wall. She did a perfect gymnast tumble right in front of the vehicle and landed on her feet.

"Major, they're coming!" The Jackal urged Cam to get into the truck. Gunner reached back and opened the door for her; then he readied his weapon. She jumped headfirst into the backseat and Bear slammed the gas pedal to the floor, causing snow and slush to spew around the rear end.

"Which way?" Bear screamed his question.

"Straight, then right!"

Bear followed her instructions, and as soon as he'd cleared the turn, he faced two Russian patrols speeding in their direction.

"Thanks, Jackal!" Bear said sarcastically.

The Jackal continued to advise them. "Just past the radio tower up ahead, there's a service road that leads into the forest. It will take you toward their processing complex, where we'll have a couple of options."

"Ghost, permission to engage," said Gunner.

"Do what it takes to get your team out of there, Major," came the reply.

Cam had caught her breath and was already rolling down the left rear passenger window. "I've got left."

"I've got right," said Gunner, who leaned out the window and released a barrage of the 6.8 mm rounds in the direction of the oncoming patrol trucks. His bullets ricocheted off the grille and hood, with one finding the windshield of the lead vehicle, smashing it open.

The trailing truck veered off to its right, leaving Bear no choice but to split them as they raced toward one another like a two-on-one joust.

Bullets stitched the front of their vehicle as the Russians were now fully aware that they were in a gunfight.

"You've got more coming," announced the Jackal.

"Roger," said Gunner as he focused his sights on the front tires of the oncoming vehicle. He let out a quick burst and his bullets found their mark.

At first, the oncoming truck veered toward its left and almost crashed into the security wall. The driver overcorrected and cut directly across the path of Bear, who slowed momentarily. The Russian driver's eyes were wide open as he pulled into the path of his partner's truck. The T-bone crash caused both vehicles to burst into flames, sending a fireball into the sky.

"They'll see that in space," commented the Jackal before giving Bear further instructions. "Turn now!"

"Got it," he said as his abrupt left-hand turn caused the rear of the vehicle to slip in the snow-covered gravel. "Now what?"

"Keep on this road. The processing complex is ahead. I don't see any security as of yet. You'll bear left around the buildings, and then you'll come to a fork in the road."

"Okay," said Bear.

"Major Fox, may I suggest staging an accident by taking the right fork? There's a retention pond that the vehicle can be driven into. Then you can double back around their tracking station and head back into the mountains."

"Sounds like a plan," replied Gunner.

Bear drove at a more reasonable speed in an attempt to avoid drawing attention as they navigated around the processing complex where the Soyuz rockets were assembled. Right after the fork in the gravel road, as the Jackal had stated, a retention pond came into view that was about forty feet below the road grade.

The three of them jumped out of the vehicle and pushed it toward the hill leading down to the water. They didn't bother to see the results, as they were now fully aware that they would be lucky to escape Russia alive.

CHAPTER 40

Sunday, April 8
The Oval Office
The White House
Washington, DC

The West Wing was immersed in bedlam. The *60 Minutes* episode forced speechwriters to tear up large parts of the president's address and start over. The media had descended upon the White House Press Room, demanding answers. World leaders lit up the switchboard, even sending their diplomats to demand an audience with the president, his chief of staff, anybody who'd hear them vent about being kept in the dark.

The White House lost control of the messaging and they now found themselves on the defensive. The issue raging through the media like wildfire was not the impending threat of IM86, but why the administration had refused to disclose this sooner.

"Mr. President," began Chief of Staff Maggie Fielding as she entered the Oval Office surrounded by her aides, on call and ready to be dispatched to deal with one flash fire or another, "I can hold off the media by ignoring them. Prime Minister Johnson and France's President Le Pen, however, deserve an explanation."

"There's no time!" shouted the president. "I'm supposed to address the nation in fifteen minutes. Can you imagine either of those conversations taking less than that? Not to mention the fact that my speech, you know, the one I've been working on for two days, is over there in the garbage can." The president pointed toward a small plastic wastebasket surrounded by yellow balls of crumpled paper, only a few of which had found the receptacle.

"Okay," she said with a sigh. "We can't worry about them being miffed, to put it mildly. I'll have my staff put them off until after your address. What about the media?"

"What about them? Do you want an executive order shutting them all the hell up? Bring it to me and I'll sign it!"

The aides in the room could be heard laughing, which drew a smile from the president.

"You wish, sir," Fielding said with a grin.

The brief moment of levity worked wonders at easing the tension in the room. The president found his chair, which had been shoved near the predominantly blue flag of the President of the United States. He slid it back to his desk and flopped into it.

With a deep breath and a pronounced exhale, he addressed his team. "Okay. You know what, I had confidence in our approach to this crisis before *60 Minutes* gummed up the works. The bottom line is we wanted to fully assess the threat before we spoke out of turn. I'll caution the American people, and world leaders, from overreacting to hyperbole and sensationalistic news. We have the finest minds on the planet analyzing this asteroid and putting together a plan to protect our planet from its approach."

"Yes, Mr. President, that's exactly right," his chief of staff said in a calm voice. She'd dealt with the president's meltdowns in the past and was glad to see that he was regaining his composure before the most important address to the nation of his young presidency. "We stick to the plan because it's solid."

"The world is in a panic because the doomsday pundits have taken over. I'm sure they've already written us off as dead and stinkin'. I've got to show them that we're one hundred percent confident in our plan, and there's no need to panic."

"Sir, one of the issues that isn't fully addressed in your address is the nuclear option. Russia, France, and China will suggest that IM86 be nuked."

"Will they?" asked the president. "I've noticed that in the list of world leaders demanding answers, you haven't mentioned the Russians. The lack of contact from Beijing doesn't surprise me. Xi

Jinping waits to speak after everyone else shows their cards. It's infuriating, but effective."

"Perhaps the Russians are waiting for you to speak?" suggested Fielding.

President Watson stood and wandered over to the windows overlooking the South Lawn of the White House. Three eleven-foot-tall windows overlooked the large area of perfectly manicured grass. He reflected for a moment and turned to his chief of staff.

"Something's not right. Do we have any intelligence on their activities at Vostochny?"

"They're still inside Russia, sir," replied Fielding. "However, I don't have any details from the Pentagon."

The president's chief speechwriter arrived in the Oval Office with two of his top political strategists in tow. The clock had reached a couple of minutes before the eight o'clock hour.

"Mr. President, your address has been uploaded to the teleprompters," he announced.

"Will I approve of the changes?" he asked.

"Yes, sir, or at least I hope so. We go live in a moment."

A production team filtered into the room and took up their positions. The president received a final touch-up of powder to his forehead, glanced at photographs of his wife, grown children and grandchildren for support, and awaited the countdown.

Three—two—one.

"My fellow Americans, this is the first time I'll speak with you from the Oval Office, and it won't be the last. My presidency is less than one hundred days old, and the world faces a threat that is like no other faced by modern man.

"In the coming days, you will learn more about asteroid IM86, a recently discovered near-Earth object that is projected to come very close to our planet. Preliminary trajectory projections indicate we are in potential danger of an impact event unless we take action.

"We have the brightest minds in the world working within NASA and related agencies. They will be collaborating with international space agencies in order to reach a consensus on how to divert this threat, with the goal of protecting our planet.

"I have implemented our government's emergency-response plans. Over the last two days, while NASA has developed a strategy to neutralize this threat, our military and law enforcement agencies have been directed to preserve order and protect our citizens from opportunists. After this address, my administration will be making a series of announcements, coupled with the signing of multiple executive orders, designed to prevent price-gouging, initiate curfews, and generally keep the peace. We will not allow a few to take advantage of the public because we face this time of adversity.

"Tonight, I ask for your prayers to give our brightest minds the strength to repel this threat, and for those who are tasked with carrying out this monumental task, the courage to do so. Like you, when a crisis arises, I fear for my children and grandchildren. At times, we have to deal with evil, and now, we have to defend ourselves from above.

"This is a day when all Americans, together with every person in the world, from every culture and walk of life, should unite in our resolve to support one another in the face of potential catastrophe.

"God bless you, and God bless the United States of America."

CHAPTER 41

Sunday, April 8
The Vostochny Cosmodrome
Amur Oblast
Far Eastern Russia

"As expected, they're reacting to the activity," said the Jackal calmly. "We've got infantry platoons and armored vehicles deploying from your south out of the residential barracks. They've cut off access to the town and have sealed off the entire compound except to the north."

"I guess that makes it our lucky day," added Bear.

"Well, actually, Sergeant, it might be. Thus far, I don't see any activity at the airport to your west. Their first efforts appear to be focused on securing the facility. The distraction will hopefully buy you time to return to your aircraft."

Gunner slapped Bear on the back and pointed toward the processing complex they'd just driven through before wrecking the vehicle. "We've just added another few miles to our hike, not to mention that it's all uphill from here. Let's go."

The three of them sought cover along the road and began the trek through the forest. The never-ending sirens wailed from the launch facility, and shouts emanated from the processing complex as orders were given to secure the perimeter. For the next thirty minutes, Gunner and his team fought through the underbrush, relying upon their GPS devices and updates from Fort Belvoir to make their way back toward the AV-280.

Bear led the way as the team entered a small clearing. "What do we have here?" he asked, using the sights on his rifle to sweep the perimeter of a small nondescript building surrounded by small geodesic-dome-shaped structures.

"Looks like weather satellites," responded Cam.

"Affirmative," added the Jackal.

Suddenly, flashes of muzzle fire winked at them through tiny slits in the block walls of the weather station. The AK-47 rounds tore into the turf in front of Bear and thwacked tree trunks behind him.

Bear ducked and rolled behind a small mound of dirt while Gunner returned fire to give him cover. Cam immediately moved to the right along the tree-lined expanse of the opening. Gunner sprinted to the left, leaving Bear to face the shooter head-on. Although it was fruitless to return fire, as the small windows would require a perfect shot, Bear did anyway to provide cover. He also hoped to keep the shooter occupied and therefore unable to alert the Russian security forces.

The west side of the building was devoid of windows, and a solitary door faced the parking lot, which contained one vehicle. Gunner decided to use a shock-and-awe approach.

Swiftly, he ran across the clearing until he reached the gravel parking area. Without slowing down, he trained his weapon on the steel door's hinges, its weakest point because it was attached to a wooden frame.

The silenced weapon emitted a hail of bullets, the rapid-fire spitting sound was muted by the frame being ripped apart. Without hesitation, Gunner ran and kicked the door open with his left foot, allowing his weapon to lead the way.

Two Russian military personnel, dressed in fatigues, huddled in the corner of the building. Gunner swept the open space and was satisfied that he'd captured the only two occupants.

"Clear!" he said into his communications mic. The female soldier was crying uncontrollably, and the male, who sat with his feet pulled up under his thighs, held his hands high in the air.

Cam and Bear entered the room, quickly removing the rifle from the proximity of the weatherman. Cam used her best Russian to determine if they'd contacted security. The woman responded that they had not because they didn't have time. They'd only received a warning notification moments before.

The team bound and gagged their hostages. It was not their day to die, despite the fact one of them, most likely the man, had opened fire on Bear.

Gunner and Cam stepped outside, under the now cloudy sky. He looked up and smiled.

"I'd like to make our way through the woods while it's still daylight," Cam began as she studied her GPS. "We've still got a tough five-klick hike until we reach the Valor, but it doesn't appear that we're being chased."

"They'll come looking for these two, or check in on them, at some point," said Gunner. "We need to get rolling."

"Do you see any benefit to taking off at night?"

"Yeah, maybe. Coming in, Bear flew low, in the canyons, to avoid radar. The biggest concern was being identified from the ground. This low cloud ceiling will help us on the way out, and darkness certainly will, too, but it won't protect us from their radar."

"The digital camo skin should, especially at night," added Cam.

"True, but they're gonna be on alert now. We shot them up pretty good, so they'll have no doubt that a special ops team was involved."

"Majors," interrupted the Jackal, referring to Cam and Gunner in the plural, "we've got inbound Kamov Black Sharks from the west. They appear to be landing at the airport, probably staging to run sweeps of the perimeter."

Bear emerged from the weather station. "I'm ready." He tossed energy bars to Cam and Gunner, who quickly opened them. The group hadn't eaten anything since they'd left the USS *Ronald Reagan*.

"I feel good. How about you boys?" asked Cam.

"I know where you're headed, and I agree," responded Gunner. "Double time. We can rest on the plane ride home."

Gunner studied his GPS device, regained his bearings, and darted into the woods, with Bear bringing up the rear.

The steady thumping of a Kamov Ka-50 helicopter was getting closer to their position. The unique coaxial rotor system emitted a deeper, more rhythmic sound than its American counterpart. The tandem-operated chopper allowed for one of the pilots to scan the ground below while the other navigated just above the treetops.

"Jackal, what's their range?" asked Cam.

"Two klicks. They are very disciplined, doing broad circular sweeps of the Cosmodrome compound, circling wider and wider with each pass."

"Can you calculate how long we have before they sweep over the top of us?" asked Cam. The trio was a mile away from their own transportation, about a twenty-minute jog in this terrain.

"Half an hour at most," came the reply. "And, Major, the Ka-50s are all equipped with their Samshit day-and-night thermal-imaging system. You'll have no cover."

"SSDD," mumbled Bear into the comms.

"Please repeat, Sergeant," instructed the Jackal.

He laughed, albeit breathlessly. The hike was taxing on his heavyset frame. "You know, *same shit*, different day."

Cam passed her partner and said, "I hate you."

"Yeah, sure you do. Secretly, you have a thing for me, right?"

"That's enough," interrupted Gunner, who became suddenly serious as the sound of the Ka-50's rotors grew a little bit louder and darkness began to settle in.

CHAPTER 42

Monday, April 9
Amur Oblast
Far Eastern Russia

Bear led the way into the AV-280, hustling into the pilot's seat and slinging his gear on the floor of the aircraft in the process. He immediately strapped himself in and hastily went through the preflight processes to lift the aircraft off the ground.

As Gunner pulled the door shut and closed up the tilt-rotor aircraft, the Jackal contacted them with a sense of urgency. "Next pass and they'll be on top of you."

Cam responded, "Roger. We heard them the last pass through. We've been damn lucky to avoid detection."

"That's about to change," said Bear as he fired up the two General Electric T64 engines. The twin turboshaft design had been a mainstay of aircraft design since 1959, and had undergone multiple technological upgrades, including increased performance and quieter operation.

The thirty-five-foot propellers quickly hoisted them off the ground as Bear wasted no time in gaining altitude.

"You've got company," said the Jackal. "Two thousand yards and closing at a higher rate of speed than its recon trips."

"Come on!" Bear urged the AV-280 upward until its vertical-lift design reached its apex. He expertly changed the configuration of the rotors to an airplane. "Hold on!"

Bear forced the aircraft to jump forward just as the Ka-50's single Shipunov dual-feed machine gun opened fire, sending armor-piercing rounds sailing past the AV-280 as it picked up speed.

"Sergeant, there are two additional Ka-50s approaching from the north in an intercept pattern. Suggest you head south to avoid."

"Roger," replied Bear, who banked slightly, following both his GPS navigation screen and the visual cues shown on his digital terrain-following system.

The AV-280 shuddered slightly as it hit some turbulence caused by slightly warmer air rising from the Amur River below them. The aircraft was designed to fly without a weapons systems officer, but Gunner slid into the seat next to Bear as he was achieving vertical lift.

The AV-280 was equipped with armaments similar to its V-22 Osprey predecessor. Gunner surveyed his options, ranging from the 2.75-inch Hydra rockets and the guided version of the Osprey's Advanced Precision Kill Weapon System.

"Major." It was Ghost on the comms. "I suggest using white phosphorous initially until the AV-280 is up to speed."

"He's right," added Bear. "In a minute, they'll never be able to catch us."

"Roger that," said Gunner. White phosphorous munitions provided both an incendiary weapon and a highly effective defensive purpose that could confuse a pursuing aircraft.

Each crewmember on the AV-280 had large multifunction computer displays with an array of information from engine and systems readouts, to navigation and weapons options. The monitors provided them a virtual depiction of their surroundings that was so detailed and vivid that it was like watching a movie in 4-D high definition.

"Major, your current flight path will lead you directly to the Russia-Chinese border. Chinese air defenses will have an impenetrable barrier of overlapping radars and surface-to-air batteries on the other side."

"Roger," said Gunner. "We've got enough trouble."

"Let me add, based upon the activity along the Sino-Russia border, the Chinese are aware of your presence."

"Wonderful," muttered Bear. "Drop 'em, Gunner."

Gunner made a series of entries on the onboard keyboard, and the white phosphorous rockets were off and away.

"Detonation!" shouted Cam, who was monitoring the external cameras on her own displays.

Bear banked hard left, only thirty miles from China, taking the aircraft to a higher altitude to avoid the terrain and gain speed.

The Jackal continued to alert the team as to the Russian military's maneuvers. "Sergeant, the Russians have scrambled intercepts along the coastline. Their 7th Air-Defense Brigade at Sakhalin is teeming with activity."

Cam sighed. She was most familiar with Far Eastern Russia and their defense placements. "They're cutting off our route to the Sea of Japan. Our only option back to the *Reagan* is to cut through China and North Korea."

"Suicide," said Gunner.

"Well, at least very bad odds," added Bear. "I can try to pull it off, but it's risky as hell."

The communications were silent as Bear initiated the aircraft's defensive countermeasures, although they had their limits. He might be able to avoid pursuing aircraft, but the ground-based radar systems were far more advanced.

"Bear, I have an idea. What about the Aleutians?"

"What about them?"

"They're expecting us to return to one of our carriers. What if we turn north, deeper into the Siberian forest? Then shoot across their coastline until we can make it into our airspace."

"I don't know, Cam. That's a long haul. We didn't plan on all of these gyrations when we calculated our fuel range."

Ghost came into the conversation. "Stand by, Sergeant. We'll lend an assist."

Bear backed off his airspeed in an attempt to conserve fuel. Plus, he was in no hurry to get shot at by the Russian air defenses in Sakhalin. They'd never survive it.

The Jackal returned to the communications. "Sergeant, I'm sending you a detailed flight path. If you can follow it to the letter, we can drop you down at the Casco Cove CGS at Attu Station."

Bear shrugged. "I've heard of it. It's like the westernmost part of the country."

The Jackal responded, "No, Sergeant, actually it's the easternmost part, technically speaking."

Bear pointed to the monitor for Gunner to see the flight-path instructions. He made some adjustments on his onboard computer so the flight navigation system could take control of the aircraft.

"Listen, Miss Jackal, I know east from west. Alaska is west. Always has been."

The Jackal showed a glimpse into her wry sense of humor. "You wanna bet?"

Cam could be heard laughing at them.

"Yeah, I'll bet you," replied Bear. "If I'm right, you pick up the tab for beer and wings."

"Fine, if I'm right," she began, "you stop questioning me."

"Hey, I can't guarantee that."

"Do we have a bet or not?"

Bear thought for a moment and turned in his seat, searching for Cam, who had suddenly disappeared from his view, yet he could hear her laughing. He shrugged and responded, "Bet."

"Okay, Sergeant King. Attu Station is actually the easternmost point in the U.S. because its located on the opposite side of the one-hundred-eightieth meridian from the rest of the country."

Bear threw his arms in the air. "Give me a break. I've never heard of such garbage."

"It's true, Sergeant. Look it up."

Cam was roaring in laughter. "I knew that. Well played, Jackal. Ha ha, Bear. You got got!"

"That's bullshit, man. She led me right into it."

Cam was still laughing. "You are such a sucker, especially for women. When are you gonna learn?"

S-400 Triumf threat detected at three o'clock. Range is one thousand two hundred feet.

Bear quickly reacted to the voice command system's warning of an incoming anti-aircraft missile.

"What the hell?" Gunner asked as he swung his head sharply, straining to look out the right-side windows of the AV-280. There was nothing there except the black of the Russian night, speckled with bright stars.

Range nine hundred feet. Evade! Evade! The robotic female voice was persistent.

"No kidding," said Bear as he took control of the aircraft and sent it into a dive toward the desolate Siberian forest.

"Where did that come from?" asked Gunner.

The Jackal responded, "They must have a surface-to-air missile battery that's unknown to our intelligence community."

Range seven hundred feet. Evade! Evade!

"I am!" shouted Bear. The missile was holding a static position in relation to the AV-280 despite Bear's wild maneuvering and flying low to the ground.

"It's heat seeking," said Gunner. "Let's give it some heat to seek that's hotter than we are."

Gunner deployed an AGM-176 Griffin B missile, a small, thirteen-pound warhead that had airburst detonation capability. It provided the AV-280 a potent deterrent capability.

"Released," he declared as the missile fell below the aircraft and its afterburner lit up the night.

The Griffin B missile raced ahead of their aircraft, soaring through the night, providing an irresistible heat-seeking trail for the incoming Russian S-400 that had been tracking them.

Range one thousand feet.

"It's turning!" shouted Bear just as a violent explosion occurred a half mile ahead of them. Bear lifted the SV-280 upward to avoid the debris resulting from the massive collision of the two missiles.

"Well done, Sergeant," said Ghost. Their commander had remained alongside the Jackal during the entire mission. "We're sending you a new flight path. I won't mince words. You'll be over open water for twenty minutes and then there's one more Russian defense system to avoid at Petropavlovsk."

"We can handle that," said Bear.

Gunner interrupted. "Jackal, have you recalculated our fuel and distance?"

"Yes, sir. It's tight."

CHAPTER 43

Monday, April 9
Over the Bering Sea
East of the Russian coast

Bear was forced to make a series of evasive course corrections in order to avoid an air barricade of Russian Coast Guard Mi-17 assault helicopters. The twists and turns employed by the seasoned pilot successfully avoided being hit by the Mi-17s' gunpods and rockets; however, they now faced a predicament just as deadly as being shot out of the sky—a lack of fuel.

"Eighty miles," he announced. "ETA less than fifteen minutes."

"How far until we're over U.S. territorial waters?" asked Gunner.

"I know what you're thinking, and it won't matter," replied the Jackal. "The line's too close and whatever happened could easily be disputed."

"Can we get any kind of ground or air support?" asked Bear.

"Sergeant, you should know the answer to that," replied Ghost.

"Hell, Colonel, at least a fishing boat. Something to pull us out of the water."

"Sergeant, by our calculations, you'll be fine to Attu Station," interrupted the Jackal. "Might I suggest a quicker descent. The Su-35Ses that are in pursuit will never catch up to you."

Ghost reentered the conversation. "Major, NORAD has scrambled F-22 intercepts in response to the incoming hostile aircraft. Once the Su-35Ses enter the Alaskan Air Defense Identification Zone, roughly seventy miles to your west, we'll engage, with force if necessary, if they enter U.S. or Canadian sovereign airspace."

The Russians were notorious for sending Tu-95 bombers on scheduled sorties over the neutral waters of the Chukotka, Bering, and Okhotsk Seas. Their forays near the northern coast of the Aleutian Islands had been increasing in recent years as they continued to test the mettle of NORAD's defensive capability.

The bomber patrols were intended by the Russians to send a highly visible message to underscore their military strength. The Su-35Ses in pursuit of Gunner's team had different plans.

Bear began to descend toward the small, one-hundred-forty-square-mile island. "I've got a visual."

Tension filled the air as the team watched the former Coast Guard station, now CIA outpost, grow larger in front of them.

Gunner looked over to Bear and nodded, offering him encouragement. Gunner suspected the water temperature was in the upper thirties in the southern part of the sea. At those temperatures, they could die of hypothermia in a very short period of time.

"We got this! We got this!" Bear shouted as he slowed to hover above the helicopter landing pad at the decommissioned Coast Guard station. He adjusted the tilt-rotor to gently drop the AV-280 down with a slight thud.

"Jeez, Louise," muttered Cam into the microphone. "Let's not do that again, okay?"

Gunner managed a laugh. "In our business, that's a promise none of us can keep."

Bear removed the harnesses and looked around the frigid landscape. He glanced around all sides of the aircraft. With a puzzled look on his face, he asked, "Hey, where's our welcoming committee?"

Ghost responded, "There won't be one, Sergeant. We're sure that your every move has been tracked by Russian reconnaissance satellites. This facility is ostensibly abandoned, although it is manned with a small team of eight who come and go under the guise of being local fishermen."

"Roger that," said Gunner.

"Major, a team will pick you up in the morning," Ghost continued. "Retrieve your gear, get some rest, and I'll meet you at Lackland for a full debriefing."

Gunner looked at his team, and then finally, after nearly being killed in Russia, he asked, "Did you get what you were looking for?"

Ghost paused. "Affirmative. Good job, all of you."

The team loaded their weapons, camera equipment, and other gear, leaving the out-of-fuel AV-280 on the helicopter pad. Bear, who honestly planned on negotiating with the colonel to keep the multimillion-dollar aircraft, bemoaned the fact that they'd have to leave it behind.

They made their way inside the former Coast Guard station and walked downward through the structure until they reached a steel security door. Gunner, who was used to working with the agency, expected them to confirm the trio's identity. Bear, who was both impatient and hungry, couldn't resist whipping out the middle finger, taunting the CIA operations team, until a loud click signaled the door was open.

Inside, they were amazed at what they found. A massive array of computers, large-screen televisions, and listening stations were spread in a semicircle facing a wall of maps. An older man of Alaskan descent approached Gunner.

"Major Fox, I'm Mr. Waters. Welcome back stateside."

"Thank you, um, Mr. Waters." *Not your real name, I bet*, Gunner thought.

Mr. Waters turned his attention to everyone in the group. "I've been instructed to make you folks comfortable until you're picked up, likely in the next several hours. I'll show you to our galley, where you can fix yourself something to eat, and if you wish, there are toilet facilities that include a couple of showers."

The group followed him down a hallway until they were left alone in a small room containing picnic tables and a sparsely equipped kitchenette.

"Do you think they live here?" asked Cam.

Gunner nodded. "Most likely on a temporary, rotational basis.

There are hidden outposts like this all over the world."

"And out of this world, too," added Bear. "I've seen pictures of the one built on the Moon. It's way bigger and nicer than this dump."

Cam rummaged through the refrigerator. "I hope you guys like salmon and crab. They've got a ton of it."

"Whadya think about the moon deal, Gunner?"

Gunner made his way to the refrigerator and retrieved a bottle of water. "I think it's like everything else that NASA and their private partners do. They have the technology, they create a concept, and then they rush into it headfirst without considering the consequences. Sometimes, I don't understand what the hellfire emergency is with those people. I mean, did they make sure it was totally safe before they expanded the outpost and populated it with families?"

Cam joined Gunner at a table with a large platter of already cooked king crab legs. She filled a bowl with cocktail sauce and offered him some.

"Speaking of hellfire emergencies, have you guys thought about what the purpose of that mission was? I mean, I get that we're in some kind of space race again with the Russians, but was it really necessary to send us in to get our asses shot off over a rocket?"

Gunner furrowed his brow and reached for a crab leg. He struggled to open it, which was why he preferred oysters. He'd become adept at popping them open when he ate them at home.

"What did you see down below? You know, under the launchpad."

Cam chuckled. "Funny you asked. I never saw anything. I was hauling my cookies across the compound to get away from their security. But I was recording as well as transmitting, just for a backup." She reached down into her gear bag and retrieved the camera. While Gunner and Bear finished off the crab legs, she replayed the footage of her escape from the Cosmodrome.

She began to shake her head. "You've got to be kidding me."

"What?" asked Gunner.

She roughly set the camera on the table and slid it toward him. "See for yourself."

Gunner looked puzzled and shrugged. He passed the camera on to Bear, who was reaching across the table for it.

"Mining equipment?" asked Bear. "We almost died seven times to get video of mining equipment? That's the dumbest thing ever."

Gunner tapped his fingers on the table, deep in thought. "Maybe not."

"Why?" asked Cam.

Gunner was about to answer when Mr. Waters entered the room. "Good news, people. Your ride is already here. Wrap it up."

"You don't have to tell me twice," said Bear as he quickly pushed away from the table. He led the way with Gunner and Cam chasing behind. All of them were looking forward to getting back to the beach.

CHAPTER 44

Tuesday, April 10
CNN Studios
Atlanta, Georgia

"The easiest way is to set a large rocket on a collision course with this killer asteroid and call it a day," said famed science commentator and television personality Dr. Bill Whitney. Then he shook his head and added, "But what a waste that would be."

There had been virtually nonstop news coverage of IM86 since the *60 Minutes* report followed by the president's address from the Oval Office. A revolving door of astrophysicists, nuclear weapons experts, astronauts, and political pundits made the rounds, providing insight as to how to deal with the threat. Interspersed between solutions, as had been the norm for decades, the blame game was on full display as politicians did their level best to find a boogeyman on Earth for the threat hurtling toward them from space.

CNN host Megyn Kelly stood in front of a large monitor with a blown-up image of IM86, digitally modified to brighten its otherwise dark appearance. Superimposed in the background was a view of Earth from space, complete with a bull's-eye on top of North America. Kelly turned to the camera as the previously taped interview with Dr. Whitney paused for a moment. Her demeanor was dour and emotional as she spoke.

"Nobody saw this coming. An asteroid over a mile wide could soon shatter our planet's atmosphere with a deafening bang, strike somewhere, anywhere it chooses, leaving a crater in the surface with the energy of several million nuclear bombs.

"Millions of people will be incinerated instantaneously. Those who aren't will succumb to the aftermath of the blast as molten debris is ejected into the atmosphere, reaching far into Earth's orbit, raining fire from above to destroy almost all life below.

"Does this sound like the preview of a Netflix made-for-TV movie? Am I being overdramatic or sensationalistic? Dr. Bill Whitney doesn't think so. In fact, I'm paraphrasing his words from an interview conducted on this network over a decade ago in which he stated that an asteroid impact like I've just described, while unlikely, is plausible nonetheless and would spell the end for humanity as we know it."

Kelly walked closer to the camera and approached the host's desk, where Dr. Whitney sat in the guest's seat, casually crossing his legs as the camera brought him into view. He was wearing a blue and white seersucker suit topped off with a bow tie. Nearing eighty, Dr. Whitney was still called upon often when major scientific events were in the news.

"Dr. Whitney, welcome back."

"Thank you, Megyn."

"Prior to your coming on with me today, I replayed that interview from fifteen years ago and couldn't help but think how prophetic it was. Do catastrophic events like this keep you up at night?"

Dr. Whitney laughed and then clasped his hands in front of him. "Admittedly, Megyn, when you're a scientist, you have a mindset that is open to all possibilities. It's like being a swimmer with a fear of sharks. It's the one you don't see that frightens you the most. That said, as a student of science, and history, I know that a catastrophic event like the one we face with IM86 has happened before, possibly multiple times, and it was sure to happen again. I look at my opinions on these subjects as warnings rather than attempts to be prophetic."

"Fair enough, Dr. Whitney; however, did you expect to see this in your lifetime?"

"An oft-repeated phrase, one that I coined decades ago, is that an asteroid impact like this one is a low probability event with enormous consequences. The laws of statistics will tell you that the probability of that ball landing thrice in a row on the number twenty-six on the roulette wheel is low probability, but it can happen. The universe is no different. The fact of the matter is, especially since we've been in an extended period of increased near-Earth object activity, that IM86 could strike the planet in three weeks, and another one could follow a month later."

"Wonderful," quipped Kelly. She furrowed her brow and leaned toward the ordinarily fun-loving and irreverent science commentator. "We know that the thought of a devastating asteroid impact makes for compelling movie scripts, and, as you say, the probability is low, yet here we are. How could this happen? How did IM86 miss being discovered sooner, or was it simply a matter of being past due for the big one, so it was our time?"

Dr. Whitney chuckled and shrugged. "Listen, nobody knows about the unknown, right? It's an oddly worded phrase that makes sense. We speculate about catastrophic events all the time. Some consider it to be pure fiction; others, like myself, study the science and history and realize they're probable. That said, the scientific community, bolstered by world governments, has taken steps to identify ninety percent of the potentially catastrophic NEOS, but that leaves ten percent. Simply put, a one-in-ten chance that a planet killer slips past our advanced technology, which is more than enough to be troublesome."

Kelly continued to quiz Dr. Whitney. "I led this segment with a taped portion of your interview on CNN in which you discussed the use of nuclear weapons as a means to divert or even destroy an asteroid that's on a collision course with Earth. What is your opinion as to how we should deal with this?"

"Well, there have been numerous scientific studies since I first started to raise awareness of the threat some twenty-five years ago. The Jet Propulsion Laboratory at CalTech has done a magnificent job of creating laboratory simulations, you know, to scale, of how to deflect, divert, or destroy an inbound NEO. However, with our increased focus on establishing a lunar outpost, an admirable endeavor, of course, we abandoned our left flank. In other words, we used our limited budgetary resources to race to the Moon and cast aside the defense of our planet."

Kelly referred to her notes but then came back to her original question, but was more pointed this time. "I understand there is a lot of debate right now about who's to blame for missing an asteroid of this size, and many believe it was simply bad luck that IM86 was trailing in the considerable shadow of Comet Oort."

Dr. Whitney interrupted her. "Megyn, searching for an asteroid is like trying to find a charcoal briquette floating in a dark room. You blindly wave your arms around in hopes of discovering it."

Kelly laughed. "I understand, however, let me get right to the point. Do you agree with the administration, and the European Space Agency, that we should use this as an opportunity to test alternatives to the use of nuclear weapons in space? Or should we attempt diversion methods first, coupled with some type of mining operation?"

Dr. Whitney became pensive for the first time. It appeared to be a question that he was uncomfortable answering, a rare occurrence for the opinionated, self-proclaimed *science guy*.

"Megyn, let me answer your question two ways. First, for the benefit of the viewing public. What you may have garnered from movies like *Deep Impact* and *Armageddon*—quite successful in the box office, but completely laughable from a scientific perspective—needs to be cast aside. Asteroids are much tougher than we expected. The computer models factor in so many variables—temperature, velocity, mass, material brittleness, etcetera. Opinions vary as to how much energy is required to divert a massive space rock off its trajectory, much less destroy it. Once that is determined, then our space agency will have to consider the short-timescale fragmentation phase versus the potential long-timescale gravitational reaccumulation phase."

"I'm sorry, Dr. Whitney, but you've lost me, and I'm sure more than one viewer is scratching their head right now."

"Okay, let me boil it down this way," he continued. "Timing is everything. Even if we could create a nuclear payload large enough to deliver a knockout punch to the most vulnerable points—plural—on the target object, then timing comes into play. Hit it too early, and the gravity of IM86 can pull it back together, except now it would be in many pieces. Hit it late, albeit dangerously close to Earth, and our chances of avoiding the worst of the impact event increase. IM86 would become more of a rubble pile rather than a reconstituted killer."

Kelly paused and then asked, "Still devastating, I presume?"

"Absolutely, but not extinction level," he replied. "The impact will be more unpredictable, as well. I mean, frankly, we'd be operating on a wing and a prayer."

"So, Dr. Whitney, bottom-line it for us. Do you approve of the administration's proposed orbital slingshot method, followed by a mission to study IM86?"

"I do because—" began Dr. Whitney in response until Kelly placed her hand to her earpiece.

She interrupted his answer. "Dr. Whitney, please, just a moment." Kelly nodded her head and spoke into her microphone. "Okay. Okay. Bring it up on the screen."

Dr. Whitney looked puzzled and then he turned his attention to the bank of monitors to Kelly's right.

"To our viewers at CNN, and CNN International, who are just joining us, we have breaking news. NASA and the Department of Defense are preparing for a press conference at this hour, which sources tell us will involve a mysterious rocket launch in Russia. Our sources tell CNN that the Russians have made an unannounced rocket launch from a remote facility in Eastern Russia. We have no further details at this time, but we are going to take you live to our correspondent at the Pentagon now."

CHAPTER 45

Tuesday, April 10
NASA Headquarters
Two Independence Square
Washington, DC

> *To reach for new heights and reveal the unknown so what we do*
> *and learn will benefit all humankind.*

The words were stenciled across the wall in the large conference room where the heads of the world's preeminent space agency met to chart NASA's course. On this day, however, they were charged with the responsibility of saving it.

"This is a game-changer as far as the president is concerned," said his chief of staff, Maggie Fielding. She was making a rare appearance outside the White House but found it necessary because the situation was fluid. The time delay associated with NASA compiling the information, creating it in report format, and delivering it to her at the White House was unacceptable. She needed to be in the room with the heads of NASA's mission directorates as they considered the ramifications of Russia's rocket launch.

"We understand," said Jim Frederick, congressman, special advisor to the president, and a former astronaut. He had been nominated by the president to become NASA's first African-American administrator, but he had not yet been confirmed by the Senate. "From the important intelligence gathered in the last forty-eight hours, coupled with this event, it's apparent that the Russians intend to explore IM86. The unanswered question remains whether they are attempting any diversion method."

215

Fielding stood from her chair and approached a window overlooking E Street. "They've cut off all communications with the State Department. We've lodged complaints with the United Nations. We've tried our usual back-channel options. Hell, we've even tried to enlist the assistance of the Chinese. They've cut us off completely."

Frederick calmly took a drink of coffee and provided his opinion. "Well, it's clear that they're trying to beat us to IM86. Either they discovered the NEO before we did, or they were prepared for this eventuality and ratcheted up their program, culminating in today's launch. Regardless, they're on their way to plant their flag on the surface of this asteroid and claim it for their own."

Fielding concurred. "That has to be it. If they were going to save the world, they'd be crowing about it. *We acted while the United States sat on its hands. The Americans were unprepared, so we did it alone.* I can hear it now."

"It's all propaganda," Frederick reminded her. "We can't stop what their ministry of bullshit says, nor can we influence what people believe. The question we face today is what do we do about it? We had a planned launch of Friday, April 20. Based upon our calculations, it will be the most opportune time to initiate the orbital slingshot because of the asteroid's proximity to the gravitational pull of the Moon."

"They'll be on the surface digging for gold and god knows what else by then!" Fielding shot back in frustration. She took a deep breath and continued. "Listen, the president is not going to sit idly by while the Russians beat us. He ran on a platform of being the preeminent space agency, advancing both our defensive capabilities through the Space Force, and continuing our rapid expansion of Project Artemis on the Moon. This is a chance of a lifetime to mine and explore an asteroid of this size. And the damned Russians are gonna beat us there!"

Frederick didn't mind taking the heat because he wasn't responsible for the course that NASA had taken in recent years. But, as he'd learned while in Congress, agency heads, even those who aren't officially in place yet, serve at the pleasure of the president. It wasn't unusual for scapegoats to be created and disappear into the night when it was politically expedient.

He turned to the experts, the career employees of NASA. "I have two questions. Is our technology for this mission better than the Russians'? Secondly, how soon can you move up the launch date?"

The room burst into chatter as the administrators began talking to one another and got their aides involved, who were sitting in chairs on the outside perimeter of the large conference room.

Finally, Nola Taylor, the head of the Space Technology Mission Directorate, spoke up. "I can affirmatively state that our program is better suited for both landing and scientific exploration. Ms. Fielding, I want you to keep in mind that placing a space vehicle of any type in the orbit of IM86 is one thing, safely landing on it is another. The Russian rocket delivery system may get them there, but the entry, descent, and landing are a huge challenge for them. Frankly, our technology is far superior."

The director of Human Exploration and Operations addressed the chief of staff. "Nola's right. Through our cooperative efforts with SpaceX and Orbital Sciences Corp, we've created orbiting labs with unmanned spacecraft that could easily beat the Russians to the surface. Our manned spaceships are second to none, although they are untested."

"Can you beat them there?" asked Fielding. "That's the question the president needs answered."

"We can't beat them into orbit, but it is possible to beat them to the surface," he responded.

An older man at the end of the table vigorously shook his head from side to side. "There's no way. We would have to move our scheduled launch up to Friday to have any chance—"

Frederick interrupted him. "Friday, as in three days? Is that even possible?"

"I don't think so," the man responded.

"Well"—Nola Taylor took the floor—"in actuality, it is. We're laying the groundwork for a launch now. We've picked our team to fly the mission. They are the best of the best. We'd have to cut their mission-simulation training short, naturally, but—"

"That's too risky," the man interrupted her. "You're putting lives—"

Chief of Staff Fielding walked toward the gentleman, who abruptly stopped speaking. "I'm sorry, who are you?"

"Ma'am, my name is Hal Rawlings, chief of the Flight Director Office. I coordinate both launch and mission control."

Frederick, the acting administrator, who'd had extensive conversations with Rawlings, added, "Ms. Fielding, Chief Rawlings, as we all refer to him by, has been with the agency since he graduated from college. He's worked in virtually every aspect of NASA's mission and launch programs. He's a true legend at NASA. Moreover, he understands NASA operations inside and out."

Fielding studied the ex-astronaut-turned-head-of-flight-operations. "If we have the best of the best, as Ms. Taylor has said, and if our technology is superior to the Russians', why is it too risky to move the launch date up by a week?"

Chief Rawlings calmly sat back in his chair, not intimidated by the chief of staff. "Ma'am, it's the mental aspect of the mission. There's tremendous pressure on everyone, from the astronauts to mission control to the people responsible for preparing the launch. You combine that with the fact we're out to save the world, and the margin for error is extremely thin."

Fielding was undeterred. She turned to Frederick. "I'm going back to the White House to relay what I've been told. I hear your concerns about pressure, but keep in mind, our president holds the fate, the very lives, of more than three hundred million Americans in his hands. If he calls upon you to step up and make this happen, I trust that you'll be able to do so."

Without awaiting a response or comment, she stormed out the door with her aides scurrying behind her.

CHAPTER 46

Five years prior
DeFuniak Springs, Florida

Gunner tried to console his wife as she fought back tears. She'd been training for the better part of a year to be a part of the first manned mission to the Moon in decades. At the last minute, she'd come down with the flu, an unusual occurrence for a young woman who was in excellent physical condition, ate all the perfect foods, and prided herself in treating her body like a temple, as the saying goes. However, flu viruses don't always differentiate between those with weakened immune systems and someone like Heather, who stayed in the best of shape. All it took was a random cough or sneeze at the grocery store or on an airplane flight, and the bug hit her.

Just days before the mission's launch was scheduled, Heather had been grounded. She'd pleaded with the launch coordinator not to use a substitute for her role as the lead astronomer on the mission. She assured them the flu virus would run its course and likely be out of her system by liftoff. However, they were unconvinced and stood by their decision. They simply could not risk putting her in closed quarters with the fourteen-man crew, possibly passing the flu to everyone on board the rocket.

She got up from the couch and wandered aimlessly across the living room of their home, which had been built in the nineteenth century by Frederick DeFuniak, the president of the Pensacola and Atlantic Railroad. The television had been muted by Gunner as the countdown for the launch had been placed on hold at T-minus two minutes. This was not out of the ordinary, as frequently technological aspects of the mission had to be checked and rechecked.

Launching a rocket into space involves lots of complex circuitry and moving parts, all of which can malfunction. Tiny failures of mechanical parts, or human error, had led to disasters like the destruction of the *Challenger* in 1986 and the *Columbia* in 2003.

On occasion, concerns over a single aspect of the launch can cause a delay, as was the case today, or even scrub the mission altogether, depending on the severity of the problem. Usually, delaying the launch allowed the threats to dissipate, as in the case of unexpected weather, or give NASA's team the opportunity to diagnose and repair the issue.

Gunner patted the sofa, encouraging Heather to return. "Come here, darling. They've promised you the first seat on the next ISS deployment. I know it isn't the Moon, but you'll take the first step towards getting there."

"I know, and that's all I expected to do on my first flight anyway. But still …" Her voice trailed off as she pouted.

A brilliant scientist and astrophysicist, Heather could've commanded a tremendous salary if she'd signed on with the private companies like SpaceX or the Jeff Bezos project, Blue Origin. She'd held out because she wanted to be a part of NASA and Project Artemis. While the private firms had designs on colonizing the Moon, the U.S. government needed to be the first to land there to stake its claim for the world's leader in space exploration.

Heather wanted to be a part of that first mission, and now she was grounded. What was even more frustrating was the fact that, as she had predicted, her flu symptoms had passed and she felt great, except for the disappointment in being forced to watch the launch from home.

Gunner grabbed the remote and fumbled for the volume button. "Look, they've continued the countdown."

Heather joined his side and wiped away her tears of self-pity. "Okay. I'm really happy for these guys. They're like family, you know. We've trained together, but it's more than that. We were going to make history by being the first human beings to live on the Moon, albeit for just a few weeks. Babe, we were going to be looked upon as pioneers."

Gunner squeezed her hand and kissed her on the cheek. He reassured her that her time would come, not knowing at that moment it would be a few years later.

And we have liftoff, Artemis One is making its historic trek to the Moon!

The excitement in the announcer's voice caused goose bumps on Heather's arms as she tightly squeezed Gunner's hand. She began to shake from excitement as the cameras caught the powerful rocket's thrusters heaving it upward into the sky.

Excitement turned to concern only two minutes into launch.

"Oh no. Gunner, something's wrong."

"What?"

"Look at the contrails. The one contrail that's supposed to follow Artemis as it reaches the stratosphere has split off."

"What does that—?"

She interrupted his question. "The solid rocket boosters have separated too early. Gunner, oh God!"

Heather began to wail as an explosion filled the screen, and then the cameras abruptly cut away. She buried her head in his shoulder and sobbed uncontrollably.

The historic, inaugural flight of Artemis One to the Moon had ended as it disintegrated.

CHAPTER 47

Wednesday, April 11
Gunner's Residence
Dog Island
Florida Panhandle

Everyone slept in after the tiring ride from the Aleutian Islands to Lackland Air Force Base near San Antonio, and the last leg was a rough helicopter ride in a torrential downpour that eventually set them down at the airport on Dog Island. Ordinarily, Gunner preferred to keep the military aircraft confined to the mainland, but the weather was so bad that he doubted any of the other residents noticed the Sikorsky drop in and immediately take off. Walking in the rain and wind for two miles to his home caused more complaining than the arduous return trip from Alaska, or the perilous escape from Far East Russia.

That morning, the sun was bright and on full display, beaming inside Gunner's home. Cam barely stirred on the sofa, and there was no sign of Bear, who'd most likely buried himself in the gym under a pile of beach towels.

Gunner made his way to the kitchen, wearing his board shorts and a NASA tee shirt that matched one that Heather had worn all the time. He was desperately trying to hold onto her even though he knew that would never be possible.

For the first year, he'd considered selling the house, as it had been designed and built on their dreams together. However, Pop had moved nearby and the place was now paid for. Besides, he wasn't prepared to let go. Not yet.

The Mr. Coffee did its job, filling the kitchen with the aroma of the dark-roasted brew. Normally, Gunner would pop a K-Cup pod into the Breville machine, but his guests would be looking for their morning *mojo* soon enough.

He walked out onto his deck and admired the white sand beach and turquoise blue water. An elderly couple stopped briefly to take pictures of the shipwreck that had revealed itself after a hurricane last fall. In 1899, it was estimated that one hundred fifteen ships had washed ashore between Carrabelle and Apalachicola. The wooden ships had crashed into the surf of the barrier islands and, over time, had been buried by sand as future storms altered the shoreline.

Hurricane Michael in 2018 had unearthed some of the wreckage, and Hurricane Harry last fall revealed several more. The tall mast ships had been part of a growing ship trade that connected North Florida with Cuba and the West Indies. Rum, spices, and sugar were frequently traded on the Panhandle in exchange for cotton and other textiles.

Gunner sighed as he reflected on their mission. He understood why the spook at the CIA outpost had purposefully kept them in the dark as to the news that had spread around the globe Sunday night. In fact, none of the military personnel his team had come in contact with had spoken a word of it as they were transferred to Lackland to meet with Ghost and a team of intelligence agents. It wasn't until after the debriefing that Ghost revealed the threat IM86 posed.

Gunner had a hunch. He and Heather had discussed the prospect of mining an asteroid many years ago. She'd had the opportunity to work for Elon Musk and had even encouraged him to join her. She believed that his Earth sciences background coupled with her desire to conquer space made them a perfect team.

After a lot of discussion, and subtle pressure on her part, Gunner had chosen to stay in the military, and Heather decided to pursue her dream through NASA. He often wondered what their life might be like if he'd followed her dream instead of sticking to his own.

Off in the distance, he could hear the sound of a Cessna. Gunner instinctively checked his watch to see if it might be Pop ferrying people to and fro, before realizing he'd taken it off before bed. Ghost had assured them that they'd be removed from the *call list*, the term used for teams of operators who remained on standby to travel on a moment's notice. Their mission in Russia had been grueling, and Ghost understood their need to decompress. To Gunner, decompressing meant not caring what day or time it was.

The sound of the plane came closer and then Gunner recognized the orange-and-white markings on the side. He'd encouraged Pop to use a different paint scheme, as his plane might be confused for being part of the Coast Guard, but his father rejected his advice, opting to keep the colors to pay homage to his hometown football team—the Tennessee Volunteers.

The plane slowed and Pop tipped his wings back and forth, acknowledging Gunner's presence on the deck. After he flew by and banked right to circle toward the bayfront dock, a sleepy voice caught Gunner's attention.

"Was that Pop?" asked Cam. "I hope he brought breakfast."

"Have you checked the fridge?" asked Gunner.

"Very funny," she growled. "There's nothing in there but beer, including three empty ones."

Gunner laughed. "Bear did that. He said that way it didn't look like we drank that much last night."

Cam joined his side and leaned against the rail. She was wearing one of his tee shirts and most likely nothing underneath. He glanced at her body, noticing her shape, but didn't give it a second thought. Of course Cam was a beautiful young woman, and a *guy's girl*, but she'd also been his best friend since childhood.

Cam glanced around. "Where's Howard?"

"He wandered upstairs to sleep with Bear. Those two probably snored in each other's ears all night."

Cam didn't respond and soaked in the beauty of the sunrise. Gunner finished his coffee and stared down the beach, watching several seagulls soar along the coast, periodically dipping down into the water to snag a fish. After a moment of silence, he looked in Cam's direction.

"Cam, what are you doing here?"

"Um, whadya mean? All my gear is here, remember?"

"You're deflecting. That's not what I mean and you know it."

Cam fidgeted and reached for his coffee mug. She took it from him, saw that it was empty, and poured the last drops onto the sand below. "Let me get some coffee." She was stalling.

"No, I'll get it and then you're gonna start talkin'. If you go inside, you'll disappear."

She pushed her hair out of her eyes and lifted her face to the sun. "Fine, but make it snappy, or I'll jump the rail and you'll never see me again."

Gunner laughed. "You mean like when we played Batman and Robin as kids? Do you remember how that turned out?"

"Yeah, yeah. Coffee, mister. Make it snappy. You've been warned."

Gunner left her side and recalled how the two of them had been inseparable. They'd dressed up in Batman and Robin costumes and were playing in the backyard. Gunner led the way as they chased an imaginary villain, climbing over a chain-link fence into an adjacent yard. Cam, never to be outdone, followed suit, only her cape snagged on the jagged edge of the fence, causing her to land awkwardly on her shoulder. As it turned out, she broke her collarbone.

As promised, Gunner quickly returned and placed the mug on the rail next to his refill. Knowing that Pop was most likely driving up to the house from the dock, he urged Cam to explain.

"Speak now, or forever hold your peace," he said with a chuckle.

"Yeah, I could've done that once before, remember. Only the whole event was my idea."

"I remember, runaway bridesmaid. You're lucky you didn't get fired off the bridesmaid team."

Cam drank her coffee and an evil grin came across her face. "He was cute."

"He was barely out of high school."

"I didn't know that!" She made a feeble attempt to defend her honor.

Gunner and Cam clinked coffee mugs and they took a sip,

reveling in the memory of a fun day for all involved.

"Spill it, Cam. Time's up."

She dropped her chin to her chest and began with a sigh. "Okay. I've been offered a job with an outfit out of Boston called Aegis. They do private security work. You know, protect rich kids. Travel to Saudi Arabia and follow some sheikh around while he gathers up more brides. Stuff like that."

"Riveting. And challenging, too." Gunner worked hard to hide his disappointment in Cam's news.

"I know. It's total bullshit. Here's the thing, Gunner. These guys pay ten times what I'm getting paid by the Air Force. Sure, there are some risks involved, but nothing compared to what we just went through. I'd be a fool not to consider it."

Gunner's mind wandered as he thought of losing the third most important woman in his life behind his Mom and Heather. He rolled his neck on his shoulder and fidgeted with his coffee mug.

Cam continued. "You're pissed. I knew it."

"No, I'm not pissed. I'm happy for you. I mean, you're right. The money is good; the stress level is waaay down. You'll get to travel. Hell, they probably have a 401k plan."

"The IRS took away 401k's, remember?"

"They did?"

Cam shook her head and ran her arm through Gunner's, pressing her body against his. "You're like my big brother, and Pop's my pop, too. You guys are all I have, not counting that beast asleep in the gym."

Gunner squeezed her hand. "Do you want me to say *go for it*? I mean, it sounds like a sweet deal."

"No, dumbass. I want you to talk me out of it!"

"Come on, Cam," protested Gunner. "I don't want to stand in the way of you pursuing something you've maybe dreamed—"

Cam slugged him, causing him to spill coffee over the rail, something that earned him a stern rebuke from below.

"Hey, watch out!"

It was Pop, who'd pulled the four-wheeler under the house and was sprayed with the coffee.

"Sorry, Pop!" Cam apologized. She turned to Gunner. "Babysitting a bunch of rich people is not my dream. But I don't want to die poor either. I'm sure as hell not gonna go find some rich guy to take care of me. I'm a soldier, always will be. It's just, dude, they pay us like shit. Look at what we do for these guys. Look at what we risk. Some pimple-faced kid on Amazon's switchboard makes triple what we do."

"Cam, I get it. What about love of country and all that?"

"Of course I love my country. And I love you and Bear, too. That's the real reason I do this stuff. We're brothers."

The elevator door opened up and Pop stumbled in with the dock cart full of groceries. "Little help!"

"Sure, Pop, we're comin'," Gunner quickly responded before turning to Cam. "If you're sure it's just about money, we have something to talk about. I need you, Cam. I mean, I have money saved that I could help—"

The offer earned him another slug. "Don't you ever do that again or I'll kick your ass onto the next island!"

Gunner frowned and rubbed his arm. "You're downright mean."

"Yup, and don't forget it. Let's see what Pop's fixin' us to eat 'cause lord knows we can't eat Doritos, oysters, and beer all the time."

"Why not?"

CHAPTER 48

Wednesday, April 11
Gunner's Residence
Dog Island
Florida Panhandle

The group had one of the best days they could recall in a long time. The phone never rang. They avoided the news. Junk food and beer were consumed in mass quantities. Everyone got too much sun and they ended the day totally wiped out.

After Bear delivered Pop to his house, he returned to talk with Gunner and Cam. The conversation between them had continued throughout the day, bringing Pop in for his words of wisdom from time to time. He'd sacrificed a lot in his life for family and country, and his insight proved beneficial to Cam.

He'd explained how he had no regrets. Sure, he thought of what might have happened if he had pursued an opportunity to go to college, maybe study law, or even attend business school. In the end, the memories he'd gained in the service were fulfilling, and he felt God had placed him in Berlin to meet his bride, Gunner's mother.

Their life together as a family had been full of fun and travel, and now he got to live a toes-in-the-sand lifestyle on Dog Island near his son.

The more the group drank, the more philosophical they got. They exchanged regrets and discussed their futures, although the concept of meeting someone was off the table, as always.

When the sun set and the all-day party came to an end, Cam pledged to turn down the offer, but the three of them focused on ways to increase the money they earned, to at least make it marginally commensurate with the risks they took.

"I've heard rumors out of Fort Bragg," began Gunner as he downed another bottle of water in an effort to nurse an early evening hangover. "The Unit finds a way to take care of their own by having a secret stash, you know, a nest egg that they can access."

"It's true," said Cam. "I dated, um, well, *befriended* a guy in Delta Force. He ran his mouth a little too much during some pillow talk, and he said they had well into six figures stashed away."

Bear groaned as he sat up in his Adirondack chair. "That's some serious change. Where did they get it?"

"It's accumulated over time," replied Cam. "They stumble across it during a mission, for example. Those guys do a lot of stuff in Central America fighting the drug cartels. The next thing you know, they stumble across a duffle bag full of cash during an op, said duffle gets mixed in with their gear, and well, whoops, all that cash ends up in their living room."

"Nobody's the wiser, right?" asked Gunner.

"Exactly," Cam replied. "Those guys follow a strict code, kinda like the SEALs. Not that different from the bond we have. I guess they turn it over to some kind of quartermaster who keeps track of how much they have and whom they disburse it to."

Bear lit a cigar, his third of the day. "Is that illegal? I mean, finders keepers, right?"

Gunner shrugged. The sweet aroma of the cigar was tempting him, but his stomach was screaming *don't even think about it.*

Cam replied, "I'm sure there is something buried in the military code about ill-gotten gains or some such. I don't know, but I do know we can't continue like this. I make sixty K a year, forty-eight after taxes. That's totally ridiculous considering what it costs to live."

Bear turned to Gunner. "I don't want to speak out of turn, but you're close to Ghost. He's been pulled out of the service to work on these special projects like Russia. Do you think he's on the O-6 military pay grade at a hundred thou a year? Or does he get paid under the table or something?"

"I really don't know, and if I asked him, he'd probably tongue-lash me," replied Gunner. He paused to think for a moment. "Listen, guys, I get it and I apologize for never considering what you guys deal with financially. I promise you I'll find the right person to address this with and see what I can do. In the meantime, you two are welcome to bunk with me until, you know, we can figure something out."

Bear started laughing, drawing a nasty look from Cam. "Nah, man. I appreciate the offer, but my girlfriend sent me a bunch of texts a little while ago. She really misses me, and all this asteroid talk got her to thinking. She wants me to come back."

Cam threw her head back and started laughing. "That so figures. She's looking for TEOTWAWKI sex."

"Huh?" asked Bear.

"You know, TEOTWAWKI—the end of the world as we know it."

"Nah, man. She really does miss me." Bear fumbled around beneath his chair in search of his phone. "Do you wanna see the text messages? She even sent me pictures."

Cam squirmed. "Oh God, no. Get away from me!"

She shot up out of the chair and Bear pretended to chase her around the deck with his phone. Gunner stretched his legs out and stared at the sky, wondering what the asteroid would look like as it crashed into Earth.

PART FOUR

ASTROMETRY

Identification Number: 2029 IM86
Right Ascension: 18 hours 44 minutes 01.1 seconds
Declination: -27 degrees 33 minutes 14 seconds
Greatest Elongation: 65.3 degrees
Nominal Distance from Earth: 0.49 Astronomical Units
Relative Velocity: 28,309 meters per second

CHAPTER 49

Thursday, April 12
NASA Mission Control
Johnson Space Center
Houston, Texas

Before a rocket can take off, NASA's Launch Control works its way through an extensive checklist. In coordination with the space agency's private contractors—including Lockheed Martin, United Space Alliance, and SpaceX—engineers, launch system coordinators, and flight crew managers work in concert to ensure a successful, safe launch.

The director of Flight Control One in the Mission Control Center, Mark Foster, nervously paced the floor as his team methodically went through the countdown process. Less than twenty-four hours ago, the order came directly from the president to ready the mission for launch.

The countdown clock began immediately at T minus forty-three hours and counting. In NASA lexicon, the term *L time* refers to the amount of actual time that has elapsed, used in a continuous countdown that cannot be modified. *T time*, or *T minus* a stated time, on the other hand, can be stopped and started regardless of a scheduled launch time.

Once the Falcon 9 rocket lifted off into space, Launch Control at the Kennedy Space Center turned the mission over to Foster's team at the Johnson Space Center. Many of the tasks ordinarily assigned to subordinates, from the traditional call to stations to conducting preliminary assessments, were handled by Foster personally. There had never been a more important space mission in history, and

Foster intended to micromanage every aspect for so long as he could keep his eyes open.

T minus twenty-seven hours and holding.

The robotic, computer-produced voice came across the communications system of both Mission Control and the launch facility at Cape Canaveral. This was the first of several built-in holds designed to halt the countdown process while the launchpad was cleared of nonessential personnel and the orbiter was loaded with cryogenic reactants into the fuel cells.

With the prelaunch process on a programmed hold of four hours during this procedure, Foster left FCR-1 and sought out Colonel Maxwell Robinson, the longtime liaison between the Pentagon and Mission Control. He found Colonel Robinson in his assigned office, which was only used during significant launch events.

"Max," began Foster, who'd been on a first-name basis since the two of them had colluded to cover up the events surrounding the ISS blackout of years before. The two of them had become co-conspirators, focused on self-preservation and protecting their careers. "I don't like this at all. Does the president not realize—?"

Colonel Robinson shut down his inquiry by motioning for Foster to join him in the office and urging him to close the door. "Stow it, Foster. We follow orders regardless of their absurdity. Honestly, I don't know what the big deal is, anyway. You guys said you're ready; what's another week?"

"It just feels rushed, and from what I've heard, it's simply because the Russians beat us to the punch. Let them have the glory, who cares?"

"Our president does, that's who," replied the colonel brusquely. "Do your duty, just like we've done before. It'll be all right. Now, how's the countdown coming?"

"On schedule, and without a hitch."

"See?"

Foster belabored his point. "This stuff is preliminary. The perilous aspects come—"

Colonel Maxwell interrupted him. "Look at it this way, Foster. If the launch had remained set for next Friday, there would've been no margin for error regarding weather delays or mechanical issues, etcetera. This way, a few hours, or even a day, doesn't necessarily alter the overall objective of this mission, which is to divert the asteroid. If you ran into difficulties next Friday, we might miss our window of opportunity to accomplish the president's goals."

Foster looked toward the ceiling and closed his eyes. He was exhausted and really needed to get some sleep. The team at Cape Canaveral was more than capable of handling the tasks that ordinarily fell under their purview anyway. The real action began at nine hours prior to launch.

"Sure, you're right," said Foster. "There is one more thing that's been bugging me, and maybe because I wasn't consulted on the decision."

"What?"

"Why didn't we take advantage of the lunar outpost? We built that monstrosity for a reason, namely as a stopping-off point for deep-space exploration. It would've made more sense to make the interim stop and then relaunch the starship orbiter to intercept the asteroid."

Colonel Maxwell rolled his eyes. He asked condescendingly, "And how long does that process take?"

"Twenty-four to thirty-six hours."

"Guess what happens during that time frame? The Russians land on IM86, hop around a few times for the camera, and stake their claim to the greatest opportunity to understand the origins of our universe we've ever had, not to mention the mining aspect."

"But, Max, do you understand how much fuel is required to—"

"Listen, this is not about conserving resources. This is about shutting down the Russians as they try to lay claim to superiority in space. If the Europeans and Japanese lose confidence in our abilities, they'll jump ship and NASA gets dismantled. Do you understand?"

Foster shook his head in disgust. He'd been threatened with this before. The answer was always push-push-push, the risks be damned. Without saying another word, he hoisted his weary body out of the chair and headed for the friendlier confines of his office, where he planned on taking a nap.

He didn't even bother to mention his bigger concern, the Pentagon's plan B, which had been a late-hour addition to the mission's payload.

CHAPTER 50

Thursday, April 12
The Oval Office
The White House
Washington, DC

President Watson couldn't stop pacing the floor. He'd hardly slept the night before as he considered the ramifications of moving up the launch. He chastised himself for placing his desire to be the champion of the so-called space race above being concerned with preparing the nation for mission failure. *Failure is not an option. Besides, how do you prepare a nation for extinction?* But, based upon the Pentagon's assurances, there was always a plan B.

"Mr. President?" announced his chief of staff as she entered the room. "Am I interrupting?"

"No, Maggie. Please come in. To be honest, I'm not really in the mood to be alone with my thoughts at the moment. The second-guessing and self-rebuke is getting old. Perhaps you can do it for me?"

The two of them shared a laugh. President Watson had never met former naval commander Maggie Fielding before interviewing her after his election of last November. She was a Washington outsider who was well respected throughout the military and known for her organizational skills.

The president had a finely tuned political machine already, honed in the trenches of a brutal primary and presidential campaign process. Politically minded thinkers were abundant in the West Wing, but it took a military veteran to herd them together into a cohesive fighting force. Because, make no mistake, there was a never-ending political war being fought in Washington, one that was far more dangerous than any threat from Moscow or Beijing.

"No, sir. I won't join your pity party, especially since you have no cause to entertain one. Your decision is rock solid, based upon the best advice from the team at NASA, and with multiple interests taken into consideration. At this point, sir, you have to rely upon people to do their jobs."

The president, who would turn seventy this summer, was known for being a hands-on administrator. From his first congressional campaign forty years ago, through his days as a governor, to becoming the leader of the free world, President Watson had become a politically astute leader known to micromanage every aspect of government he controlled. To his credit, he quickly learned that the job of President of the United States was too large for his normal modus operandi, which made his first hire, Maggie Fleming, all the more critical.

"Maggie, when I entered the Oval Office for the first time following my inauguration, I faced challenges that had been building up for decades. We are a nation divided, and I felt it was my duty to bring Americans together. I knew I would not always make perfect decisions or say all the right words, but I vowed to stay true to my principles."

"Mr. President, you do realize that you've only been on the job for eighty-some days, right? You've got three and a half years left to implement your policies, and with your current popularity, you might as well figure on two terms."

The president chuckled. "I like your optimism. Would you mind talking to those mopes down the hall who stress over the political ramifications of everything I say and do?"

"No, thanks," she replied. "They hate me because I always have to tell them no!"

The president took a sip of coffee and reviewed some notes on his desk. "Are the Russians ever gonna have the balls to respond to our inquiries? And where is the United Nations in all of this? They'd be screaming bloody murder if we launched a rocket into space under similar circumstances and then quit returning phone calls. Are they that afraid of Putin?"

The president was agitated, and all of the things on his mind began to pour out at once.

"They are, but we're not, sir. Our intelligence team came out of Far East Russia with confirmation of their intentions. I trust in the judgment of our people at NASA. They are confident that, for one, the Russians don't have the technological capability of landing on IM86—safely anyhow. And, secondly, we can overtake their head start with tomorrow's launch. We'll just have to be patient while this plays out."

President Watson picked up an outline of the launch sequence provided to him by the acting NASA administrator. He glanced at his watch and read some more.

"Assuming we're still on time, they're in the middle of a T minus nineteen hours hold. According to this summary, they've begun final preparations of the spacecraft's three main engines and other apparently mundane tasks." He set the paper down and looked over his glasses as he asked, "I take it they'll contact you directly if there's a delay or hiccup?"

"Yes, sir. In fact, I wanted to address this with you. As you know, liftoff is scheduled for seven in the morning. As is customary, launches from the Cape take place in the early morning hours to avoid the high-level winds that tend to whip up along Florida's Atlantic coast as the day wears on. We can tap into the agency's closed-circuit live feeds rather than watch it on one of the news networks."

"That sounds good," interjected the president. "I don't want to hear the talking heads' news commentary anyway. Have them make a staffer available to explain what's happening."

"Yes, sir. Would you prefer to watch in the Situation Room, or shall I set up multiple monitors in here?"

"How about the Roosevelt Room? I'd like my wife to be with me, as well as the communications team and probably the press secretary."

"Anybody else?" asked Fielding.

The president rolled his eyes. "I suppose we should have the political folks and the speechwriter. I'll need to have them prepare a statement in advance for my review, to be delivered from the Rose Garden if weather permits."

His chief of staff began making notes and then sent a text to her aides. After she was finished, she took a deep breath and exhaled.

"What is it, Maggie?" he asked.

"Sir, we're receiving reports, um, more like feedback from our governors that people are restless. Don't get me wrong, I believe you've done everything in your power to exude confidence in this crisis, and our messaging has been spot-on. It's just that ..." Her voice trailed off.

"There's still a modicum of doubt in our approach," the president said, finishing her thought for her.

"Yes, sir. It has nothing to do with you and everything to do with the nonstop media coverage that has stoked people's fears. The drama on the news is scaring the crap out of people."

The president leaned back in his chair and shook his head. "High drama results in high viewership. High viewership results in higher ad buys. Can you think of any higher drama than an extinction-level event?"

"No, sir. Unfortunately, we can only do so much through our communications team to assuage their concerns. A successful launch tomorrow will go a long way toward calming down the public." Again, Fielding's voice trailed off.

"I sense there's a caveat to your statement," said the president.

"Yes, sir. If the mission is unsuccessful, or even marginally so, then we have to be prepared to deal with society's reaction."

The president knew what Fielding was alluding to. During the campaign, the president had run a campaign based upon unity— bringing the American people back together as one nation, not two separate politically charged groups. He'd said many times during the campaign that the country was one bad news story away from societal collapse. The arrival of IM86 was certainly a *bad news story*.

"I think I know where you're headed with this, Maggie."

"Good. Sir, the media is distracted. Congress is in Easter recess. I think it would be prudent to have the White House legal team begin drafting executive orders for your signature, you know, in case they're necessary."

"Do you think I should sign them now, in the midst of the countdown? Won't that show a lack of confidence in our own decision?"

"No, sir. Not now, but after, just in case it doesn't work."

The president rose from his chair and paced the room. The Great Seal of the President sewn into the carpet on the floor of the Oval Office might not withstand a four-year Watson presidency. He began to reel off a list of directives that he wanted carried out.

"Bring our troops home, quietly, Maggie. I want to circle the wagons in case the Russians or Chinese decide to take advantage of this crisis to attack us. I was disturbed by the intelligence report in this morning's Daily Briefing regarding Russian submarine activity. They're off our coastlines more than normal."

"Sir, the intel didn't indicate they were positioning themselves in any type of attack formation. Vice Admiral Lewis of the 2nd Fleet reported two Typhoon-class nuclear-powered ballistic-missile submarines had been lurking along the continental shelf near Bermuda, but that's not out of the ordinary."

The president grimaced. "I don't like the timing. They screw with us all the time, constantly testing the fences with their nuclear bombers in the Pacific Northwest. Now's not the time to play games."

"Yes, sir, I agree."

The president continued. "Have the legal team prepare the continuity-of-government orders, including a martial law declaration. Naturally, some of these things won't be required initially, but I'd prefer to have them on our desk and ready. Make arrangements to evacuate my wife to Cheyenne Mountain. I'd suggest, no, I'm ordering you to do the same for your husband."

"He'll be fine," Fielding responded.

"You did hear me say *order*, right, Maggie?"

"Yes, Mr. President," she replied with a smile. "Sir, I have an additional suggestion that might seem odd on its face, but it can help you accomplish your purpose without unduly raising alarms in the media and the public."

"What do you have in mind?"

"Currently, the Homeland Security Advisory has designated the terror threat level at yellow, or elevated. They've always maintained that we're at a significant risk of terrorist attacks. On several occasions, as you know, the level has been raised to orange—a high risk of terrorist attacks."

"Do you want to go to orange?"

"No, sir. I believe, with the help of our friends at the FBI, we can make a case for a red designation, a severe risk of terrorist attack. We'll use the recent discovery of the terrorist cell operating in Southern Arizona as our point of reference. The FBI director can make the case that the threat continues throughout the Southwest, thereby justifying the increase in the threat level."

The president stopped pacing. "Do you think that this will fly under the media's radar?"

"Not necessarily, but it'll be a minor story in comparison to tomorrow's launch. We can make the announcement after the evening news, minimizing its exposure. By raising the level to red, the National Guard can be activated, FEMA takes on a bigger role in its preparations, and you can have greater powers in anticipation of a martial law declaration."

The president smiled. "Good thinking, Maggie. We prepare for the worst, without causing panic in the streets with our actions. Make it happen."

CHAPTER 51

Three years prior
Kennedy Space Center
Cape Canaveral
Atlantic Coast of Florida

The night before the scheduled launch of STS-199 to the International Space Station, Heather was restless. She missed Gunner, and her stay in the small, hotel-like astronaut crew quarters at the Kennedy Space Center was lonely without him.

Heather tried desperately to sleep, but her excitement before her first trip into space was overwhelming. She also had anxiety. STS, an acronym for space transportation system, had shuttled astronauts to and from the International Space Station for years.

Heather had been promised a seat on STS-200 with an all-American crew scheduled for flight four months from now, rather than the international contingent she was hitching a ride with tomorrow.

The launch of STS-199 had been delayed from a month ago when hail damage from a severe thunderstorm damaged the external fuel tanks. The mission was scrubbed and repairs were effectuated.

The resulting rollback of STS-199 led to a change in launch schedules. Heather was pulled from STS-200 and added to the current mission. While she was excited about joining NASA's first mission into space since the demise of Artemis One, new challenges were heaped onto her shoulders, including learning Russian.

She had a working knowledge of basic phrases and greetings, something she and her best friend, Cameron Mills, had in common from their days in college. They used to practice Russian and enjoyed teasing guys when they went on double dates together. Although most of what they said was gibberish, when they spoke Russian in front of their dates, some found it infuriating, and others, one guy in particular, found it adorable.

That guy was Gunner Fox. Cam introduced the two and they hit it off immediately. Both had a love of flying, although Heather's goals were a little loftier than Gunner's. The two fell in love and were married.

Now, on her last night on Earth before her dreams came true, she lay in bed staring at the decades-old popcorn ceiling, wishing she could remove it and stare at the stars. She glanced over at the nightstand to the small plastic cup that contained two Ambien sleeping tablets given to her by the flight doctor. Heather had taken Ambien before as a tool to recover from jet lag, but she didn't really like the effect it had on her.

Nonetheless, as part of her preflight training, the medical team suggested biting a smaller portion of the tablet to see how her body reacted to it. NASA had considered everything as they created a regimented schedule for their astronauts.

They also must have assumed that some of their astronauts would have difficulty sleeping. Heather tossed and turned that night as she mentally struggled to clear her mind of the myriad possibilities thundering through her head. Assuming a safe trip into orbit, not necessarily a given considering the demise of Artemis One and prior space shuttle missions, Heather would be away from Gunner for three months.

In addition to the emotional feelings that consumed her mind, her brain was clouded by the intense desire to be technically perfect on the mission. She wanted to fly to the Moon, and she looked at this initial space station mission as an opportunity to prove she was worthy. A perfect mission might result in a quick turnaround to be included on Artemis Two scheduled for later that year.

The goodbye process with the astronaut's loved ones was very emotional, and somewhat insensitive when the brief, *launch-minus-one day* encounter took place. Earlier in the day, Heather had experienced her first *wave across the ditch*, as NASA called it. After being grounded from Artemis One due to a flu bug, Heather understood why the procedure had been established.

After her final training had been completed in Houston the week prior, Heather left for Cape Canaveral. The final goodbyes took place across a road, the proverbial ditch, where all she could do was wave to Gunner. The procedure had been established to prevent the astronauts from carrying a virus or illness into space, so the quarantine was an absolute necessity.

He'd been so supportive of her as the days to launch ticked away. As a fighter pilot, he understood risks. After the explosion of Artemis One, the couple had had many serious discussions as to whether she should continue in her career. In the end, they reminded each other that you get one life, one opportunity to achieve the highest goals within your reach. Despite the risks, Heather was an astronaut, just as Gunner was a fighter pilot. They'd accepted the risks and lived their lives accordingly with the full support of their spouse.

His support was unconditional, as was his love. His words of encouragement and devotion rang in her head. *You're not just a star, darling, you're my whole damn universe.*

It made the separation from Gunner, however, much more difficult and threatened to distract her from the task at hand—spaceflight. Heather had to make peace with her decision to leave Earth. Her mind had to get right with the fact that she'd be leaving Gunner for three months, but it was for the right reasons—helping humanity.

She looked at the thought process as tying up the loose ends of her life because you never knew what might happen. But then again, you never knew what was going to befall you on the drive to the grocery store, either. That thought allowed her to feel at peace with leaving. The emotional roller-coaster ride was over.

She was eventually able to fall asleep, but she dreamt of every minute of the launch and then the feeling of exhilaration she anticipated once she arrived at the ISS.

Because, after all, every day was a good day when you're floating.

CHAPTER 52

Present Day
Friday, April 13
Kennedy Space Center
Cape Canaveral, Florida

On the surface, the scheduled launch of Orbital Slingshot One, dubbed OS-1, was like any other mission at the Cape. Proven procedures and safeguards were built into the prelaunch activities, complete with redundancies and cross-checks. This mission wasn't necessarily any more complicated than any in the past, except it was full of several firsts.

OS-1 was being prepared for liftoff from Launch Complex 39B at NASA's modernized spaceport at the Kennedy Space Center. Since 1968, Kennedy had been NASA's primary launch center for manned spaceflights. From the first Apollo flights through the present, the facility at the Cape Canaveral Air Force Station had witnessed highs and lows in man's quest to explore space.

The center of activity at Kennedy was the Launch Control Center. The four-story building on Merritt Island handled all spaceflights with human crews on board. After liftoff, the control of the vehicle was turned over to Mission Control in Houston.

The launch director for the flight of OS-1 was a seasoned veteran of NASA spaceflights, former space shuttle commander Wanda Lawson. Lawson had taken over after her predecessor resigned due to the Artemis One tragedy. Although no negligence had been found during NASA's internal investigation, the demands and accusations leveled upon the former launch director during congressional hearings proved to be unbearable, so he resigned.

Lawson, as the launch director, coordinated all aspects of the mission. She communicated frequently with Director Foster at Mission Control in Houston, keeping him abreast of prelaunch procedures and the status of the crew. Lawson bore the heavy responsibility of making the final determination of whether the launch was a *go* or *no go*, one that was reached after consulting with every member of her team.

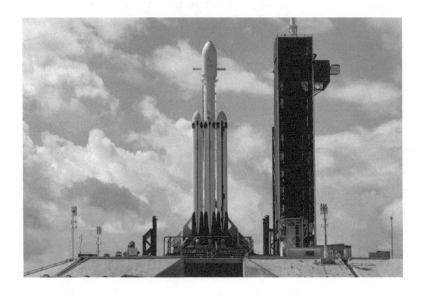

T minus six hours and holding.

The same robotic voice heard at Mission Control in Houston filled the air at the Launch Control Center. This was a built-in hold at this stage, which typically lasted two hours, or only one hour if a mission was scrubbed during this portion of the countdown.

Several important variables were considered by the Mission Management Team and Director Lawson. The weather was one factor, although the pressure was on to get OS-1 on its way to save the planet, needless to say.

A final check was made with the flow director and the booster test conductor as the external tanks were prepared for their propellants. This flight's distance and duration were unusually long, as OS-1 was tasked with intercepting IM86 farther away from Earth than any manned space mission had traveled.

T minus three hours and holding.

Tension was building in the Launch Control Center as several critical aspects of the prelaunch procedures took place at three hours prior to scheduled liftoff.

The NASA manager overseeing the development of SpaceX's commercial crew ferry ships, as the long-range missions were called, had approved the private company's proposal to strap in the astronauts atop the Falcon 9 rocket assembly early at T minus three hours, followed by a last minute *load-and-go* procedure for fueling the rockets.

This newly adopted process, made at the behest of SpaceX, provided for the launchers to be fueled in the final hour of the countdown sequence. Rather than filling the external tanks at the six-hour mark, which was customary for other rocket designs, such as the Atlas 5 and Boeing's CST-100, an automatic countdown sequencer command was designed to chill the kerosene and cryogenic liquid oxygen, allowing it to flow into the Falcon 9 rockets in the final minutes before the firing sequence.

The Falcon 9 burned a mix of kerosene and liquid oxygen chilled to near each of the fluids' freezing points. This densified the propellant, allowing more fuel to be loaded into the Falcon 9's tanks, thus giving the rocket's Merlin engines enhanced thrust capability.

The combination had been tested on unmanned, tethered flights, and the team at SpaceX believed that they had the perfect configuration to place OS-1 on an intercept course considering the advanced launch date.

The crew had departed for the launchpad. There were thirty-eight active astronauts that made up the NASA Astronaut Corps. That didn't include two dozen astronaut candidates who were training at the Johnson Space Center in Houston. Of the thirty-eight, nineteen were either assigned to the ISS or the lunar outpost as international active astronauts. That left nineteen active astronauts and eighteen *management astronauts*, those who remained employed by NASA but were no longer eligible for flight assignment, to choose from for this mission.

All of them volunteered, and through a stringent process of elimination, a crew of eleven was chosen to manage OS-1. The crew, chosen because of their work experience and educational backgrounds in engineering, physical science, and mathematics, were trained in the orbital slingshot method of diversion.

At the Johnson Space Center, elaborate simulators were created to recreate the gravitational conditions and orbital mechanics necessary to produce the slingshot effect. This was a first as well. Thus far, aerospace engineers had worked with computer-simulated models. They'd never attempted to recreate the gravity-assist process using a flight-crew simulator, much less using it on a celestial body.

Nonetheless, the crew of eleven performed the task flawlessly, and assuming their predictions of mass, velocity, and energy were correct, then the mission could be accomplished.

This crew of brave Americans checked their cockpit switch configurations. They performed air-to-ground voice checks with both Launch Control at Kennedy and Mission Control at the Johnson Space Center.

The orbiter's crew hatch was closed and sealed shut, followed by a leak check. They were ready.

CHAPTER 53

Friday, April 13
Kennedy Space Center
Cape Canaveral, Florida

T minus twenty minutes and holding.

Another built-in hold that lasted ten minutes was instituted as Launch Control completed its final preflight alignments and measurements. At this point the orbiter's onboard computers were set to launch configuration. The orbiter cabin vent valves were closed, and the backup flight system was set to launch configuration.

The entire prelaunch process takes forty-three hours. In that time frame, at an estimated sixty thousand miles per hour, asteroid IM86 had traveled a distance of three million miles closer to its target—Earth.

Time was of the essence.

Director Lawson moved from station to station within Launch Control—questioning, confirming, and double-checking protocols with all members of her team. Satisfied that OS-1 was still a go, the countdown clock resumed, ticking ever so slowly to liftoff.

T minus twenty minutes and counting.

Now minutes felt like hours as everyone waited in nervous anticipation. Dozens of NASA personnel worked methodically through the prelaunch tasks, being diligent, as always. The eyes of the world were upon them as America entered the fray, prepared to destroy the enemy that barreled through space toward Earth.

T minus nine minutes and holding.

Another built-in hold, one that was excruciating to the lay public but customary as part of the prelaunch countdown. Now Director

Lawson would make her final decision regarding the launch window. And she made her final go, no-go poll. The test director, the mission management team, and the launch director spoke one by one with their subordinates as they listened for the hoped-for response—*go*.

With a sigh of relief, she made the call. The robotic voice made the announcement.

T minus nine minutes and counting.

The team started the automatic ground launch sequencer. Flight recorders were activated. At seven and a half minutes before launch, the orbiter access arm was retracted.

Anticipation began to build, causing the massive roof air-conditioning units to work overtime to keep the Launch Control Center cooled down as heat poured off nervous bodies.

At five minutes, the auxiliary power units were started and the solid rocket booster safety devices were armed.

Another minute passed. IM86 was closer, and NASA was closer to launching their solution. Two important tests were conducted— the orbiter aerosurface profile test followed by the main engine gimbal profile test. Both were critical to the launch. When it was announced that both tests were successful, nervous applause filled the Launch Center. They were within three minutes.

The gaseous oxygen vent arm was retracted as SpaceX finished loading the fuel. The Ground Launch Sequencer program switched the main fuel valve heaters off. From this point forward, the GLS was in control of the flight, leaving everyone in Launch Control to become spectators, like the rest of the world.

The crew's commander instructed his crewmates to close their visors in preparation for launch.

T minus thirty-one seconds and counting.

With no technical issues having been reported by the GLS, the *go command* was given for the auto sequence start, an important moment when the GLS hands off primary control of the countdown to the Falcon 9's onboard computers.

"Go for launch," Director Lawson calmly said into her microphone. The team at Launch Control let out a cheer.

Then the robotic announcement came over the speaker system.

Ground launch sequencer is a go for auto sequence start.

T minus sixteen seconds and counting.

Shouts of joy and excitement filled the air from outside the Launch Center. Thousands of people screamed their encouragement, beneath a sea of red, white, and blue American flags waving over their heads.

USA! USA! USA!

The launchpad sound-suppression system was activated, not that anybody would've heard the rockets igniting over the chanting. Several members of the Launch Center team began to cry, tears streaming down their faces in a show of raw emotion as the magnitude of the moment began to overtake them.

Then came the final countdown, that period of ten seconds that every kid waited for when their heroes took off into the last frontier to conquer the unknown.

The main engine hydrogen burn-off system was activated, marking the final ten-second countdown.

T minus ten seconds. Nine. Eight. Seven.

CHAPTER 54

Friday, April 13
Gunner's Residence
Dog Island

Gunner didn't want to watch the liftoff of the Falcon 9 rocket from the Cape. Not because he was an ostrichlike, head-in-the-sand kind of guy, but because he'd held a high level of contempt for NASA for years. He blamed the space agency for taking away his wife, and his life.

Despite making his feelings known to Pop the night before, his persistent father had shown up anyway with a basket full of homemade beignets, the deep-fried nuggets of sweetened dough made famous at the Café du Monde in New Orleans' French Quarter.

Gunner rolled over in bed as the aroma filled the house. Even Howard, a notorious late sleeper, heck, an all-day sleeper, managed to hoist himself up and turn the sniffer into the air.

"It's still dark outside, Pop." Gunner bemoaned the early hour. He dragged himself out of bed and staggered into the bathroom to get his business out of the way.

Howard stirred long enough to find the warm spot abandoned by Gunner, and settled in to sleep some more. After all these years, he'd learned that the smell of something that good rarely ended up in his bowl.

"Launch is scheduled for seven eastern. It's six a.m. in paradise, son. Up and at 'em!"

Gunner pulled a sweatshirt over his head and made his way to the kitchen. Pop had already started a pot of coffee and was spreading the beignets out on a platter.

"I'm pretty sure I told you I wasn't interested in watching this—"

Pop cut him off. "Son, I'll never forget watching the coverage of Apollo 11 as a boy. Neil Armstrong and Buzz Aldrin were American heroes for what they accomplished on that mission to the Moon. What we are about to witness today is a crew who'll quite possibly be saving the world. This isn't some kind of movie or make-believe story. It's real stuff and we need to be a part of it. All Americans should want to support them."

Gunner sighed. Of course, Pop was right. He usually was. When Gunner wanted to sulk and be left alone, Pop kicked him in the ass. When Gunner wanted to drown his sorrows in a vat of Oyster City Beer, Pop reminded him that he could be called to duty at any time. And when Gunner appeared to throw caution to the wind a little too much, it was Pop who tried to remind him that he had something to live for—no easy task.

The two munched the still-warm beignets, piling on the powdered sugar to add to the delicious flavor. After the coffee was made, Pop glanced at the clock on the microwave and panicked.

"It's almost time!" He ran over to the coffee table, which held the remotes, some empty beer bottles, and an iPad. He shook his head in disgust and powered on the monitors. "Fox News?"

Gunner replied with a mouth full of beignet, "Nah, CNN. They're better for stuff like this."

He wandered over in front of the television. He gazed upon the awesome sight of Falcon Heavy, the most powerful rocket in the world, by far. Pop turned up the volume on the monitor, and the CNN reporter described the scene.

"This incredible rocket has been modified to send the orbiter and its crew deeper into space than any other in history. Its first stage is powered by three Falcon 9 nine-engine cores, whose twenty-seven Merlin engines will generate over six million pounds of thrust at liftoff. To put this in perspective for our viewers, that's the equivalent of eighteen Boeing 777 aircraft."

"I've got the chills," said Pop. He rubbed his arms and appeared to get a little teary-eyed. "I mean, look at that thing."

T minus thirty-one seconds and counting.

The reporter continued. "This is an important moment as we await Launch Director—"

A female voice could be heard, obscuring the reporter's sentence.

Go for launch.

A spontaneous cheer erupted at Launch Control, which put Pop further into an emotional state. He began to applaud.

"Man, oh man!" he said excitedly.

Ground launch sequencer is a go for auto sequence start.

T minus sixteen seconds and counting.

The CNN cameras, rebroadcasting the feed provided by NASA, focused in on Falcon Heavy as the hydrogen burn-off system was initiated. The screen split as their cameras panned to the many thousands of onlookers waving their flags, not trying to hold back their tears of joy.

T minus ten seconds. Nine. Eight. Seven. Six. Five. Four.

Pop joined in the final countdown with millions of others around the globe.

Three. Two. One. Zero!

Solid rocket booster ignition and we have liftoff of Orbital Slingshot One!

"Woo-hoo!" yelled Pop, startling Howard, who jumped out of bed and began his quintessential hound-like howling bark combination that was irresistible. Pop grabbed Gunner's arm and began to hop up and down like a child, his exuberance eventually rubbing off on Gunner.

A test pilot of Gunner's caliber had certainly experienced the kind of rush that astronauts felt, only they hadn't traveled as far into space. Gunner tried, and it had almost killed him. However, Pop's enthusiasm was infectious, and Gunner quickly got caught up in the moment.

He studied the telemetry that was superimposed in the bottom left of the screen. Gunner's mathematical mind quickly appreciated the sheer power of the massive Falcon 9 engine cores. That amount of thrust was surely exerting a tremendous amount of gravitational force on the crew.

Power and telemetry are nominal.

OS-1 was one minute into flight. The cameras picked up the sound of the rockets forcing Falcon Heavy in a northeasterly direction away from Florida's Atlantic Coast toward the island of Bermuda.

Gunner closed his eyes for a moment and recalled that day in DeFuniak Springs when Heather had declared that something was wrong with the launch of Artemis One. He tried to remember.

"Two minutes," he mumbled aloud.

"What?" asked Pop.

Vehicle is supersonic.

The calm voice of someone at Launch Control was providing periodic updates of Falcon Heavy's progress. The CNN reporter began to provide the benefit of his knowledge.

"You can hear the applause building to a crescendo at the Cape, both within the confines of Launch Control and from the tens of thousands of Americans who've lined the highways surrounding the Kennedy Space Center." He began to well up in tears as he looked around at his fellow news reporters; all of them were truly caught up in the moment.

Maximum dynamic pressure achieved.

"I apologize for my emotions, ladies and gentlemen," the reporter began, in between sniffles. "Maximum dynamic pressure, or max-q, is an important part of lift off. At this point, the rockets aerodynamic loads are at their highest, a very good sign."

He could barely be heard over the shouts of delight from those who'd made their way to Cape Canaveral.

Gunner was apprehensive as he focused on the telemetry displays. Falcon Heavy was approaching ten thousand miles per hour. It had shot up through the stratosphere, quickly approaching the dark layer that surrounded the earth, where oxygen dissipates and space begins—the mesosphere.

It was also approaching the two-minute mark. The visions of Artemis One flashed through his mind. The sadness Heather had felt when she saw the inaugural lunar mission fail in spectacular fashion.

The CNN announcer described this stage of the launch. "We're at two minutes now, and the power will begin to drop in the side boosters to decrease loads on the center core." He paused for a moment.

BECO.

The Launch Control announcer spoke calmly into the communications system.

"To our viewers worldwide, BECO is an acronym for booster engine cutoff. It marks an important point in the launch process, as you can now see via this split screen that the two side booster engines have separated from the rocket. These side boosters have begun their return to the launchpad at Cape Canaveral.

"There! You can see on your screen that the side boosters have safely fallen away from Falcon Heavy and their grid fins have deployed. The side booster's engines have refired, and their guidance systems will carry them back to Earth to be used on a future mission."

"Wow! Wow! Wow!" exclaimed Pop as he wiped the tears away. He'd abandoned any attempt to control his emotions, allowing them to pour out as the excitement continued to build to a crescendo.

Gunner exhaled for the first time in a minute. They were past the two-minute mark. He managed a grin and leaned down to scrub on Howard's back, whose tail hadn't stopped wagging since liftoff.

"The center core has powered up once again and has achieved a speed of ten thousand miles per hour." The CNN reporter, having managed to regain some sense of professionalism, continued to describe the process for the viewers.

The mission time clock clicked away as they approached three and a half minutes.

MECO.

"Ladies and gentlemen, *MECO* is an acronym for main engine cutoff. The three Falcon 9 engines have done their job, and with the drop-off of the main engine, the orbiter will begin to operate under its own power as it soars into space on its mission to intercept asteroid IM86!"

Separation ignition.

Gunner smiled. It was gonna be all right.

He'd learned a lot about the process of launching rockets into space from Heather. Many a night was spent as she explained to him that it was safe, despite what they had witnessed during the Artemis One launch. She'd done her level best to convince him that her first mission into space, to the ISS, would be the two-hundredth time NASA had carried out a launch. She tried to explain the odds, and that they were better than driving down the highway.

He recalled her words. The promises of safety. The convincing nature she had when she wanted something bad enough.

And then Gunner was grabbed back into the present as the image of Orbital Slingshot One disappeared in a flash of bright, hot-white light.

CHAPTER 55

Friday, April 13
Gunner's Residence
Dog Island

"Wait. What's happened?" Pop walked up to the large screen and tried to reach into it, as if touching the rocket would provide him answers. He stood there for a moment in stunned disbelief.

The news feed switched back to the CNN newsroom, where the hosts were speechless, and the panel of experts were fighting back tears.

"Ladies and gentlemen, we've lost the feed to the OS-1 spacecraft. We're not sure if, um, we're hoping that some kind of malfunction has resulted in the camera being disabled."

Gunner calmly set down his coffee mug and stormed onto the deck, rubbing his hands through his hair as he tried to process what he'd seen. He knew there was a difference between a camera malfunction and an explosion. He'd blown up plenty of aircraft to recognize a catastrophic failure.

"Gunner, what just happened?" asked Pop through the open door. The tears streaming down his face had changed from an emotional high to ones of utter devastation. He could sense it in his gut as well.

Gunner leaned over the rail and shook his head without answering. He couldn't bring himself to answer. The anger that he'd suppressed for so long was beginning to well up inside him again.

"Son?" His father was pleading with him.

Gunner manned up and turned to Pop. He stretched his arms out and gave his father a hug, the first one the two men had shared in a long time.

After a moment, Pop broke away and looked into Gunner's eyes. "It's gone, isn't it?"

"Most likely, Pop. We'll wait to hear something official, but, um, it doesn't look good."

"But they were on their way. I mean, all the hard stuff was over. It's not like before, right? They were past all that."

"Yeah, Pop. They were." Gunner turned away and walked back to the rail. He gripped it with both hands and squeezed the teakwood until his knuckles turned white. He looked up and down the beach, which was devoid of the usual seashell hunters and hand-holding strollers. Everyone, it seemed, had been captivated by the launch, and now, he presumed, they were mourning the dead.

Pop walked back inside and began to flip through the channels, hoping to find a news report that definitively gave him answers.

Gunner already knew in his gut what had happened. He wasn't sad; he was angry.

The sound of his phone ringing caught his attention, but he ignored its incessant demands to be answered. *No, I don't want to talk about what just happened.*

Minutes stretched into more than an hour. Periodically, Pop would walk onto the deck and report some kind of update and the opinions of a talking head who purported to know why the OS-1 mission ended.

By nine a.m., the finger-pointing and blame game had begun.

NASA overloaded the orbiter's fuel tanks.

SpaceX misrepresented their capabilities.

Rumors were the president was obsessed with the Russians and forced the launch to be moved up a week.

We weren't ready.

Gunner spoke to Pop briefly and took a shower. For ten minutes, he allowed the hot water to pour over his head, hoping to erase the memory of another mission failure. By the time he got dressed and emerged from the bathroom, Pop had recovered and was now focused on the media topic du jour—*now what?*

"Look here, son. They're already working on a plan B."

Gunner snickered and said sarcastically, "I'm sure they are."

"No, seriously, we're a great nation and you can't keep us down. I say jump back in the saddle and ride."

"Sure, Pop," said Gunner, agreeing but not really agreeing. He glanced at the clock. It was already ten a.m. He opened the refrigerator and retrieved a beer, convincing himself that it was *beer-thirty.*

"Son, your phone has been ringing and they've been leaving voicemails."

"Yeah, you know, I just don't feel like talking about it. Listen, Pop, I need to head into town. Do you need anything?"

"Into Apalach? I've stocked your pantry and there's more beer in the downstairs cooler."

"Nah, I just have an errand to run."

Pop knew his son was lying. "Gunner, come sit down and talk with me for a minute."

"No, Pop. I really need to go."

"You mean run away, right? Escape? Go anywhere but have the conversation I want to have with you."

Gunner swigged some of his beer and set it sharply down on the wooden table that served as a kitchen island and dining table. The bottle hit so hard that beer foam began to rise up the neck.

"What's there to talk about, Pop? It's a repeat of past failures. It'll probably happen again and again. I mean, how many good people does NASA have to kill until they get it right?"

Pop scowled. "They are lessons learned in blood, but necessary."

"And that makes it okay?" Gunner didn't like to argue with his father, but maybe he needed to let him know how he felt.

"No, of course not," Pop replied. "But you can't take your ball and glove and go home. You don't quit. You pick up the pieces and try again."

Gunner gritted his teeth. He was beginning to get the sense that Pop was discussing more than the explosion that ended the flight of

OS-1. Before he could counter his father's statement, Pop continued.

"You can't let a setback, a failure, stop you. You chase your destiny. If it involves risks, then so be it. That's what it takes to insure you achieve your goals, or at least progress in that direction."

Gunner didn't want to hear any more. He stomped toward his nightstand and retrieved his phone. He glanced at the display and saw that he had nine missed calls. He set the phone to mute and shoved it in his pocket.

He could not, however, mute Pop, who continued. "Son, if risk is the price of progress, what's required to save humanity?"

"Apparently, eleven more dead astronauts," he snidely replied.

"Yes, son, that's right. The ultimate price. Death. Death is the result of pursuing the nearly impossible. But, as they say, with great rewards comes great risk."

Gunner's phone began to vibrate in his pocket again. He reached for it and then decided against it. He just wanted to get away.

"Pop, how many lives will it take? How many?" Gunner suddenly became emotional and the tears filled his eyes. He turned his head away from Pop and made his way to the stairwell, not wanting to bother with the elevator.

"Son, please don't go," pleaded Pop. "I'm sorry. We can talk about this later."

Gunner waved his hand over his head. "I'll be back later."

"Where are you going?" asked Pop, but Gunner was gone.

CHAPTER 56

Friday, April 13
Apalachicola, Florida

It was all Gunner could do to lay off the throttle as he navigated his boat away from his bayfront dock and through The Cut. Despite his melancholy mood, he was still very much aware of the dolphin pod that had taken up residency in the nearby waters around the two barrier islands.

Once he was clear of The Cut, he opened her up. The Donzi lurched forward and quickly reached seventy-five miles per hour, and it began to crash wildly into the incoming waves. Gunner didn't mind the rough ride, as he simply wanted to go fast. As fast as he could toward the middle of the Gulf, and away from everything.

He was miles from shore and glanced behind him to see that Florida was fading from view as sea spray obliterated his line of sight. Then he looked down at his gauges and realized his fuel was low. *Dammit! Really?* He was in no mood to call Sea Tow to get a five-gallon refill at four hundred dollars per hour.

He stopped the boat and allowed it to idle, rocking with the waves as they rolled in toward shore. It was a beautiful day, weather-wise, but it was more than glum as it related to his state of mind. For the first time, he actually wanted to speak with Dr. Dowling at Eglin. All of the pent-up emotions demanded to be released—the memories that he'd suppressed for so long.

He rocked along for a moment, his brooding being interrupted one time by a fixed-wing Cessna flying nearby, ambling low to the water along the coast in the direction of Mexico Beach. Gunner took a deep breath of the salt air that he loved so much, and held it, allowing its intoxicating taste to soak into his body. The warm sun gave him new life, and he tried to force himself into a better frame of mind.

Gunner immediately felt bad about leaving Pop the way he did. He powered up the boat and turned it back toward Dog Island. He retrieved his phone from his pocket and was about to send a text when another call tried to come through. He hit decline, immediately sending it to voicemail. He opened up the message app and typed out a text while driving with his knee.

GUNNER: Hey, Pop! I'm sorry I was being an asshole. Can I buy you a beer and a dozen on the half shell as an apology?

Several moments later, his good-natured and, thankfully, forgiving father replied:

POP: No apologies necessary. I get it. See you at the dock.

CHAPTER 57

Friday, April 13
Apalachicola, Florida

Pop and Gunner hugged it out when they met up at the dock. The two talked briefly and then put the whole ordeal behind them. Gunner made his way into Apalachicola Bay and pulled into the City Dock, where they worked together to tie off the boat. It was approaching noon when they marched up Avenue D to The Tap Room.

The doors were open and Kenny Chesney was belting out the lyrics to "No Shoes, No Shirt, No Problem" on their sound system. The stage was set for a raucous Friday lunch crowd; only there was one problem—no customers.

Usually, the Friday bar patrons were getting geared up for the weekend, as the oystermen were looking to spend their pay in style rather than downing the usual six-pack on the dock, a ritual that capped off the other days of the workweek.

But not today. The restaurant was empty except for Sammy Hart and one of the servers standing behind the bar, staring up at the continuous news coverage of the tragedy. The two were so consumed by the reporting that they didn't see Gunner and Pop belly up to the bar.

"Hey, Sammy," said Gunner, catching his amateur therapist's attention.

Sammy snapped his head around, revealing the dour look on his face. "Hey, sorry, gentlemen. It's just that …" His voice trailed off as he pointed his thumb over his shoulder.

"I know, we saw," interrupted Gunner. "Let's have a couple of

Hooter Browns and two dozen raw, please, sir."

"Sure."

"Extra horsey for mine," added Pop. "Tabasco, too."

"You got it, Pop."

Hart turned to put in the order and then poured their draft beers. He avoided small talk, somehow sensing that Gunner didn't want to discuss the tragedy. Instead, he cut up lemons and limes to restock the bar, anticipating an afternoon crowd that even he knew might not materialize.

Gunner's phone buzzed again, and he pulled it out of his pocket. He set it on the teakwood bar covered with multiple layers of shellac.

"Son, are you gonna see who's been calling you? It's probably Cam or Bear. Or are you back on the call list?"

"Not supposed to be, Pop. Not until Monday."

"What about Cam or Bear? They're your friends. Don't you want to—?"

Pop didn't finish his sentence as Gunner raised his hand to stop him. He reached for his phone and began to scroll the recent calls to look at the numbers. Cam and Bear had called, but they only represented two of the thirteen attempts. The others were from numbers he didn't recognize.

"I'll call them back later," Gunner said as he stared at the other calls. "These area codes are, um, two-oh-two, that's DC. The other is five-seven-one."

"Virginia, I think," offered Pop. "It could be McLean, Alexandria, Reston. I don't know."

Gunner shrugged and put the phone back on the bar. As if on cue, it began to buzz again. *Jesus!* He angrily grabbed the phone and looked at the display. Two-zero-two.

Hart arrived with the oysters and set the guys up with another round of beers. Pop stayed focused on the news, reading the closed-captioning that revealed more about the catastrophe.

Gunner stared at the tray of oysters, wondering about the origin of the old saying *the world is your oyster.* He'd always understood it to mean that a person could achieve anything they wanted to in life, which hearkened back to the conversation he'd had with Pop after his shower. Gunner looked at it another way.

Oysters get eaten. What did that say about a world that claims to be someone's oyster? Or whatever. Gunner didn't really give a crap, he just wanted to take his mind off, well, everything.

The satellite radio station had a brief pause between songs, causing Gunner to change his focus to his surroundings. That was when he heard footsteps approaching the bar. He adjusted his seat slightly to get a view of the approaching new customer through the mirror. It was a clean-cut man, with tanned skin and dark sunglasses. He was wearing a starched white shirt and khaki pants.

When the man sat next to him at the bar, Gunner's eyes slyly glanced down at his shoes. They weren't Sperry Top-Siders, something he'd seen worn by most of the bankers and lawyers in town who donned khaki pants. These were shiny, black and belonged on somebody with a coat and tie.

"Good morning, gentlemen," he began without looking directly at Gunner or Pop. "Do you recommend the oysters?"

"They sure do," answered Hart, Gunner's *guardian of the gate*. "I'd be glad to get you a dozen."

"No, thanks. I'll have an iced tea."

The three lone guests at the bar sat quietly for several awkward minutes. Pop continued to be affixed on the television, Gunner looked straight ahead, mindlessly counting the number of liquor bottles on display, and the newcomer casually rotated a beverage napkin on the bar.

Gunner suspected the man was out of place. He didn't order food. He didn't order a sweet tea, a definite red flag in the South. And his shoes were too shiny. After another beer was delivered, Gunner decided to have some fun. He acknowledged the man to his left for the first time.

"So are you two-oh-two or five-seven-one?"

The man chuckled. "How did you know?"

"Well, your shoes are a dead giveaway, and my damn phone quit ringing right before you walked in."

The man drank from his tea, which was now watered down with melted ice. "Two-zero-two, Major."

"You know me, obviously. Do you have a name?"

"Nope. Just a message."

"Okay," said Gunner, his curiosity piqued.

"Your country needs you," the man said dryly.

Gunner laughed loudly, pulling a mesmerized Pop away from the television. Gunner took another long drink from his pint of beer. "That's what they all say. Sorry, though, I gave at the office."

"That's disappointing."

"Who are you? Even better, what are you?"

"Have you heard of the CIA, NSA, FBI? The list is long."

"Yeah, of course."

"They don't know who I am. That should actually reassure you."

Gunner started laughing again. He elbowed Pop and whispered to him, but loud enough for the visitor to hear him, "I kinda like this guy."

"Who is he?" asked Pop, leaning forward to assess the man next to Gunner.

Gunner shrugged again. "Beats me." Then he turned to the stranger, who'd clearly been sent to recruit him for something. "Well, mister no-name, no-title, no-three-letter-designation, I'm listening."

"Major, I'm gonna put this in very technical, patriotic terms for you. Your country is in a pickle."

Gunner burst out laughing, snorting his last chug of beer through his nose. Pop joined in the laughter, and Hart fumbled around for a towel before he quickly wiped the residue of Gunner's outburst off the bar top.

As Gunner recovered from the laughing fit, he glanced up at the television screen. They were showing the photos of the astronauts who died on this mission, and the twenty-four who'd perished on prior space missions. The graphic immediately put a damper on his newfound jovial mood.

Gunner closed his eyes and shook his head. "No. Leave me alone."

Hart picked up on Gunner's changed mood and immediately switched to another news network.

The man persisted. "Major, I'd like you to hear me out."

Hart became protective of his friend. "You heard the man. I think you should leave."

The man sighed, grimaced, and began to walk away. Gunner glanced up at the television monitor and furrowed his brow as footage obtained from a boat in the middle of the Atlantic Ocean was being shown. It was replayed twice, revealing the moment the OS-1 exploded. Gunner tilted his head, squinted his eyes, and stood from his seat to get a closer look at the monitor.

"Wait!" he shouted to the man.

The recruiter stopped in his tracks, but didn't turn around. Staring at the front doors, he simply said, "You don't know what we want."

Gunner glanced over at Pop and then back to the screen, which was frozen in time, showing the point the mission ended.

"Doesn't matter. Tell them I'll do it."

THANK YOU FOR READING
ASTEROID: DISCOVERY!

If you enjoyed it, I'd be grateful if you'd take a moment to write a short review for each of the books in the series (just a few words are needed) and post it on Amazon. Amazon uses complicated algorithms to determine what books are recommended to readers. Sales are, of course, a factor, but so are the quantities of reviews my books get. By taking a few seconds to leave a review, you help me out and also help new readers learn about my work.

And before you go …

SIGN UP for Bobby Akart's mailing list to receive special offers, bonus content, and you'll be the first to receive news about new releases in the Doomsday series. Visit: www.BobbyAkart.com

VISIT Amazon.com/BobbyAkart for more information on the Asteroid trilogy, the Doomsday series, the Yellowstone series, the Lone Star series, the Pandemic series, the Blackout series, the Boston Brahmin series and the Prepping for Tomorrow series totaling thirty-eight novels, including over thirty Amazon #1 Bestsellers in forty-plus fiction and nonfiction genres. Visit Bobby Akart's website for informative blog entries on preparedness, writing, and a behind-the-scenes look into his novels.

Made in United States
Troutdale, OR
05/16/2024

19903713R00181